BARDD

The Welsh Guard Mysteries:
Crouchback
Chevalier
Paladin
Herald
Bardd

The Gareth and Gwen Medieval Mysteries:
The Bard's Daughter (prequel)
The Good Knight
The Uninvited Guest
The Fourth Horseman
The Fallen Princess
The Unlikely Spy
The Lost Brother
The Renegade Merchant
The Unexpected Ally
The Worthy Soldier
The Favored Son
The Viking Prince
The Irish Bride
The Prince's Man
The Faithless Fool
The Honorable Traitor
The Admirable Physician

THE WELSH GUARD MYSTERIES

BARDD

by

SARAH WOODBURY

To Brynne and Alex
With love

A Brief Guide to Welsh Pronunciation

Names derived from languages other than English aren't always easy to pronounce for English speakers, and Welsh is no exception. As far as I am concerned, please feel free to pronounce the names and places in this book however you like. I want you to be happy!

That said, some people really want to know the *right* way to pronounce a word, and for them, I have included the pronunciation guide for Welsh sounds below.

Enjoy!

a an *ah* sound, as in *cat* (Catrin)
ae an *eye* sound (Caer)
ai an *eye* sound (Dai)
c a hard *c* sound (Catrin)
ch a non-English sound as in Scottish *ch* in *loch* (Fychan)
d as in *David* (Dafydd)
dd a buzzy voiced 'th' sound, as in *there* (bardd)
e an *eh* sound as in *bet* (Medwyn)
f a *v* sound as in *of* (Caernarfon)
ff as in *off* (Gruffydd)
g a hard *g* sound, as in *gas* (Gruffydd)
i an *ee* sound (Dw i)
l as in *lamp* (Hywel)
ll a breathy /sh/ sound that does not occur in English (Llywelyn)
o a short *o* sound as in *cot* (Conwy)
rh a breathy mix between *r* and *rh* that does not occur in English (Rhys)
th a softer unvoiced sound than for *dd* as in *thick* (Arthur)
u a short *ih* sound (Gruffydd) or (Tudur), or a long *ee* sound if at the end of the word (Cymru—pronounced *kumree*)
w as a consonant, it's an English *w* (Llywelyn); or as an *oo* sound as in *book* (Bwlch)
y when it is located in any syllable before the last one, it is an *uh* sound (Hywel). At the end of a word it can be *ih* as in *Llywelyn* or *Gruffydd*, or *ee* as in *Cymry*.

Cast of Characters

Catrin – lady-in-waiting
Rhys – quaestor; member of the King's Guard
Edward – King of England
Eleanor– Queen of England
Baby Edward – Prince of England (soon to be Prince of Wales)
Edmund – Prince of England, King Edward's younger brother
Margaret – lady-in-waiting
Isabella de Beaumont – lady-in-waiting
Hywel – Catrin's brother
Tudur – Catrin's brother
Gruffydd ab yr Ynad Coch – Tudur's bard
Simon Boydell – captain of the King's Guard
Elizabeth – Simon's wife
Oswald Boydell – Simon's brother
Emma Boydell – Simon's niece
John Boydell – Simon's cousin

William de Beauchamp – Earl of Warwick, steward to King Edward
Robert Burnell – King Edward's adviser
Otto de Grandison – Justiciar of North Wales
John de Vescy – King Edward's adviser
Humphrey de Bohun – Earl of Hereford
Miles de Bohun – Humphrey's uncle
Stephen FitzJohn – Nephew to the Earl of Warwick
Owen de la Pole – Marcher lord
Joan – Owen's wife
Moriddig – Owen's bard
Adam – Moriddig's brother
Patrick – Moriddig's son
Hugh – Owen's steward
Mary – Hugh's wife
Jane – Hugh's daughter

<u>The King's Guardsmen</u>
Rhys
Mathonwy
Ralph
Fulke
Jehan
Bertran
Donald
Edgar
Roger
Harold
Thomas
George

A Note about Bardd

Welsh musical traditions predate the medieval period, as evidenced not only by the poems and songs left to us by bards throughout the ages, but by the Welsh language itself. In fact, the English word *bard* is derived from the Welsh word *bardd*. And thus, the title of this book.

The tradition of a bardic class can be traced to Celtic times when no distinct line was drawn between a druid and a bard. With the conversion to Christianity, the role of the bard became more court poet and less seer. Bards were required to be literate and thus became the secular equivalent to monks.

A medieval document called *The Triads of Britain* details the three primary tasks of a bard:

> *One is to learn and collect sciences.*
> *The second is to teach.*
> *The third is to make peace*
> *And to put an end to all injury;*
> *For to do contrary to these things*
> *Is not usual or becoming to a bard.*

Within native Welsh society, the bard's role was to act as the repository of tradition, including history, poetry, and music. The bard was an educator of the people, and his duty, culturally speaking, was sacred. The laws of Hywel Dda, codified in the tenth century, delineate the bard as a member of the king's household, part of whose duty was to sing of the sovereignty of Britain.

Wales had a particularly well-developed written tradition, even in what has been known colloquially as the *dark ages*. Literacy in Wales dates back to the Britons' conversion to Christianity during the Roman era. In fact, throughout the medieval period, Wales had "a self-confident literary culture" with "a highly developed form of prose writing."[1] Wales's legal system was not conducted in Latin, but in Welsh, and Wales's vernacular literature as a whole was unusually sophisticated for the period. Historian Huw Pryce writes further that in Wales,

> ... both the legal and the poetic strands of native culture were closely connected and thereby reflect the status of law as part of a wider body of traditional learning, known in Welsh as *cyfarwyddyd*, which also included poetry, narrative tales, history, and genealogy.

As champions of that history, bards were members of a class unto themselves, such that, even as late as 1596, Edmund Spenser wrote that "bards were held in so high regard and estimation ... that none may displease them, for *feare to runne into re-*

---

[1] Pryce, H. (2000). Lawbooks and Literacy in Medieval Wales. *Speculum, 75*(1), 29–67. https://doi.org/10.2307/2887424

proach through their offense, and be made infamous in the
mouths of all men."[2]

In 1284, after his conquest of Wales, King Edward recognized that power ...

____

2 Spenser, Edmund (1596). *A View of the Present State of Ireland: Discoursed by Way of a Dialogue between Eudoxus and Irenaeus.*

1

King Edward's voice sliced the air. "I will see his tongue cut out!"

Rhys froze in his tracks a few paces from the entrance to the king's pavilion, which was surrounded on all sides by fields of tents, stalls, stages, and pavilions, all awaiting the beginning of the music festival that was set to begin that afternoon. It was from this magnificent pavilion that the king had spent the last week conducting business, and from here that he would continue to do so during the festival.

Fortunately, the only one to see Rhys's hesitation was Math, who was on guard at his usual spot outside. For a moment, the two men stood side-by-side, Math facing outward and Rhys inward.

"I assume you saw our wayward bard safely away?" Math said in Welsh in the lowest of undertones.

"He is already across the Dee. We ourselves could be hanged if what I've done is discovered. Do you regret joining with me?"

"Never." Math's answer was immediate and impassioned, indicating he was more certain than Rhys about what he'd done.

Rhys didn't know how the king had arrived at the idea of a grand music festival, a gathering of bards known as an *eisteddfod* to the Welsh. Rhys hadn't been in the room when it was first discussed. But whether his own idea or someone else's, the king had latched on to it with an urgency that would not be denied. He'd gone to Vale Royal Abbey to present the monks there with a silver cup created from Llywelyn's melted seal; he had a plan to tour all his new Welsh castles between now and Christmas Day; but somehow, he was taking a fortnight out of that short amount of time to order a thousand bards from all over Wales to play at Overton-on-Dee.

Rhys had overheard some members of the court complaining that it made no sense. The king liked music, but he didn't like it *that* much. To Rhys, however, it was plain as day that the king's purpose here was exactly the same as it had been in Caernarfon, at Llyn Cwm Dulyn, at Nefyn, and at Vale Royal Abbey: to announce from the mountain tops that Wales was conquered and would never rise again. One by one, their holy objects, their sacred sites, their history and traditions, were being taken by the king and turned to his own ends. The Welsh were never getting them back.

In all his cunning, King Edward knew that before the people could see this truth, he had to impress it upon their bards. When they dispersed after this festival, they would do the job for him.

And Rhys, God help him, would be standing at the king's side every step of the way.

Putting on a cloak of confidence he didn't feel, Rhys strode into the pavilion as if nothing was amiss. There, he found no revelers or hangers-on, just a half-dozen men, frozen as he had been a moment ago, at the king's ire. These men included Edward's steward, William de Beauchamp, the Earl of Warwick; Robert Burnell, his chancellor, visiting from London; and John de Vesci, his secretary.

At Rhys's arrival, King Edward's gaze locked on to him. "Come here!"

Rhys held his bow until he'd halted at the king's throne. "Yes, my lord?"

"Is this man's translation of that minstrel's song a true one?"

Rhys looked down at the older man the king indicated. He was slight in body, and his hood was pressed to his chest to further accentuate the respect he was paying the king while on his knees. He gazed back at Rhys with eyes as wide as serving platters.

Rhys returned his attention to the king. "My apologies, my lord, I did not hear what he said."

"Tell him!"

Though his voice trembled, the man obeyed, perhaps realizing only now the danger inherent in being the first to bring this new form of treason to the king's ear. He spoke first in Welsh and then translated his words into French, *"Cadwaladr is a spear at the side of his men; In the forest, in the field, in the vale, on the hill; Cadwaladr is a candle in the darkness walking with us; Gloriously he will come, and the Cymry will rise ..."*

"And who was it that sang thusly?" King Edward showed no signs of calming.

"One Trahaearn ap Deiniol, a bard from Llandecwyn." The man named a place in southern Eryri, what the English called Snowdonia, some twenty miles southeast of Caernarfon.

Rhys bent his head respectfully. "Yes, my lord, that is a true translation. I heard about the song myself and have already looked into Trahaearn's tent. He appears to have fled."

In the aftermath of the events at Vale Royal Abbey, following hard on the heels of those at Windsor, Rhys had found a way forward through this duty to the king. He knew his service for what it was, and he had resolved to fulfill it absolutely to the best of his abilities—right up to the moment that duty conflicted with what he knew in his soul was the greater good.

He'd determined as well that the best way to deceive his Norman masters about the big things was to speak the absolute truth about the small ones.

Not that this incident was necessarily *small*. What Rhys wasn't telling the king specifically was that he had not only heard *about* Trahaearn singing that morning, he had heard *him*. It just so happened that the bard had pitched his tent not far from Rhys and Catrin's. They hadn't been asleep, but had been lying in each other's arms, putting off their duties in the royal court for another quarter of an hour. Just before dawn, Trahaearn's baritone had filled the air, throwing his listeners into disarray.

Rhys had risen from his bed in a flash, flung on breeches and shirt, and was out the door before the last notes of the song faded.

"What in the name of all the saints do you think you're doing!" Even as he had laid into Trahaearn, Rhys had started tossing a few of Trahaearn's possessions into a satchel he'd found at the end of his pallet.

"My duty. To Llywelyn. To Gwynedd. To Wales." Trahaearn had been insistent. "How can we not sing as we have always sung?"

"You can't be that naïve! Sing whatever you want after you leave this place, but you must know the world has changed. Do you not realize the position into which you've put everyone who heard you? I have learned that I can serve our people better by living than dying, and I'm not dying for your stupidity today!"

"Worse, if we don't report you, somebody else definitely will." Catrin had arrived with a portion of cheese and bread for the road.

"I am not afraid of a martyr's death," Trahaearn said proudly. "It would show all the world who Edward truly is."

"Those of us who fought against him already know." Rhys pressed the now-full satchel to Trahaearn's chest. "Was not Llywelyn's death enough? Did you not hear how Dafydd died? Have you not seen that this king is capable of *any* cruelty?"

"More specifically, how do you feel about the removal of your tongue?" Catrin had been more blunt than Rhys. "Run. Now. Before it's fully light."

Trahaearn hadn't wanted to listen to Rhys, but Catrin's comment had finally forced the issue home. As it turned out, she had been right about the danger to Trahaearn's tongue too.

Now, as the king glared around the tent, his eyes were as hard as Rhys had ever seen them. Then he turned to Simon, who was standing stiffly off to one side. "Send men to find me this minstrel. When we open the festival this afternoon, we will begin by making an example of him."

2

Day One

Catrin

Towards noon, Catrin gazed out over the sea of faces gathered in front of the main stage, set at a sharp angle to the viewing stand, from which the king and the royal court would watch the festival's various competitions.

One thousand bards had come. That was the number reported by Huw, or rather, *Hugh,* the man charged with the organization of the festival. While he was Welsh and had been christened Huw, in recent years he had anglicized his name. Honestly, it hardly sounded any different to Catrin however he spelled it, but it appeared to be an important distinction to him. Given that he was steward to Owen de la Pole, who, in his younger years, had been known as Owain ap Gruffydd ap Gwenwynwyn, the change shouldn't have been surprising.

In point of fact, they now had only nine hundred and ninety-nine bards, since Trahaearn had successfully escaped. Any joviality in the festival participants, even if forced at times these last few days, was gone. If by now every single one of them wasn't in fear for his life, he should be. As far as Catrin and Rhys knew, nobody had seen them entering Trahaearn's tent shortly after the incident. At the very least, nobody had reported them. The man who'd reported Trahaearn to the king hadn't been a bard but one of the many merchants who'd come to the festival, running a stall that sold scented candles.

It was a fine line the two of them were walking—a knife's edge really. One slip and they might find themselves on the ground bleeding out.

Catrin hadn't asked Hugh what he thought of this new world he was living in. No man of Wales got to choose the lord he served. He followed where his lord led, and Owen had led Hugh into King Edward's arms. In truth, she couldn't begrudge Hugh whatever he did in his attempt to survive the transformation of Wales that had taken place, even as she hated it. She herself had refused to change her name to *Catherine*.

But today, if never before, she could appreciate the extent to which Hugh was caught between two worlds.

Hugh looked up from his ledger where he had been recording the names of the bards in attendance and the order of events. "Where is Moriddig, by the way?"

"I haven't seen him." As she spoke, Catrin realized the question had been somewhat rhetorical. She could hardly be expected to know where Moriddig was if Hugh didn't. Moriddig was Owen's bard in the same way Hugh was Owen's steward. If anyone should be keeping track of him, it was Hugh.

He looked back to his ledger. "We have very little time to get this right. He is supposed to walk at the front of the line. Does he really want to give Gruffydd the opportunity to lead the other bards all by himself?"

He was referring to Gruffydd ab yr Ynad Coch, who at one time had been the most renowned bard in Gwynedd, if not all Wales, since he'd sung for Llywelyn ap Gruffydd himself. Now, he served in the household of Tudur, Catrin's brother. It was a reduction in status for him, but since he was still alive when so many others were dead, she hadn't heard him complaining. He was also Moriddig's chief rival for the station of preeminent bard of Wales and for the chair of this *eisteddfod*.

From what Catrin knew of Moriddig, it was extremely unlike him not to put himself at the front and center of any ceremony or festival in which he was participating. He was *always* front and center. Admittedly, what was happening now was only the rehearsal for the main event. He still should have been the one holding the staff of chief bard and leading the procession towards the viewing stand, where in a few hours the king would be sitting.

Unless Moriddig had chosen to cede that position to Gruffydd? On the whole, that seemed as unlikely to Catrin as it was to Hugh.

Although secure in his position as Owen's household bard, Moriddig, like every other bard present, had been summoned to Overton-on-Dee by King Edward. And just as when the king had called the archers of Wales to him at Nefyn in July, he was offering a rich prize of silver for the winner. However, the point of the event, also as it had been in July, was less about the festivities *per se* than to make an accounting of all the bards of Wales.

Over the centuries, accomplished bards had been revered, in addition to being well paid by the lords who sponsored them. Now, instead of counting archers, King Edward would be recording the name of every bard. Most importantly, he had brought them here to ensure they understood to the very core of their being that their previous way of life was, for all intents and purposes, gone. If they hadn't understood that before Trahaearn's misadventure, they knew it now.

No more could they sing what they were moved to sing. No more could they compose ballads lauding the achievements of great Welsh warriors from the ancient past like Cadwaladr, the last Pendragon. No more could they convey the stories of heroic deeds to a new generation. No more were they the repositories of Welsh history and learning. Most importantly, they explicitly could *not* lament the loss of their country to the English or bewail the assassination of Llywelyn, their former ruler. From now on, they could sing praises to God; they could sing praises to the king; they could sing of the love of women or the beauty of the landscape.

There was nothing more offensive to the king's ear than to hear a song that ended *and the Cymry will rise.*

King Edward hadn't yet elucidated broadly the potential consequences of violating this stricture. But, as had been the case this morning, severe penalties had been implied. These would fall upon not only the bard who violated the rules, but also the lord who allowed him to sing an offending song in his hall and every person who listened to such a song and did not report it immediately to the king or one of his designated authorities.

Thus, Trahaearn had represented a grave threat to every person who'd heard him singing. It was no wonder the candle-maker had reported him. He'd been rewarded with a handful of silver pennies too, which was possibly more money than he would make in his stall during the entire fortnight.

None of the Welsh noblemen still alive in Wales needed to be reminded of the dire consequences of disobedience. Over the last two years, King Edward had laid waste to their brethren. Men like Owen de la Pole and Tudur, Catrin's brother, had survived the initial purge. They were thus fully cognizant of what was required of them going forward. And since any nobles still on their feet owed their station entirely to the king's largesse, it was unlikely any would be willing to commit treason this soon into their renewed tenure.

It went without saying as well that any of the Norman lords who'd been given land in Wales were even more beholden to the king than their Welsh counterparts. Certainly, none had any allegiance to a past when Wales had been independent. They, in fact, were instrumental to King Edward's plan to ensure it never would be again.

"Why don't I try to find Moriddig for you?" Catrin turned abruptly to Hugh.

"You would do that for me?" Hugh put a hand over his heart. "I would be grateful, my lady."

"It would be my pleasure." The words came easily because they were sincere. It wasn't that Catrin had any desire to speak to Moriddig. Rather, in looking over the once-great men before her, she found herself unable to stomach the extent of their diminishment even for one more moment.

3

Day One
Catrin

Catrin set off towards the rows of wagons and tents—upwards of a thousand of these as well—that occupied the fields around the festival grounds and housed everyone attending.

Trahaearn had pitched his tent two more fields over, so few had been close enough to hear him singing. Catrin and Rhys had been nearby because they valued their privacy and didn't mind having to walk farther than most to reach center of the activities. By contrast, Moriddig had found a spot closer in.

Because bards were traditionally wanderers, those with more resources than Trahaearn lived out of a covered wagon they drove from community to community, event to event, and which contained their worldly possessions. Even renowned and well-compensated bards like Moriddig and Gruffydd were still required to move from place to place, accompanying their lord while he circumnavigated his domain. With over twenty administrative centers just in Gwynedd,

Llywelyn had been known to travel from one *llys* to the next every few weeks in order to maintain his relationship with, and oversight of, every person in his country.

"Where are you off to?"

Catrin practically jumped out of her boots as her brother fell into step beside her. Hywel had come to the festival as a member of Tudur's retinue. As she'd just noted, their eldest brother was the sponsor of Llywelyn's former bard, the very Gruffydd ab yr Ynad Coch now leading the procession. *Gruffydd, son of the Red Magistrate.*

Gruffydd's father had been one of Llywelyn's legal advisors, which was how Gruffydd had come to royal attention. In Wales, lawyers and bards were both expected to be literate, so it wasn't uncommon for employment in these areas to run in families. It helped that Gruffydd's voice was also one of the finest imaginable. His position as Moriddig's primary competition this week had been well-earned.

"Moriddig didn't come to the rehearsal, so I volunteered to fetch him."

"Perhaps he mistook the time." Hywel was six inches taller than Catrin, so he had to shorten his stride to match hers. Only two years apart in age, they had been natural allies as children. They'd fought, teased, and supported each other until, at the age of sixteen, Catrin had been married to a Norman and gone to live in England. Hywel had also spent their growing up years as Rhys's best friend, since the two men were almost exactly the same age and had been thrown together essentially since birth.

The twenty years they'd spent apart hadn't changed how much she and Hywel loved each other. As with Rhys, adulthood and recent suffering had served to deepen their bond. Also like Rhys, Hywel was among the few people in this world Catrin could truly trust.

Now she scoffed. "Gruffydd is there. The only way Moriddig isn't there too is if something has happened. Perhaps he is unwell."

Hywel grinned and added in a snide tone, "Perhaps he became so puffed up with his own importance that he actually burst. Against all expectation, we are about to find ourselves rid of his pompousness forever."

Catrin put out a hand. "Don't say that. Never say that." She had spied Moriddig's wagon and picked up her pace, not liking the deserted feel of the place. If he were anywhere, he should be here.

"Don't tell me you actually *like* him?" Hywel easily kept pace.

"Of course I don't like him, but I have seen far too much death in recent years, not to say these last few months, to wish it on anyone, even someone I don't like. I certainly don't need to see any more." Her words were heartfelt, but just speaking them out loud prompted Catrin to trot the last few paces to Moriddig's wagon.

The entry at the back was blocked by canvas, with the strings tied in a tight bow holding it closed. Every other time she'd passed before now, the flaps had been hooked open to the wooden frame. Catrin rapped her knuckles on the side. "Moriddig? It's Catrin, Rhys's wife. Hugh sent me to find you. They are about to start the rehearsal! They're waiting for you." That might not be true anymore, but her words were designed to elicit a response, if anything would.

When no reply came, Catrin put her ear to the canvas door. The fabric wouldn't be thick enough to prevent her from sensing movement inside, but there was nothing to hear. In fact, the feeling in the air was still that of absence, like walking into an abandoned building and knowing without having to peer into every nook and cranny that it was empty.

"He isn't here," Hywel declared. "We should look elsewhere. Perhaps he is with his lord."

"I suppose he does have rooms at the castle, though didn't he have to give them up to someone in the king's party?" Catrin wrinkled her nose. The castle was where the king would sleep tonight, even if he was holding court in his pavilion at the festival grounds. She didn't want to walk all that way only to find Moriddig wasn't there either.

But then, just as Catrin was deciding she had no choice but to try somewhere else, Moriddig's brother arrived with a smile and a raised hand in greeting. He looked nothing like Moriddig, tall and thickset where Moriddig was slight. Though he had the physique of a workman or soldier, his hands were smooth, more accustomed to holding a pen than a blade. Like many men, as a symbol of his relative wealth, he wore a signet ring on his left hand and was dressed in finely woven clothing, which included a hood of a particularly beautiful blue color.

His name had once been Cynddelw, which his Norman masters had no notion how to pronounce. Now he was Adam, which was much simpler for them, and maybe that made Adam's life easier too. Really, it was a wonder Moriddig hadn't changed his name to something the Normans could encompass, like *Morgan* or *Marcus*. Both were pronounced essentially the same in English as in Welsh.

"I thought I might find you here," Adam said in his typically friendly fashion. "I've just come from the festival. Hugh told me you offered to look for Moriddig. He's not here either?"

"It does not appear so," Hywel said.

Adam put his hands on his hips. "Where did he go? I can't believe he would intentionally miss the rehearsal. He knows how important it is. *Moriddig*!"

Hywel bit his lip. "I would think if he could answer, he would have come out by now."

Adam wrinkled his nose, which was pretty much the only expression of annoyance he ever allowed himself. Catrin had found him to be generally of a sunny disposition, greeting everyone with a smile and a kind word. His job required it, since he was the one to smooth all the many feathers Moriddig ruffled over the course of a day. He also made sure Moriddig got to events on time, didn't overspend his money, and ate regular meals.

Prior to Edward's conquest, when Wales had been independent, household bards had been among the most trusted advisors in a lord's retinue. Some acquired as much wealth as a steward or other nobleman. Special dispensation had even been made for them within Welsh law. Thus, it was completely natural that a bard of Moriddig's standing needed someone like Adam to look after him. Bards were notorious anyway for being unreliable about everything but their work. Moriddig was actually more organized than most.

Adam was still lamenting. "We breakfasted together, and then he said he was going to warm up his voice before coming along to the rehearsal. He didn't want me to walk with him because I made him nervous. He said he would meet me there. We talked about timing his arrival so he was among the last to arrive but not the very last." The look he shot Catrin wasn't even sardonic. "It is important to maintain his status in that way."

"I was loath to enter the wagon uninvited, but I'm sure he wouldn't mind if you did," Catrin said.

"Mind? Of course he will mind. He hates being interrupted and always thinks he's right." Adam grinned as he spoke, implying that this was something to laugh about, rather than to find annoying. Then he began working at the strings holding the door closed. "Let's see if he left his *crwth*. That might tell us if he at least *intended* to attend the rehearsal."

A *crwth* was a particularly Welsh six-stringed instrument, like a lyre, but played with a bow. It was at the center of any bard's musical repertoire.

Adam finally got the strings untied and flung open the sides of the canvas door. The *crwth* was indeed hung on its hook. Below it were Moriddig's booted feet, toes pointed at the ceiling, since he was lying face up and unmoving on the floor of the wagon.

Moriddig wasn't going to lead the assembled bards at this festival today—or, in fact, ever again.

4

Day One

Rhys

Osborn Boydell, Simon's elder brother, had reached the front of the line. After waiting over an hour, it was his turn to bow before King Edward. "My king, may I introduce my family."

The more these Normans smiled at each other and made polite talk, the more impatient Rhys became with the entire endeavor. Because of his role in Trahaearn's escape, Rhys had spent the morning fearing that at any moment someone might point a finger at him, and he would find himself in chains. That constant anxiety had made it difficult for him to remain alert through all the bowing, scraping, and droning on about the majesty of the king. That said, the longer the day went on without the capture of Trahaearn or Rhys's own arrest, the less likely either were to occur.

A stooped man of forty, Osborn was one of several minor lords of this region of England who had gathered to greet the king.

Every day, he had been among those in attendance, along with his cousin, John. While younger than both Simon and Osborn, John was nonetheless the senior member of the Boydell family. His seat was at Dodleston, ten miles north of Overton.

As was common in Norman families, inheritance was based on primogeniture, and John's father had been the eldest brother in his generation. Rhys's Norman friend, Miles de Bohun, was in a similar situation. His elder brother had inherited the title of the Earl of Hereford from their father. That brother had died, leaving the title and lands to Miles's nephew, Humphrey, who was only slightly younger than Miles himself.

Still, like Miles, Osborn was doing well for himself. Last year, Queen Eleanor had appointed him steward of her new manor right here in Overton-on-Dee. In fact, it was on the manor's lands that the *eisteddfod* was taking place, and it was in the manor itself that Queen Eleanor had chosen to spend the fortnight with her ladies.

Through typically questionable means, the queen had acquired the land from its former owner, Robert de Crevequer. He was a nobleman sprung from an ancient Norman family, but one that had fought on the rebel side in the battle of Evesham during the Second Baron's War. None of the locals seemed to remember Robert fondly, except for his one service to the area, which was convincing the king to grant a charter to Overton to hold a weekly market fair.

Osborn's ancestors had also come with the Conqueror, but a more nervous man could not be found for a hundred miles. Today, he had brought his seventeen-year-old daughter, Emma, to the audience. He was hoping the king would give his approval during the coming week for an appropriate match for the girl. With her blonde hair, pale skin, and blue eyes, she was at the height of her beauty. It was fortunate for Osborn that Edward did not have a wandering eye. If one of his ancestors had been the king today, he might have taken her for himself.

Simon's children were much younger than his brother's, so he was not yet fretting over their future in quite the same way as Osborn. Through Simon's royal service, first to Prince Edmund and then to the king, he had enough wealth to bestow a dowry on the daughter he had, and a satisfactory estate of his own six miles to the east of Overton to leave to his eldest son.

Rhys was thinking now that the reason the king had granted Overton its market fair in the first place was because he knew the queen had designs on the estate. And he had chosen Overton as the site of the *eisteddfod,* so the queen could assess her new manor and its surrounding lands in person. The royal household was always one for killing two birds with one stone.

Not even a month had passed since the death of King Edward's son, Alfonso, so Rhys could hardly expect him to look on a man with a beautiful eldest daughter and four sons with favor. He also might still be smarting from the perceived treason of Trahaearn. Nonetheless, the king greeted them all with something of an avuncular look, inspecting them in order from Emma on down to the baby in Osborn's wife's arms. "Welcome, Osborn. And thank you for your service to the crown. It has not gone unnoticed. My wife is very pleased with the preparedness of the estate for her arrival."

Osborn's hand went to his chest. "It is the greatest honor of my life to serve her and you, my lord."

He spoke the truth as he knew it, as Rhys constantly had to remind himself. This encampment was so close to Wales he could practically taste it on the wind, but the whole Boydell family was as Norman as it was possible to be. There was a reason why this part of the world was known to the Welsh as *Maelor Saesneg*—English manor.

The Boydell estate, where Simon had grown up and which Osborn had inherited, was located another mile to the south. Osborn was fortunate that he wasn't expected to feed a thousand bards for a fortnight from his own pocket. Still, with the gifts, honors, and taxes arising from this event, the upcoming winter might be a lean one. He had to know that many who were associated with the queen in business matters came out the worse for wear, Robert de Crevequer among them.

All the more reason to make a good match for Emma. In the end, if everything went well, he might find himself in a better position than when he'd started.

The line of supplicants waiting to enter the king's presence had grown with each hour that passed. At one point, Simon had caught Rhys's eye and given him something of a beady look. Rhys returned it with as innocent an expression as he could muster and then endeavored not to laugh at Simon's snort of feigned disgust.

And then Hywel appeared at the entrance to the pavilion.

As a younger brother of a nobleman in favor with the king, Welsh or not, Hywel could join the line, but he couldn't just walk to the front and ask for what he wanted. There were at least twenty people between him and Rhys, and that could have been a hundred for all the difference it made. No matter the urgency, it just wasn't *done*. He could look at Rhys, however, standing as he was a step or two behind the king and, with a few motions of his fingers, tell Rhys they'd found a body.

Until two years ago, they'd served together in Llywelyn's court, which meant they'd been trained by the same men and learned the same hand signals as a means of communicating during a mission. Hywel then stepped outside again and disappeared from view. Rhys followed his shadow as he walked along the outside of the pavilion until he stopped at a point directly behind Rhys. Once Rhys took two steps back, they were separated by a matter of a few feet and the thin fabric.

While neither Rhys nor Hywel had the rank to come and go as they pleased, Simon was the captain of the king's guard. Always observant, he sidled over. "Has something happened? Did they find Trahaearn?"

"I don't know yet." That Hywel had somehow found Trahaearn and that he was dead was the first thought that had occurred to Rhys too. He took one more step back and tapped the side of the tent twice. "What news, Hywel?"

So far, nobody else had noticed their peculiar behavior. Rhys was also happy to note that Simon hadn't been able to read Hywel's hand signals. It would be disappointing to discover they'd become common knowledge.

Hywel obliged, speaking in Welsh, not realizing Simon was there to listen. "It's Moriddig, Owen de la Pole's bard. He's dead. Catrin is there already. We need you to come now."

5

Day One

Catrin

At the sight of Moriddig's dead body, Hywel had gasped, "I spoke in jest. I swear it!"

While Catrin respected those who had a strong connection to spirits and faeries and the world that couldn't be seen with the naked eye, she had never had the gift of *the sight* herself and would not have said her brother did either. But his earlier banter had become potent premonition, and she herself had taken one look at Moriddig's body and known he was dead. There was always an aura—or maybe a lack thereof—around a corpse that made it feel different from a man who was merely asleep.

Immediately, she had turned to Hywel and said, "I need Rhys."

"I don't want to leave you—"

"I will be fine. I have done this before, as you well know, and we need to begin as we mean to go on. That means Rhys. Last I saw, he was on duty in the king's pavilion."

It was because of Rhys's work that she had been left on her own during the rehearsal. Festival or no festival, treason or no treason, the king was seeing to formal business. No matter where he traveled, the work of the court went on. Catrin could have been attending to Queen Eleanor or baby Edward, but both were napping, and the queen hated to be hovered over while she slept. If they had found Moriddig alive, Catrin would have returned to the manor afterwards. Now she was going to be late—perhaps very late—and she hoped the queen would see her excuse as a good one.

As Hywel set off for the king's pavilion at a rapid walk, Adam was still refusing to accept what his eyes should have been telling him. "Moriddig! Wake up!" He tugged on one booted foot. When that garnered no response, he grunted unhappily, "How did he get this drunk between breakfast and now that he can't be woken?"

"Does he often drink to excess in the morning?" Catrin hadn't meant to start in on the questions already, but the circumstances seemed to call for it.

"Not recently. Last year he was drinking quite a bit, but he has been better these last few months. I wouldn't have thought he'd want to be impaired for the rehearsal or for his performance this afternoon before the king!"

Unfortunately, while Catrin had been distracted by the issue of Moriddig's sobriety, Adam had boosted himself into the wagon. He hadn't even used the stepstool left at the back for that purpose.

Catrin hadn't realized what he intended until he was already inside. While to her, it was obvious that Moriddig was dead, she hadn't actually spoken the thought out loud, not even to Hywel. With her brother, she hadn't needed to.

By the time she was able to say, "Adam, you don't understa—" he had discovered the truth for himself. After a choked exclamation of surprise, he sent up a high, keening wail.

"I'm so sorry, Adam, but you must quiet yourself!" This was definitely not a conversation to be had while Catrin was still outside the wagon. She grabbed the stepstool, since her clothing was not designed for clambering, and got herself into the back of the wagon too, settling on the opposite side of Moriddig's body from Adam.

"He's dead! He's dead!" The pain in Adam's voice was bottomless.

"I know he's dead, but it would be preferable if you didn't announce that fact to the entire encampment before we know how or why." It was the kind of thing she thought Rhys might say. "Maybe his killer is close by and waiting to see what happens upon his discovery."

Adam's keening cut off like the slamming of a door. "His killer? What are you talking about?" He had barely encompassed the fact that Moriddig was dead. The idea that he had been *murdered* was so far beyond him that he just stared at her, open-mouthed.

Moriddig's wagon was one of the most impressive Catrin had seen, as befitting his station as the household bard in the retinue of Owen de la Pole. A raised platform bed took up one side, and it was on the edge of the bed that Catrin was sitting. Adam had settled opposite, on one of the wooden boxes that would be secured to the side of the wagon with netting while on the move. Moriddig was lying in a narrow corridor that ran from the front of the wagon to the back. He was a small man, short and slender, so he fit in the space in a way that a much larger person like Adam would not have.

While Adam gazed at her in shock, Catrin took a moment to unhook the canvas flap that exposed the back of the wagon to the world. As she did so, she was pleased to see that nobody was within hailing distance, even after Adam's loud grieving. Everyone who had set up his tent or wagon in this field should be at the rehearsal. Those who weren't participating were likely watching.

Besides, in an encampment this large, shouts, curses, and barking dogs were commonplace, not to mention drumming, strumming, and singing. The extent to which everyone was accustomed to an excess of noise had acted to their advantage this morning. Trahaearn hadn't been the only bard starting early. It was impossible to have a thousand bards, with all their families, friends, and retainers, in one place without a certain degree of chaos. Some bards, particularly those younger and less accomplished, might have come to the festival alone, but most would have at least one person with whom they shared the road. In that, this encampment was little different from one associated with an army.

"Your brother did not die of a natural cause. You can see that from how he is laid out here on the floor, like he's waiting for burial. A man doesn't die with his hands folded on his chest."

"He could have been sleeping and died in his sleep!"

"When there's a perfectly good bed right here?" Catrin had known by instinct that Moriddig was dead before she climbed into the wagon. Now that she was beside him, he had obvious wounds around his neck that Adam in his grief had failed to see. "He was strangled, Adam."

Adam reared back, denial in every line of his body.

Catrin looked at him pityingly, and maybe it was that expression, more than her words, that had him looking at his brother more closely. "Sweet Mary. No!" He threw himself across his brother's body, hanging on like a drowning man to a floating log.

With Adam lost in his grief, Catrin gently lifted Moriddig's right arm at the wrist. His body was warm and barely stiff. That meant he had died recently, within the last two to three hours. Catrin herself would have liked to examine the body more fully right there and then, but she couldn't move Adam yet. It would have been better had she found a way to stop him from climbing into the wagon in the first place.

But since she couldn't begin again, and Rhys hadn't yet arrived, what was left to her were more questions. "I'm sorry to inquire so soon about this, Adam, but can you tell me again when you last saw Moriddig?"

"At our morning meal!" He pushed up from his brother's body, wiping at the tears on his cheeks with his fingers. As it turned out, asking a question had got him thinking instead of upsetting him further.

Until that point, Catrin had been worried he would start wailing again. "What hour would that have been?"

"I can't say exactly. Mid-morning sometime?"

"Now it's mid-day, so … three hours ago?"

"That would have been when we breakfasted. It was probably closer to two hours ago that he left. My brother didn't rise early since he keeps late hours when performing." He paused. "Kept. My brother kept late hours."

"Thank you." Catrin bent her head in appreciation. "We will ask who else might have seen him after you."

It would have been more polite to let Adam grieve in peace, but Catrin wasn't in the business of being polite, not with a murder victim in front of her. She certainly wasn't about to leave Adam alone with the body. In her experience, which admittedly wasn't all that extensive, men were usually murdered by someone they knew.

Adam had to be at the top of that list, never mind that his grief appeared very real and raw right now. With his reddened eyes and tear-streaked cheeks, she found it hard to believe that he could have murdered his brother. At the same time, his tears could have been the result of regret at what he'd done. Moriddig had been the preeminent sibling and Adam at times hardly more than his servant, even though he was the elder. Just because Adam murdered his brother, that didn't mean part of him—or even all of him—mightn't regret doing it.

With that, she'd just accused, tried, and convicted Adam with no evidence whatsoever. Probably, if she put her mind to it, she could come up with an equally plausible scenario to explain why one of Moriddig's rivals, like Gruffydd, murdered him instead. Or even his lord, Owen. This was the reason Rhys discouraged speculating. It could take an investigator down distracting paths.

"Did Moriddig have any other family? A wife, perhaps?"

"After his wife died, he never remarried and had only one son. Padrig." The answer came quickly, followed almost instantly by the correction: "Patrick. He is a bard too, as you might expect. A good one. That's who I was with after I ate breakfast with Moriddig."

This too would be easy to confirm, and for now Catrin took Adam at his word.

Then Adam let out a moan. "I'll have to tell him. He will be as distraught as I am."

"Moriddig and Patrick got along well?"

"Always." This answer was instinctive, and she saw the moment he realized it wasn't entirely true and that he needed to modify that thought as well. "Most of the time. You know how fathers and sons are. Moriddig was perhaps harder on him than he should have been. You have a son of your own, I hear."

"I do."

Adam nodded, as if that settled the matter.

Catrin had one son, Justin, from her first marriage, and her husband had been overly hard on him at times. It was fortunate for Justin that he had taken to the physical and mental tasks of a nobleman with more ease than some. Catrin hoped that one day, perhaps even this month or the next, she'd be able to tell Rhys, who had no children of his own, of a new pregnancy. She wasn't pregnant yet, and she reminded herself that they'd been married less than two months, only since the last days of July. The middle of September was hardly time enough to fall pregnant, especially at her age.

Adam knew nothing of these issues, and his tears had abated during her questioning, revealing the intelligent and fundamentally competent man she knew him to be.

"Was anything taken from the wagon that you can see?"

"Are you wondering if he came upon a thief, who killed him?" The idea seemed to cheer Adam. Then he swallowed. "I can't see anything missing. If the killer looked through the boxes, he was very neat. But—"

He paused long enough for Catrin to prompt him. "But what?"

Adam pointed to Moriddig's hand, near where she was sitting. "Moriddig's ring is missing."

"Was it one he always wore?"

"Yes. It was in memory of his wife, who gave it to him. He took it off only to play the drum, and even then he put it on a chain around his neck."

Moriddig wasn't wearing such a chain now, though that would have been a useful weapon by which to strangle him. As it was, when Catrin inspected Moriddig's hand more closely, she thought she could make out an untanned circle of skin at the base of the fourth finger. "Do you know anyone who would want to kill him?"

Despite his grief, Adam barked a laugh. "Only every single other bard here."

6

Day One

Rhys

They'd worked hard to disguise that anything was amiss, so Rhys made sure he moved casually after Hywel, without giving the appearance of hustling. As he did so, he suppressed a surge of guilt for being impatient with his job for even one moment. Anyone who'd ever been under attack—and that number included a significant portion of the men in the pavilion—knew the idiocy of wishing for action. A lack of action meant a man lived through another day. Rhys was clearly an idiot.

He left the pavilion with the hope of not disturbing those within, and he thought perhaps he had succeeded. To an outside observer, Rhys and Simon had conducted a short conversation, after which Rhys departed with neither fuss nor urgency. And then, since Math was still the one on duty standing guard outside, Rhys picked him up to come along too. Simon had known already to choose another of the guardsmen to take Rhys's place. Now he would just have to find two.

Since April, when Rhys had renewed his service to the king, he and Simon had come to rely on each other again. Rhys hadn't meant it to happen. After almost dying at Cilmeri, he had been actively avoiding attachment. But somehow, in the following five months, Rhys had acquired not only a wife but close friends again, one of whom was Simon, another Hywel, and a third, Math.

It was odd, and oddly wonderful, to be striding along with the two of them. Rhys had enjoyed mingling with any number of Welsh folk at the festival, finding himself happy to be surrounded by people speaking his native tongue. But none of them were companions in the way of Hywel, his oldest friend in life, and Math, his newest.

"What is the king going to say about this?" Hywel asked in an undertone and in Welsh.

"I don't yet know what *this* is, do I?" Before now if Rhys were to think about Moriddig at all, he would have said that he hadn't liked him very much. In truth, it was hard to imagine anyone *liking* the man. At the same time, he certainly had never wished him dead. "All you've said is that you found Moriddig's body. Though, if Catrin is there, and she sent for me, she's thinking he was murdered."

"He ate breakfast with his brother this morning, and then three hours later we find him dead on the floor of his wagon."

"Is there a chance it was just his heart failing?"

"He lies flat on his back with his hands folded on his chest, like he's asleep."

"Except he's dead," Rhys said, only partly as a question.

"That sounds like the body was arranged after death," Math put in. "A guilty conscience?"

"I can't know anything until I see it," Rhys said heavily, thinking about how many people Moriddig's death was going to affect, whether or not he was murdered. Given his stature in this community of bards, his loss was going to upset the entire event.

For starters, the king wasn't going to like the distraction from his agenda. If Moriddig had hated being upstaged, the king refused to abide it. He was already in a foul mood, knowing that the men he'd sent after Trahaearn had so far failed to recover him. Math and Rhys could only be grateful they hadn't been chosen for the task. Rhys thought it was a kindness on Simon's part and, possibly, a mistake. They were the only ones among the king's guard who spoke Welsh. Still, it was the guardsman George who'd been assigned to lead a troop of mounted soldiers from the military escort that always traveled with the king. If they didn't find Trahaearn within the next few hours, they were never going to find him at all.

The king might be furious, but Rhys privately thought it was a blessing, and not just because he didn't want to see Trahaearn's tongue cut out. The festival was already a pile of pitch wood waiting for a spark. Bards, as a whole, were independent folk, never mind that they sang for great lords. They had always been set apart from normal society and its rules. Uniquely among members of a Welsh royal court, they were tasked with speaking the truth as they saw it, and woe betide the lord who offended a bard and was subsequently memorialized in song.

Trahaearn's flight and the king's wrath might cow them for a time, as might Moriddig's death. King Edward would undoubtedly try to turn both to royal advantage. All of a sudden it occurred to Rhys that he might not even want Moriddig's killer found: *one of Wales's preeminent bards is dead? Only nine hundred and ninety-nine more to go.*

"I still find it interesting you're not questioning that there will be a killer," Rhys said, putting aside his ruminations for now.

"You didn't see the body," Hywel said. "Catrin knew it the second she saw it. It was she who sent me to you, of course."

And that could engender another spasm of guilt on Rhys's part, if he let it. Fortunately, they arrived at the wagon instead.

Catrin had seen them coming, and by the time they stopped in front of her, she had sat herself on the top step, her chin in her hands like she was a girl of seven. Her manner appeared relatively cheery. Again, how shameful was it that he'd so conditioned his new wife to murder that she could treat it with such nonchalance?

Though she'd positioned herself in such a way that it wasn't easy to see past her, Rhys could still make out the soles of a pair of boots that must belong to Moriddig.

"Where's Adam?" Hywel asked before Rhys could. As her brother, he was typically unconcerned about her feelings.

"He went to find Moriddig's son, Patrick. We're not going to be able to keep Moriddig's death a secret for very long, if even another hour. I asked Adam to bring him here, since they are the first to whom we'll need to speak." She made a motion with her head to indicate the depths of the wagon. "You should have a look at Moriddig before Adam gets back, Rhys." She then hopped down so Rhys could climb the stepstool in her place. "I know how you like to see things for yourself, so I won't say anything more until you do."

"You know me too well." He patted her shoulder as he went by.

"I wouldn't say *too* well."

At another time he would have grinned. Instead, Rhys ducked under the canvas entry and surveyed the body. Moriddig's narrow nose was pointed at the ceiling as Hywel had described. At first glance, the bard could have been asleep—until Rhys bent closer to see that Moriddig's neck was arched unnaturally and, even in the relative darkness of the wagon, the bruising of the tissues was clear.

"Strangled?" Math settled on the other side of the body without being invited. He really was growing on Rhys. "A crime of passion?"

"I can't answer that until we discover who did it," Rhys said.

Catrin came up the steps again. "Afterwards, the killer put thought into his position. Check his mouth. There's something in there. I didn't want to pull it out until you arrived. Adam didn't note it." She settled herself beside Math, while Hywel took his turn crouching on the top step. If someone passed by, they might wonder what was happening, but Hywel's station could keep them from asking.

Now that Rhys was looking closer, he could see the bit of paper stuck to Moriddig's lip. And because the body was in the early stages of rigor, he was still able to open the jaw wide enough to extract the rest which filled his mouth.

Math bent closer. "Strangled *and* suffocated?"

"Don't tempt me to speculate, Math." It was a bit of censure, but kindly meant. Before coming here, Rhys should have detoured to his tent to acquire his small leather wallet with some tools of his trade, including a pair of tweezers. As he hadn't, he was left with tugging on the paper with two fingers, as delicately as he could, so as not to rip it. "It depends on how much paper was used. It could have been stuffed into his mouth after death."

Just thinking about it made Rhys want to vomit. He hated having anything pressing at the back of his throat.

"Is it a message?" Hywel's face was bright with interest.

"And if so, to whom?" Math said. "Moriddig? Or the one who would find him."

"How could the killer have been sure who that would be?" Catrin said.

"Likely, you are the last person he'd expect," Rhys said, somewhat absently. Once he coaxed the thin piece of paper out of Moriddig's mouth, he carefully spread it flat on his knee, inadvertently smearing a bit of the ink writing as he did so, since it was moist from Moriddig's mouth. The paper was a handspan wide and equally tall. In volume, it shouldn't have been enough to choke Moriddig. For all that Rhys didn't like jumping to conclusions, Hywel was probably right that this was meant to be a message, not a murder weapon.

Even smudged, Rhys could make out a verse written in a fine hand, worthy of the bard Moriddig had been. He scooted to the end of the wagon, into the daylight, and began to read. At first, it was only to himself, but then he spoke the words out loud, having realized that what he was reading was too important to be kept from the others, even another moment.

> *Can you not sense the turmoil amongst the oaks?*
> *Do you not see the path of wind and rain?*
> *And that the world is ending?*
> *Cold my heart in fearful breast*
> *For the lion of Wales, that oaken door*
> *our warlord, our dragon-king*
> *Our Llywelyn ... is dead.*

The words were heartrendingly beautiful and utterly treasonous. The paper was signed Gruffydd ab yr Ynad Coch.

7

Day One

Math

"Nobody can know about this." Catrin had come to the end of the wagon to look over her husband's shoulder. "Nobody but us."

"And the killer." Math climbed out of the wagon after Rhys and Catrin, suddenly grateful that Simon had not come with them and that Catrin had sent Moriddig's brother away when she had.

Hywel, whom Math really hoped they could trust, was already on the ground. Although Math had been born the greater lord, his family had chosen the losing side in the last war and had refused to switch sides, even when the end was plain to see. As a result, Math's brother had ended up in an English prison. Hywel's brother Tudur, on the other hand, had defected to the king and had achieved a certain degree of favor. Even if Catrin had explained quite fervently that Llywelyn had told him to do so, Math didn't necessarily believe it.

"You don't mean the murder, do you?" Hywel said. "Just the poem."

"Just the poem," Catrin said. "We don't need to give the king another bard to mutilate, whether or not he murdered Moriddig."

"What do you mean *whether or not* he murdered him? It's his poem, stuffed into the mouth of the man he killed!" Hywel let out a sharp breath. "To think my family is sponsoring him at this festival. If this gets out, it could be the end of us too."

"Hywel." Catrin put a hand on her brother's arm. "You know Gruffydd, better than most. Does strangling a man after the morning meal really seem like something he'd do? Have you ever even seen him angry?"

Catrin's words caused Hywel to stop and think. "I guess not. He's a jovial fellow on the whole. Generous, always. Much like Adam."

"If Gruffydd decided to murder Moriddig," Math said, not sorry to be able to counter Hywel too, "it would have been in the heat of the moment. And if he did murder him, would he really be stupid enough to incriminate himself by stuffing his own poem into his mouth? Whatever Gruffydd may be, he is not stupid."

Hywel was starting to nod. "I have always found him to be honest. If he had murdered Moriddig, he would have walked into the king's pavilion and announced his guilt. He wouldn't be subtle about it."

"We don't want him to have done it, that's clear." Rhys cut through their talk. "We can come up with every reason on earth why he couldn't have. But it is wrong of us to dismiss this. We all have faced demons these last two years. It is safe to say that Gruffydd has as well."

Hywel was still thinking. "Maybe he didn't even write the poem. Anyone could have signed his name to it."

"It couldn't have been just anyone," Rhys said. "The style is very much Gruffydd's, and few would have had access to a poem we know for certain Gruffydd is not sharing widely."

"So the killer is someone who hates Gruffydd *and* Moriddig," Math said. "If the murderer is not Gruffydd, I can't think of a better way to take down both."

"Imagine if anyone other than us had found the poem?" Catrin's expression turned pensive. "Imagine if Adam alone had found it. He was on his way to the wagon; Hywel and I arrived only a few moments before he did."

"He would have shouted for Gruffydd's head from the ramparts," Hywel said, as sure of Gruffydd's innocence now as he had been a moment ago of his guilt. "The king would have had him hanged, drawn, and quartered before dinner, practically before Gruffydd even knew of what he was accused."

"I don't like to rely on luck, but we were lucky," Catrin said.

"Again." Math shot a meaningful look at Rhys and Catrin, thinking of their intervention with Trahaearn. It had been an eventful day, and it was barely past noon.

"I read you the poem because, once heard, it cannot be forgotten," Rhys said. "I do believe Gruffydd could have written it."

"It does sound like him," Hywel admitted, "and if we hadn't found it in the mouth of a murdered man, I couldn't have been more proud to have him in my brother's household."

"We will start by asking him," Rhys said.

Catrin's reply was to point to the paper in her husband's hands. "Put that away right now."

Rhys did as his wife bid, not asking why, especially since she was already stepping past him to greet Adam and Patrick, who were just arriving. Math had also been so intent on the conversation that he hadn't noticed them coming. It was a poor performance, on the whole, for two of the king's guards to be caught so unaware.

Adam had his arm around the shoulders of his nephew, who took after him physically far more than his father. It was obvious to anyone looking at the pair that they were related.

While Catrin held out her hands to Patrick, Rhys stayed facing away, his back to the newcomers so he could fold the paper into a small square without them noticing. Then he handed it to Math, who took it unquestioningly, accepting that he was less likely to be noticed by Adam, since Rhys was the real authority here in terms of the investigation. Math didn't believe for a moment that Rhys would pass off the paper so he wouldn't be caught with it and would in no way be surprised to find that he wanted it back just as quickly. Rhys was like that. He would be trying to protect *Math*.

Once again, they were in this together, however one described *this*.

Even so, since Math was dressed identically to Rhys, in armor that didn't exactly provide him with a plethora of pockets, he at first didn't know what to do with the paper anymore than Rhys had. After a moment's consideration, he tucked it into the bracer on his forearm. He'd already built a secret sleeve within the leather for a tiny knife blade. He'd never been called to use it, but one could never be too prepared.

"My father really is dead?" Patrick stared into the back of the wagon.

Initially, Hywel had shifted to block his view, but then, at a look from Rhys, gave way enough for the young man to see his father's unmoving form.

"I am so sorry for your loss," Rhys said.

Patrick reached out a hand towards his father's foot but then drew it back. "My uncle told me he was dead, but I didn't believe it until now."

Rhys put a hand on his shoulder. "I must leave you now to speak to my commander and likely the king. After that, I assure you we will do everything in our power to discover who did this to him."

Patrick turned his head to stare at Rhys, his brown eyes disconcertingly wide. "Wh-who did what to him?"

Rhys hesitated as he looked past Patrick to Adam. "You didn't tell him?"

"What could I say?" Adam put up both hands in a helpless gesture. He looked like he'd aged ten years, so drawn and white was his face. "I couldn't tell him the whole of it."

In the pause that followed, Math took it upon himself to stand eye-to-eye—and man-to-man—with Patrick. The two of them were close in age, and he thought the truth might be easier coming from him. "Your father was murdered. We don't know the full circumstances; in fact, we don't know anything about Moriddig's movements this morning other than what Adam was able to tell Catrin. Did you see your father this morning?"

"No." Patrick was swallowing repeatedly. Math had thrown a whole raft of information at him. Fortunately, he latched onto the last sentence, as Math hoped he would. "He hates to be disturbed in the morning. I learned that a long time ago."

"What about last night? He often stayed up late ..." Math let his voice trail off, asking a question without asking it, wanting Patrick to fill in the rest of the thought on his own.

"I'm not sure what he did. What does it matter since he was seen this morning?"

"We are just trying to get a sense of his movements." *And yours* went unsaid in Math's mind.

Patrick obliged with a definitive answer. "He and I practiced long yesterday afternoon, separately and together, and then had a meal. Afterwards, I was invited to a gathering of other bards from Powys, younger ones, not my father's concern. I was with them until after the midnight hour. Then I went to my tent."

"Alone?" Hywel asked softly, speaking for the first time since Adam and Patrick had arrived.

"Alone, my lord," Patrick said firmly. "I know better than to become distracted in the midst of an *eisteddfod*. If my father saw me with a woman, he would have my head!" Then he stopped and swallowed hard. "He would have had. Poor choice of words."

For a bard, a poor choice of words or a slightly incorrect turn of phrase could be the difference between maintaining his position and being thrown out of his lord's household on his ear. Moriddig himself had always been one for flowery phrases, august proclamations, and using ten words when two would do. Prior to the conquest, a Welsh bard went through a decade of training as an apprentice, memorizing tens of thousands of lines of poetry, in order to finally achieve the lowest status of bard. As a result, bards had a habit of working what they'd memorized into daily conversation.

The highest-ranking of all bards were the *pencerdd,* the master bard for the kingdom, followed by the *bardd teulu,* the household bard.

For Gwynedd, the *pencerdd* was Gruffydd ab yr Yfan Coch.

For Powys, it had been Moriddig.

8

Day One
Rhys

Rhys halted outside the king's pavilion, a strange pause settling on him. He'd given himself the task of lying to Simon and the king again, during which time Hywel and Catrin (original poem in hand) would speak to Gruffydd, and Math would remove the body to a place where they could better examine it.

This moment was to be remembered, when life was simpler. His announcement was sure to throw all who heard it into disarray, and right now it was known to just a few. *Right now,* Moriddig was dead only to his brother and son. Everybody else still thought he was alive and getting ready to sing for the court as he'd done the previous evening.

Moriddig had viewed himself as special in a way Rhys found more usual amongst the most elite jousters or archers. As a rule, within a lord's personal guard, or the religious/military orders like the Templars, men had to work as part of a team towards a common goal. Rhys had felt that way when he had served Llywelyn, and he still felt that way (almost despite himself), as a member of King Edward's guard.

There was a reason a Welsh leader's personal guard was called a *teulu,* which translated best to *family*. As the captain of King Edward's guard, Simon had been working hard to foster that same feeling amongst a very disparate group of men, knowing as well as any soldier that a war was not won when each man fought for himself and his own glory. That was for the ancients. Or for Danes.

Bards worked much the same way. There was little more enjoyable than watching a number of bards come together to sing or play just because they could. Because it was fun for them too.

An *eisteddfod*, like a martial tournament, could bring out the competitive side of the bardic tradition, with each man focused on advancing his own standing and acclaim. Rhys hadn't seen much of it this week, however, except in men like Moriddig, who just couldn't seem to help lording their station and abilities over others. In general, the best bards took on the role of teacher and saw it as their duty and honor to raise up a new generation of musicians. Sometimes a bard took on an apprentice, or had a son to train, enjoying a reflected glory in the accolades accorded the younger version of himself.

This camaraderie had been particularly evident this week. If one man's life was on the line for daring to sing about a forbidden topic, then all of their lives could be in danger. Trahaearn had violated that compact.

By now, news of his flight had spread throughout the encampment, and the unity of purpose, even among the highest ranking bards, was in full effect. It was for this reason Rhys was honestly surprised Moriddig had been murdered. The community of bards was genuinely that: a community. Moriddig, for all his prickliness, was one of them. On the whole, Rhys was quite sure the bards had never before felt this vulnerable. Just on his walk back to the king's pavilion, he'd heard one bard assuring another he was going to do as he was told while they were here because he wanted to live to sing another day.

Rhys caught Simon's eye within moments of his arrival in the pavilion. He didn't walk directly to him, but navigated through the throngs of hangers-on with a smile here and a nod of greeting there. Simon's brother, Osborn, was still present, standing next to his cousin, within reach of the king. Given their favorable reception today, it might even be that Emma would leave the festival an engaged woman.

"How bad is it?" Simon met Rhys halfway across the pavilion, and they walked together a few more paces to some tables covered by the remains of a meal Rhys had missed.

"Moriddig was murdered. Strangled, unquestionably. As we speak, Math is moving the body so I can better examine it out of sight of any prying eyes."

"Is it too early to ask if you have any suspects?"

Rhys coughed a laugh. "We just found the body, Simon. Give us an hour at least!"

"I suppose, with a thousand bards here, you have a thousand suspects." As Rhys had hoped, Simon responded with a smile and a clap on the back. The moment of joviality thus masked his glaring omission.

"It might appear so at first blush, but most people are murdered by someone they not only know but know well. It is one thing to kill a man in the heat of battle. It is another to come into his wagon and strangle him. Whoever did this will have left clues to his identity. We just have to find them."

"Was there no obvious evidence at all?"

"Two things. According to his brother, Moriddig's ring is missing, so we can't exclude theft as a motive. The second is that Moriddig had a piece of paper stuffed into his mouth. The writing on it is illegible now, so we don't know if he tried to eat it to prevent the killer from finding it, or if the killer stuffed it into his mouth as part of the murder." Again, under the principle that the best lies were founded in truth, the four conspirators had agreed that this was the story Rhys had to tell.

"That's ... unusual." Simon frowned. "Are you implying this killer is literate?"

Rhys looked at his friend a bit sideways. "Every bard here can read and write, which means many members of their families can too."

"I had no idea. A first for me, certainly." Simon gave a shake of his head, reminding Rhys that he was such a good leader because he was willing to admit ignorance. To be fair, as a Norman, he would have no way of knowing that Wales had a rich tradition of literature and laws long before his people came to Britain. "The fact that the killer can read and write is therefore not going to help in finding him. You're telling me this will take time."

"As I'm not standing here with the man in chains already, it will definitely take time. As you said, I have a thousand men to sift through!" Rhys pushed down any more thoughts of Gruffydd and his poem. He needed the true story so far back in his mind that he almost forgot it. That's how he'd suppressed his lies about the death of King Edward's son, Alfonso. It might even be, in the years to come, that he himself wouldn't be able to truly recall what part of the story they'd told was the truth and what was lies. He knew, better than most, what an infinite capacity humans seemed to have to lie to themselves in order to preserve their own existence or personal integrity.

Simon sighed. "At the very least, you'll have dozens of people to question."

"That is unfortunately true, but first—" Rhys took in a breath, "—it was my thought to speak directly to the king."

Simon bared his teeth in something of grimace. "Are you sure you don't want me to give him the news in your stead?"

"I appreciate the offer and will give way if you think I should, but I think I should begin as I mean to go on."

"God help us all." It was meant as a jest, and Simon shot him a grin before making his way back to the king's side.

They had a brief conversation, and then William de Beauchamp stepped to the fore to clap his hands. That was the signal indicating the general audience was over. It was not without precedence for the king to send everyone away while he attended to matters of state.

There was some milling about as people departed, which allowed Rhys to come closer unremarked. He wore the king's livery and, for all intents and purposes, was as notable as one of the posts holding up the canvas roof. There was a moment where he and Prince Edmund exchanged a glance. Truth be told, they'd mostly avoided each other since Edmund's arrival at the king's encampment. There would have to be a reckoning between them, but with another murder investigation before Rhys, it wouldn't be today.

Once everyone not vital to the court was gone, Rhys bowed to King Edward, "My lord, I have some grave news."

"Simon implied as much. Spit it out. I'm sure I'm not going to like whatever it is." The king's tone was as dry as only Edward's could be.

"I fear that's the case, my lord. I heard you say last night that you enjoyed the singing of Moriddig, Owen de la Pole's court bard. A moment ago, I saw with my own eyes that Moriddig has been murdered."

As was typical for him, King Edward contained his expression, sitting for a breath or two with his elbow on the arm of his throne and his fingers to his chin. Then he said, "How?"

"He was strangled, my lord."

With that, the tension that had momentarily crept into the demeanor of the men around the king eased, even as William asked, "It wasn't poison, then?"

Rhys understood the reason for the concern. Poison as a means of murder was difficult to guard against, especially herbs that were slow-acting. King Edward had been poisoned in the Holy Land, and even if that had been at the hand of a man he thought to be a diplomat, the fear remained. Although the king didn't know it, his son Alfonso had been poisoned too. That was the secret Prince Edmund and Rhys were keeping from him.

By contrast, with his guard around him, plus all these other men who served him, nobody with the intent to strangle the king was ever going to get close enough to do it.

"No, my lord. The bruises on his neck are clear," Rhys said. "I can have Simon look to confirm."

The king waved a hand. "That won't be necessary. I trust you."

I trust you.

Rhys disguised his moment of emotion with a bow. He was honored by the trust. He couldn't help it. And also disgusted that he wanted and needed it from one of the men he hated most in the world. As he came up, he briefly met King Edward's eyes and knew two things without having to ask: the first was that Moriddig's death would not be deemed enough of a crisis to warrant a discontinuance or postponement of the festival. The second was that the king really did trust him and wanted him to continue as his *quaestor*.

When they'd been at Vale Royal Abbey, Rhys and Catrin had briefly considered running away to some part of Wales or the world where nobody knew them. A significant portion of Rhys had wanted to. In the end, they had decided it wasn't really possible. As he turned away from the king, Rhys once again told himself that while God had not seen fit to save Llywelyn, He had saved Rhys and put him right here, right now, for a reason.

Simon joined him at the entrance to the pavilion. "This is a moment where I am not your superior, my friend. You are the king's quaestor. What do you need, other than Math, whom you have already appropriated? Do you have enough help?"

Torn, Rhys pressed his lips together in thought. He did have too much work to do in too short a time and only one of him to do it. But the poem had him worrying about opening wider his circle of trust. "Hywel was with Catrin when she found the body, praise be, and they are going to make a start. I do have Math, as you said. If necessary, I was hoping I could borrow one or another of our men when they are off-duty."

"Of course." Simon bobbed his head.

"Then let's leave it there for now. The dead man was Welsh, even if he served a Norman, and I know my people well enough to know that no Norman is going to get the whole truth out of them. First, before I examine the body, I will tell the bards gathering at the main stage what has transpired. Rumors will have started by now anyway, and maybe I can head off the worst of them. Although Math should be on the way to the castle even now, I would ask that you go too and personally speak to Owen de la Pole, if you will. This is news he must hear immediately but wouldn't want to hear from me."

Simon *tsked* under his breath. "You give me all the best jobs."

"I will pray for you, as always, as I walk away."

Rhys was grinning as he did exactly that.

9

Day One

Catrin

Catrin's brothers had been in Nefyn for King Edward's tournament there, and thus had witnessed her wedding to Rhys. Although she hadn't seen Hywel since then, it was still less than two months since they'd spoken. As they'd been apart for twenty years before that, she was still getting used to having brothers again. There had definitely been times during all those years in England where she had felt abandoned to her fate. And still, given that they were suddenly embroiled in another investigation, if she couldn't have Rhys at her side, Hywel really was the next best person.

Hywel himself might also still be getting used to having a grown woman for a sister. On the one hand, he had left her with a dead body as if it were nothing. On the other, a dozen times since the two of them had been walking together on their way to find Gruffydd, he'd looked at her out of the corner of his eye.

Finally, she said, not without exasperation, "What?"

He put one hand up, somewhat defensively. "I was only think-ing that marriage to Rhys suits you."

She softened. "It does; it really does."

"I knew when we sent you to England all those years ago that you might not be happy. It wasn't that I didn't care, but I didn't know what it meant. I regret being so cavalier with your life."

"You've said as much to me before," Catrin said gently. "It was my life, and even if much of it I would have preferred not to ex-perience, I had to find happiness where I stood. Those twenty years gave me a son, and they also brought me to where I am today. Rhys and I both have struggled with our present circumstance, Rhys more than I, but—"

"Serving the king, you mean?"

"That surprises you?"

"If it is a struggle for him, he doesn't show it."

"He'll be glad to know that. At times it feels like a lifetime has passed just since our wedding, not to mention since April."

"I'm not sure that's a good thing! And it sounds like a story you need to tell me."

That Hywel hadn't realized the extent of Rhys's grief was a testament to how profoundly Rhys was swallowing it down. "Maybe not today." Catrin gave him a small smile.

Hywel gave way, thankfully unaware of how momentous that story might be, were she ever to be able to tell it. Catrin and Rhys had shared a meal with Hywel and Tudur when they'd first arrived, at which time they'd related something of the events at Windsor and Vale Royal Abbey. They hadn't been able to speak the whole truth of what had happened to Prince Alfonso, not even to her brothers. Even so, she was sure her sorrow at the melting down of Llywelyn's seal had bled through the telling.

"Let me see. You investigated murder in Caernarfon; and then more murder at Nefyn; then the death of the king's son in Windsor; and finally those deaths at Vale Royal Abbey." He ticked the items off on his fingers. "And now Moriddig is dead too. I can't decide if this number of strange incidents should be normal for a royal court, which I never noticed until you became involved, or if this is something new."

"I wasn't in the royal court before two years ago either." Catrin frowned. "I imagine, as with anywhere, people of all ages die. I have never taken the time to separate those deaths that occur in warfare or childbirth from murder. After a while, they just wash over you like swells in the ocean. Rhys says most murders aren't that hard to solve because it's one man going at another with a knife in a tavern brawl. This one, like the others we've seen of late, appears to be more than that."

"I'm looking forward to watching you work."

They arrived back at the rehearsal, which was currently ongoing for the nine hundred and ninety-eight bards who had survived the day so far. Sensibly enough, Hugh had decided he couldn't keep everyone waiting any longer and had begun without Moriddig, as he would have to do from now on. The rehearsal had progressed to the point that the remaining senior bards, Gruffydd among them, had paraded past the king's currently empty seat. They had then clustered to one side to watch the rest of the bards bow to the empty throne and then move on.

The entire ceremony would be repeated later this afternoon before sunset, with the king and the court present. The weather was even cooperating. The king's viewing stand was roofed, as was the stage, but no pavilion could hold a thousand people at once—and that was just with the performers. Like the tournament in Nefyn, this was an event attended by thousands more people, including tinkers and merchants, gamblers and thieves, and common folk in large numbers. It was not an event to miss, even for those who hadn't been commanded to attend.

It occurred to Catrin that, for all that this festival was about the bards, it was the common audience who was the real object of the king's strictures. It was their way of life the king intended to transform, beginning with the music they heard.

Since Gruffydd was a member of their brother's household, Catrin and Hywel didn't have to disguise their approach or make up an excuse to talk to him. Hywel took the lead, striding right up to Gruffydd and greeting him with a clasped forearm, after which he introduced Catrin.

Gruffydd took Catrin's hand and bowed over it. "It was a shame our lives were deprived of your beauty all these years. You were much missed. But we are delighted to have you returned to us."

It was typical flowery bard-speak to the sister of his patron. They were just three friends, talking as friends do. None of the nearby bards did more than glance their way.

"Thank you, Gruffydd," Catrin said, before adding in an undertone, "You may be less delighted when you hear why we are here."

Hywel motioned with his head, and they got Gruffydd to move some ten paces farther away, stopping near the stone wall that demarcated this particular field. Once there, Catrin, who'd taken Gruffydd's poem back from Math and secreted it in her purse before leaving Moriddig's wagon, pulled it out.

He started reading, and immediately his face paled. "Where did you get this?"

"Is it yours?" Hywel wasn't giving an inch, no matter the apparent extent of Gruffydd's shock and that Hywel had agreed earlier that Gruffydd wouldn't have murdered Moriddig. Gruffydd was his man, or at least his family's, so any wrongdoing on Gruffydd's part would reflect directly back to them. He had to be sure.

"Yes, it's mine." Instead of matching Hywel's intensity, Gruffydd let out a slow breath. "Let me show you." With something of a surreptitious look at his fellow bards, all of whom were looking away, he pulled a piece of paper from within his jacket. "Here's the whole poem as it is so far."

"There's more?" Hywel practically snatched the paper from his hand. Then, as he began to read, his stance softened considerably. "I have never read its like."

"It will be beautiful when it's done," Gruffydd said softly, "if it is ever done and if it can ever be sung."

"It must be." Catrin spoke fiercely. "To this day, nobody has sung of him. It is your task. You must finish it."

"I do know that, but—" He made a helpless gesture in the direction of the stage where Hugh had put up his hands to gain everyone's attention. "How?"

"You will find a way." Somehow, Catrin was sure.

"Not if he's hanged for murder." Hywel was still reading the lines on the paper.

"What did you say?" Gruffydd had moved to stand very close to him, half-shielding him from the view of anyone in the field. Even if Trahaearn hadn't fled this morning, King Edward had made it clear he would give short shrift to any bard who violated his edicts. If a Norman connected the poem to Gruffydd, and how could he not since he'd signed it, Gruffydd could find himself condemned by sundown. By now too, Gruffydd was catching on that something more was wrong here than the finding of his poem, which was bad enough. "What is this really about?"

Catrin studied the bard, uncertain how much she was ready to say. Hywel, to his credit, controlled whatever impulse he may have had to treat her like his little sister and answer for her. Then, in the periphery of her vision, she caught sight of Rhys arriving. He must have finished speaking to the king, and his task now was to inform the rest of those assembled here that Moriddig was dead.

In a moment, she would run out of time to tell Gruffydd the news herself, and she definitely wanted to watch his face when she did. To that end, she put a hand on Gruffydd's arm, to ensure he was looking at her when she spoke. "Moriddig was murdered this morning."

Then Hywel added, on his own recognizance, "What's more, my friend, we found this piece of your poem stuffed into his mouth."

10

Day One
Math

Moriddig's body was already in the wagon, so all Math had to do was hitch a horse to it and move it. Before Rhys left, he had insisted that both Patrick and Adam stay behind with Math. If Rhys's first task was to speak to the king, it wouldn't do at all for either man to be wandering the festival, spreading the tale of Moriddig's loss before those in authority were aware of it.

Math trusted nobody more than Rhys. Math himself, for all that he was a member of the king's guard, conversed with the king rarely, and only when King Edward asked him a direct question. Maybe that would change in time; Math's service was less than two months old. He had reached this point because he'd been willing to stand out when it mattered—namely at that archery contest at Nefyn. Despite being admitted to the king's guard as a result, he was in no hurry to stick his neck out again.

For now, despite the fact that Patrick and Adam sat silently weeping on the wagon seat, Math was feeling adequately entertained. He would have to ask forgiveness at his next confession for being glad he had something to do besides stand outside the king's pavilion. As it turned out, constant vigilance was both boring and exhausting at the same time. He was quite sure Rhys felt the same way. The king required able and accomplished men to guard him, but the duty itself was at best routine. At worst, it was cripplingly dull.

Math walked at the front of the wagon, leading the horse. They had deliberately collected Moriddig's own horse from the corral for this purpose. Some of the onlookers they passed might be wondering why they were moving Moriddig's wagon in the middle of the day, but Adam and Patrick were a familiar-enough sight that nobody should be thinking about it very hard.

Yet.

Everyone would know soon enough that Moriddig was dead, at which point, those who'd witnessed the removal of the wagon would be at the center of gossip Math could hear even now:

"I can't believe Moriddig was murdered!"

"Who could have done such a thing?"

"Do you think his body was actually in his wagon when it passed us?"

"I never liked the man myself, but far be it from me to speak ill of the dead."

And so on.

The question before them, as Math had come to see since he'd joined the king's guard and begun his association with Rhys and

Catrin, was how exactly they were to sift through everything they would be hearing over the next few days for the truth amidst the lies. People *would* lie, too, about far more than the murder. Everyone kept secrets and hid shameful things, some of which had occupied them while someone else had been murdering Moriddig.

"We'll need to turn here," Math called behind him to Adam. "We want the castle, not the church."

"But surely—" Adam broke off to reorient his thoughts, "— with the king in residence—"

"The church doesn't have a room set aside for examining the body, and Rhys needs one." Math appreciated Adam's concern. He didn't want to offend the king either, but that didn't change the reality before them. "Moriddig was Owen's man; he should lie in Owen's castle, whether or not that's where the king is also laying his head. Rhys investigated deaths in Caernarfon and Nefyn while the king was present. Rhys is *his* quaestor. It matters not whether the castle is the king's own or Owen's."

This particular castle had been built a hundred years or more ago by the patriarch of Simon's family, after which time the King of Powys had taken the castle for himself. It was more than a little ironic that Owen was doing everything in his power to make everyone forget he was half-Welsh, when it was his Welsh ancestors who'd overcome Simon's. Undoubtedly, that long-ago king was rolling over in his grave to see his descendants bowing and scraping to those who'd been his enemies.

Math served the king now because he had no choice. Clearly neither did Owen de la Pole. But although Owen's lands had been bestowed on him by the king, he could never be fully trusted. A man who had betrayed one liege could equally betray a second. Math's family, except for a momentary lapse early on, had been staunchly behind Llywelyn to the bitter end. Everybody knew it, knew he was Welsh, and didn't expect him to somehow become Norman overnight as the Poles had done.

Owen's allegiance had never really been to Wales, even if his father had nominally sworn himself Llywelyn's vassal. Owen's mother was sister to Roger le Strange himself, one of the chief conspirators responsible for the murder of Llywelyn at Cilmeri. Math wasn't sure Owen even spoke Welsh fluently. As far as Math could tell, Owen was fully aware of what everyone thought of him and didn't care.

The castle had remained in Owen's family all this time, and these days was just one of many within Owen's remit. That wasn't to say Simon's family bowed to him, despite losing their castle. Neither Simon, his brother, nor their cousin John owed personal allegiance to anyone but King Edward. John Boydell had received his lands directly from the king as a descendant of the original Boydell who'd come with the Conqueror. In fact, the Boydell family could claim kinship through marriage to the royal family.

That the king would retire at night to Owen's castle during this fortnight was as much a matter of convenience as a mark of Owen's standing. Queen Eleanor and baby Edward were staying at her manor, of which Osborn was steward, implying that the Boydells were equally trusted.

The castle was built on high ground on the eastern bank of the River Dee, with a grand view to the west (and thus Wales). St.

Mary's Church, where the service for Moriddig would occur, was built on relatively flat land within the town, some distance to the southeast. The festival was taking place in a cluster of fields to the east of the castle and town. There were also flat lands around the river Dee, but these were marshy and unsuited to wagons and tents.

As they arrived at the main castle gate, Math didn't bother speaking Welsh. "We request admittance," he said in French, and then he added, *s'il vous plaît*, as something of an afterthought.

"What is this about, Adam?" The guard at the gate stepped forward. "I thought you were staying at the encampment."

"We were."

Math had seen the guard take in the sigil on his tunic. Anyone could see that he served the king and truly he should have recognized Math anyway, since Math had been in and out of the castle all this week, guarding the king as he slept. And still, his eyes narrowed distrustfully. "Has something happened?"

"Yes," Math took charge again. "But it is for your lord's ears to hear first. I am Math, a member of the king's guard and companion to Sir Reese de la Croix." He didn't like pronouncing Rhys's name the Norman way, but he was hoping for cooperation. Math was not a Norman name, but it was understandable to Normans, more so than his full name, *Mathonwy*.

"At once." The guard motioned that they should drive into the outer bailey. Math would have to let Rhys know that the mention of his name had a greater effect on the guard than the king's!

The circling wall around the castle was built of wood and, from the dryness and weathering of the planks within view, hadn't been renewed recently. The keep, on the other hand, had been converted to stone, and portions of the bailey had been laid with flagstones, so any rain wouldn't turn it to mud.

"Lord Pole is here; I will tell him you have arrived and have news for him." Having left another man to take his place at the gate, the guard set off at a loping run for the great hall, which was the largest building in the bailey.

At that point, Patrick began to openly sob. Adam helped him down to the ground and then said to Math, "I'll take care of him. He needs a restorative drink."

At Math's nod, the pair disappeared into the kitchen, a building near the hall but standing apart from it. Math was thus left alone to wait for Owen, during which time he could feel the wondering eyes of the various workers in the bailey, otherwise going about their business. Finally, the door to the great hall opened and the half-Norman lord stepped out. Owen was similar in age to Math, not even thirty, though with his receding hairline, he looked much older.

He gave no explanation for the delay but said abruptly upon approaching Math and the wagon, "I spoke to the king this morning. Does he want me back in his pavilion?" The query was almost aggrieved. In truth, his voice always sounded to Math like it had a bit of a whine to it.

"My apologies, my lord. I am here on an entirely different matter." Math bent his head in an attempt to be respectful. He figured if he apologized continually, he might be able to mask his disdain. "I am sorry to report that your bard Moriddig is dead, and his body lies within his wagon. I am charged with finding a place to leave him until such a time as the body itself can be examined." He intentionally didn't mention Rhys's name yet or that Moriddig had been murdered. Owen would know Rhys, but Math didn't know if Rhys's animosity towards him was returned and wanted to leave the news that it was Rhys himself who would be examining the body until later.

Meanwhile, Owen was openly gaping. "I can't believe it! I spoke to him yesterday evening. He really is dead?"

"If you would look this way, my lord, you can see for yourself." Math gestured towards the back of the wagon. Moriddig *was* dead, and no amount of disbelief on the part of Owen or anyone else was going to change that fact. Math opened the flaps to reveal Moriddig as they'd left him, still flat on his back, though now covered by a sheet. Owen was tall enough to see the way Moriddig's nose made a bit of a tent of the linen.

"I see." Owen gazed at him through several breaths before turning back to Math. "I suppose you'll be wanting to put him in our dead house to prepare him for burial." *Dead house* was the Norman term, borrowed from the Saxons, for a laying-out room. Math enjoyed how bluntly to-the-point it was. "But what's this about examining it?"

It was only in that moment that Math realized he should have been more forthcoming. He was just opening his mouth to explain about the murder when Simon rode through the gatehouse with a clatter of hooves. As Math's superior, Owen turned to him immediately, beating the stable boy to Simon's side and holding the reins as Simon dismounted.

"My bard is dead." Owen's tone implied the very fact of it was offensive.

Simon bent his head. "I'm afraid so, my lord. My apologies for not coming sooner but I was delayed with the king." As excuses went, it was a good one and certainly not something about which Owen was going to argue. "He was murdered this morning. The king has tasked Math and me, as adjutants to Sir Reese de la Croix, with discovering why."

11

Day One
Catrin

"Was it—did it—was it the poem that killed him?" Such was Gruffydd's shock that he actually stuttered. For a bard of his standing, that was unheard of.

"No. The current evidence points to him being strangled." Then Catrin clarified more bluntly. "Someone strangled him."

Gruffydd let out a puff of air. "Moriddig and I didn't always see eye-to-eye—" he made a motion with his head, "—well rarely, anyway, and not just because he was so short, but I would never have wished him dead! Least of all by my poem."

Hywel stabbed a finger towards the paper still in Gruffydd's hands. "How did it get into his mouth?"

"I don't know!" Outrage, which Catrin had never seen in Gruffydd before, suddenly flared. "I certainly didn't put it there."

Hywel glowered at him. "You have to admit it looks bad."

"I can't help that."

"When was the last time you encountered Moriddig?" Catrin thought it was time to bring the level of emotion down a notch.

"I saw him this morning sitting with his brother at the morning meal. Then he left. I had just arrived, having arisen later than perhaps I should have done. I did not see him again." Conveniently, he'd just confirmed Adam's story.

"What did you do after the meal?" Catrin asked.

"I played, as I do every day." He waved a hand in the general direction of the stage. Hugh was now speaking to the last group of a hundred or so bards. These would be those in the lowest echelon, mostly apprentices. Moriddig's son should have been among them, but he was still with Math. "I confess, I was somewhat resentful of the requirement to spend half the day here. I was told attendance was mandatory."

"As were we," Hywel said. "Why did you think he didn't come?"

Gruffydd shook his head. "Moriddig's standing is such that he is able to decide what is or is not worth his time. He is Owen de la Pole's man, and Owen has the king's favor, which means Moriddig, at least, can do precisely as he wishes." Gruffydd spoke of Moriddig as if he were still alive. Because they were speaking in Welsh, he could have said *Owain*, in reference to Owen de la Pole. Instead, he'd pronounced the lord's name the English way.

Catrin didn't begrudge Gruffydd the tinge of derision in his voice either. She heard the same undertone in Rhys's whenever he said Owen's name too. "Was anyone else with you?"

"My apprentice, Rory."

Catrin tipped her head to hear the name. "From Ireland?"

"He has an Irish mother. The Normans are able to pronounce Rory better than Rhodri, so he keeps to it."

"He wouldn't be the only one." Hywel spoke without emphasis, merely stating the plain fact.

Catrin gazed towards the cluster of young bards. "Can you point him out?"

"At the back, there, in blue. Red hair."

Hywel grunted. "My eyes aren't what they once were."

"I see him." Catrin was standing on her tiptoes. "Can he attest to your whereabouts?"

"Didn't I just say so?" Gruffydd cleared his throat. "If you need more, you can ask Rhiannon, my wife. She was with us all morning too, even walking me here before returning to our wagon."

"She didn't trust you to make it to the rehearsal on your own?" Catrin said.

Hywel's mood had improved dramatically with the elaboration of Gruffydd's alibi, and he was the one to laugh. "She did not. And for good reason."

At Catrin's sour look, Gruffydd hastily put up one hand. "She isn't worried about my fidelity! Nothing like that. If I'm left on my own, I have been known to wander about. I might get an idea for a new song and never arrive at the place where I was supposed to go." He paused. "She's been worried for a while about me losing my head, figuratively speaking. Now she fears I might actually lose it."

"She knows about the poem, then?"

"She does."

Rhiannon was suddenly at the very top of the list of people Catrin needed to talk to. "Does Rory?"

"Yes."

"Anyone else?"

"No. The fewer people who know about the song before it can be sung, the better." That was all very well and good to say, but Gruffydd had shared it with three people. They'd now added four more. It was looking less a secret by the moment.

"Have you ever had an argument with Moriddig?" Catrin said.

Hywel scoffed openly at the question, causing Catrin to say, somewhat dryly, "I gather that's a *yes*?"

Gruffydd didn't reply immediately, instead folding his poem and stowing it away again in his jacket. "If you already knew the answer, why did you ask?"

"I needed to hear you say it. Even without the poem, you could be the prime suspect in the eyes of virtually everyone. Moriddig had rivals, and you were chief among them."

"Far better to hear all about it from you now," Hywel said. "That way we can dispense with the issue straight away."

Gruffydd seemed to accept that logic. "We have been rivals, as you know. Except for when we were very young, I was always the better, as you also know. Moriddig was the elder of us, and he resented the way I pushed at him. I made him better, in truth. That is not to say we didn't strive to out-perform each other. But I like to think that in our later years, we'd come to an understanding." He looked from

Hywel to Catrin. "Don't be fooled into thinking that Moriddig agreed with everything the Poles stand for, just because he served them."

"What exactly do you mean by that?" Catrin said. "What else are we supposed to think?"

"You will have noted, for example, that he never changed his name."

"I wondered about that," she admitted. "It seemed odd, given *Owen, Adam, Patrick,* and *Hugh.*"

"The language we speak, the words we choose, have the power to move the world." Gruffydd gestured broadly to indicate the company in the field. Catrin, Hywel, and Gruffydd were still off to one side. "Isn't that why we are here? The king is determined to curtail the power of the bards. He knows what we are. Why do you think we haven't had a nationwide *eisteddfod* since before the first Welsh war?"

"To keep us divided," Hywel said.

"As you say." Gruffydd acknowledged the answer with a tip of his head. "Moriddig knew whom he served. Owen's father was a clever man, albeit as ruthless as they come. He's a shadow of his former self now, the last of the great Welsh lords of his generation, not even well enough to wait upon the king. I hear he resides permanently at his castle at Powis. By contrast, Owen is a lesser man. Llywelyn told me once that King Edward's bargains are never what they seem at first, and the Welsh always come out the loser. Moriddig knew it. Owen will discover it soon enough."

Catrin's lips twisted. "The way you describe Moriddig is a far cry from the way he presented himself to the world."

"That was deliberate. He wasn't prepared to lose his position, not until he had someplace else to go. I assure you, in his heart, he was a Welshman."

Hywel still looked skeptical. "It is by a man's actions, not his words, that he is defined."

"Not when he's a bard," Gruffydd said. "I know people perceive me in much the same way. I serve your brother, after all, who some would call a traitor."

Few had the temerity to say those words out loud to Catrin, though they'd been whispered in circles that continued to resist the king. "They say that about me and Rhys too, I'm sure."

"And me." Hywel rubbed his chin. "I suppose, in that case, I can believe what you're saying about Moriddig. Even so, there's something bothering me about the poem: why is the one you showed us different from the one we found on Moriddig?"

"I don't conceive a ballad all at once." Gruffydd had a bit of impatience in his voice, as if this fact should have been obvious. "Any song takes time to perfect. That was an earlier version. And perhaps I should have said as well that it is not a version I shared with Moriddig—though I did share the poem with him."

Catrin found herself gaping.

Gruffydd shrugged to see it. "I told you we'd come to an understanding. Several months ago, we talked about the possibility of him finding a new patron, although last I heard nothing was confirmed. It would not do to offend Owen, because that would mean offending the king."

"You are sure you didn't leave the poem with him?"

"Definitely not." Gruffydd shook his head with fervor. "I knew what I had written, and he did too. He didn't even ask to keep it."

"So what happened to this bit after you wrote it?" Hywel said.

"I save all my drafts, in case I want to go back to an earlier version. The paper in Moriddig's mouth should have been in a locked trunk in my wagon. Someone must have broken in and taken it."

"Who might have done that?" Hywel said. "And when?"

Gruffydd turned his palms face up in an elaborate pantomime of ignorance. "How should I know?"

"Has someone broken the lock on your trunk?" Hywel asked.

"No." Gruffydd looked rueful. "So maybe he had a key."

"Did you note anything awry within your wagon in the last few days?" Catrin said.

Gruffydd appeared to waver without answering.

"Though one of the greatest bards who ever lived, Gruffydd is not, shall we say, *tidy*." Hywel explained before Catrin could ask what she wasn't understanding. "Are you certain the paper ever went into your trunk? Could you have left it on the floor in a moment of inattention?"

"I—" Gruffydd shook his head. "You know how I am when I'm writing. I forget things."

"So you could have?" Catrin said.

"Yes."

"Don't you have a steward like Adam to clean up after you?"

"Better, he has a wife," Hywel said dryly, "but Rhiannon is not allowed in the wagon unsupervised. She might move some of his things."

For a moment, Gruffydd looked genuinely sheepish. "She is very forgiving, is my Rhiannon."

"Why did you sign the paper?" Catrin asked. "Just admitting you wrote it could have you in chains. You had to know that."

Gruffydd's chin came up. "I sign every draft, every paper, no matter its condition or the state of the poem, bad or good. As I was taught. As is my right."

She had touched a nerve. "If you did not murder Moriddig, you made it easy for the person who did to blame you."

"I know." Gruffydd readily admitted it, but his head remained high. He was not going to change who he was. And maybe, despite what he'd said about Moriddig growing and changing, he couldn't. It wasn't Catrin's place to make him.

Nor was it Hywel's. It seemed her brother's opinion had turned completely around between when they'd discovered the poem in Moriddig's mouth and now. "If you finish this song and sing it for us, just once, whatever you may or may not have done will be forgiven."

Gruffydd swallowed hard. "You aren't going to tell the king?"

"We are not." Catrin might have added to that if they could just live long enough to hear Gruffydd sing the song as he was meant to, he would live forever a hero to the Welsh. "And I say this knowing I am committing treason."

"What about Rhys?" Gruffydd's eyes went to where Rhys was conferring closely with Hugh. She could feel the announcement of Moriddig's death coming, like an oncoming storm. "He feels the same?"

"He does." Catrin motioned towards her husband. "He will have told Simon that we found a paper stuffed into Moriddig's mouth, but that the writing had been smudged and was now illegible."

Gruffydd wasn't yet able to believe her. "If it is discovered that he knew about my poem, it would threaten his position in the king's court."

"Yes, it would," Catrin said.

"It would threaten all of our positions," Hywel said.

"He would do that for me?"

"Not for you, not if you, in fact, murdered Moriddig. He would do it for Llywelyn." Catrin made a motion with her head. "For him, even in death, he would do anything."

Gruffydd's eyes remained on where Rhys was now standing on the stage, his hands up, asking for quiet. "I suppose, if the stories I've heard about Cilmeri are true, he already did."

12

Day One

Rhys

Rhys first had to explain to Hugh why he'd come. At the initial telling, the steward flat-out didn't believe him. And then, once Rhys went through the details again, Hugh had to blink back tears.

"I'm sorry," Rhys said. "I wish I didn't have to tell you this way."

Hugh brushed at his eyes with his fingers. "I wish you didn't have to tell me at all." After a few more breaths, he got himself under control. Turning away from Rhys, he retook the stage and then raised his hands above his head to get everyone's attention. It took a moment for the assembled bards to give it. The brief interlude where nobody had been instructing them had encouraged them to think the rehearsal was over.

Now, however, Hugh wanted to make sure every single man present heard what he had to say. "I have just been informed that one of our number, the esteemed bard and my good friend, Moriddig, has died."

With that, every single person turned to his neighbor and expressed his immediate reaction, preventing Hugh from saying anything more. Amidst the noise, one of the renowned bards from the south, a man named Cadwgan, who had to be one of the favorites to win at least some of the contests at the festival, came out of the crowd and onto the stage to stand beside Hugh. He put a wooden whistle to his lips and blew hard.

Until his death, Moriddig had been given precedence at this festival for more reasons than just because Owen was his patron and the festival was located in the former Kingdom of Powys, which Owen's father had once ruled. Moriddig had possessed an amazing voice, and his mastery of the various instruments a bard was required to learn was unparalleled by any man here, with the possible exception of Gruffydd, whom Rhys could see talking even now with Catrin and Hywel.

Cadwgan, meanwhile, had to be a close second. Coming from the south, he had long experience with Normans and their restrictions. He might, in fact, be the most palatable choice to win the chair as a result, if their Norman masters were doing the judging.

Rhys caught Catrin's eye, and she motioned to him that all was well. Growing up with him as she had done, with the same father as Hywel, she knew the hand signals of Gwynedd's *teulu* too. For a moment Rhys saw her in pigtails with dirt on her nose.

Then the moment passed, and Cadwgan had quieted the crowd (as much as a group of a thousand people ever could be quieted). Moriddig had been respected, but Cadwgan was better liked. "I have just heard this news too and am grieving with you. I give you now Sir Rhys ap Iorwerth, a man whose great deeds should have long since earned your respect."

Cadwgan bent his head and gave way to Rhys, who was so surprised he initially didn't step forward, a bit stunned by the accolade. It was as if they remembered him. As if they knew about Cilmeri. It had also been a long time since anyone had spoken his name fully, with the patronym *Iorwerth*. In the king's court, he was Reese or Sir Reese. If respect had to be forced, then it was Reese de la Croix, referencing his participation in the crusade. Nobody had ever even alluded to the fact that he was the sole survivor of the ambush where Llywelyn had lost his life, and that it had been he who'd carried Llywelyn's headless body to Abbey Cwm Hir for proper burial.

Then the moment passed. Rhys cleared his throat of the unexpressed emotion and stepped to the fore. "Thank you for your attention. I must thank you in advance also for your patience. My news is more than what Hugh or Cadwgan has expressed: Moriddig was not only found dead on the floor of his wagon this morning, he was murdered."

A collective gasp rippled amongst his listeners. Rhys immediately put up a hand, calling for their renewed attention, and they gave that to him, too. "We may need to speak to every one of you in the coming days. If you encountered Moriddig more than just in passing, ate with him, spoke with him, played with him; if you noticed anything amiss or awry, or if you have even a stray thought at the back of your mind, one you might not otherwise think important enough to share, please share it with me anyway. A murderer cannot be left to roam free among us. The king has charged me with finding him and bringing him to justice."

On the whole, Rhys would have preferred not to bludgeon them with mention of the king. In the coming days, they would be hearing plenty about what the king wanted. Despite the accolade from Cadwgan, Rhys's authority among them came not from a shared history and understanding of what had happened to their country, but because he was the king's man. He wouldn't pretend otherwise.

He knew for certain now, with Gruffydd's lament, that Trahaearn wasn't alone in his defiance. Half these bards or more could be secretly writing forbidden songs. While there were always going to be those who cooperated with the Normans, like the candle maker, wanting what they could get out of them regardless of how many of their countrymen they hurt, he didn't see them as the majority. Not yet.

A man in the second row put up a hand. "I'd like to know how he was killed."

"I will not be sharing that information at this time as I barely have had a chance to examine the body."

The man subsided, though his expression indicated dissatisfaction with Rhys's answer. Rhys couldn't help that. It was the only answer he was willing to give.

"Are any of us in danger?" That came from someone more at the back. "Our wives are here with us; our children."

"That is a good question. My wife is with me as well. Given the circumstances of his death, we believe Moriddig himself was directly targeted."

The first man cut in, derision in his voice, "You *believe*—"

Simon's authority would have been useful at this point, but questions like this were why Rhys had evoked the king in the first place. He cut off the commenter before he could finish his sentence. "King Edward's wife and son are here too. He has decreed that the festival will continue. He is staying, so we are all staying."

Rhys could feel the unrest just below the surface. They had known intellectually that they couldn't leave, but now they knew it for certain.

Then Catrin hooked her arm through his, having left Hywel and Gruffydd on the edge of the crowd. "What you may not know is that my husband has experience investigating death under difficult circumstances. He served Prince Edmund in that capacity during his time on crusade in the Holy Land; he fulfilled the same position afterwards as part of Llywelyn's *teulu*; and now that he has been remanded to the king, he is once again a quaestor in royal service."

Rhys liked the way she'd put it, implying that Rhys's current position was not his choice, any more than the bards before him had chosen to be here. It was a way to remind them that he was as Welsh as they and as much caught up in trying to survive this new world Edward had created as every one of them.

Catrin's words did appear to ease some of the immediate resentment in the faces of the men closest to Rhys. Now he added, "What I can tell you is that Moriddig's death was not a random act.

We were not attacked in the night by marauders. Whoever killed him knew what he was doing."

"Moriddig was ever one for making enemies," a different man said, one whose age approached Moriddig's.

"One of them was even me, at one time." Gruffydd had come the front of the crowd too, choosing to stay on the ground before the stage. He'd also gone straight to the heart of what many might already be thinking.

Catrin spoke again: "Gruffydd was the first of you to be questioned about his whereabouts during the time of Moriddig's death. Whatever his disputes over the years with Moriddig, he did not commit this heinous act. Over the next hours and days, we may be coming to each one of you in the same fashion, to ask where you were this morning and what you knew of Moriddig."

Rhys might not have excused Gruffydd publicly like that, but he saw the benefit of not allowing the new *de facto* leader of the bards to be undermined unnecessarily. And while he was hopeful he wouldn't actually have to question all thousand bards, they needed to know it was possible and that all would be expected to cooperate.

He could tell by the way many in his audience were shifting from one foot to the other that he'd lost their attention. Most here had already been standing for longer than was comfortable, since they'd delayed the rehearsal from the start waiting for Moriddig. Maybe he'd said enough for now. Gesturing to Hugh, who might have a few last-minute admonitions, he merely added, "The opening ceremony will be held later today as planned."

Then Rhys, Cadwgan, and Catrin left the stage.

Gruffydd met him at the bottom of the steps. "My apologies if it was not my place to speak, Rhys. I was only trying to help."

"As was I," Cadwgan said.

"You did help, both of you, and I appreciate the effort. In the coming days, I will need all the help I can get."

"Do you really think it was one of us?" Gruffydd asked.

"I think it likely," Rhys said.

Cadwgan looked away, not towards the gathering of bards, but in the direction of the king's pavilion. The flags of England were clearly visible, outstretched in the breeze. "We are all strangers in our own land."

Gruffydd put a gentle hand on his shoulder. "Maybe none, in the end, more than Moriddig."

13

Day One

Math

Owen de la Pole narrowed his eyes at Simon. At first, Math assumed his ire was because of Rhys's name, but then he said, "Murdered? This must be a jest."

"I'm sorry to say that it is not—"

Simon cut himself off as Owen grabbed the step stool, which they'd reset in its usual place for travel, and climbed into the back of the wagon. Then, with a flourish, he tossed away the sheet that had been covering Moriddig's body.

"Oh."

Math glanced once at Simon, who came very close to rolling his eyes, and then climbed in after him. Owen might disturb the body. Or maybe, Owen was the murderer, in which case he could be making sure he'd left nothing behind to link him to the crime.

Ten years earlier, Owen had plotted with Dafydd, Llywelyn's brother, to murder Llywelyn. It wasn't until months later that Llywelyn had learned the truth. Anian, the Bishop of Bangor, had violated the sanctity of the confessional to tell Llywelyn what Owen had confessed, believing the intervention of the snowstorm that had prevented the murder was an Act of God.

Although the attempt on his life had failed, time had revealed it to be the beginning of the end for Llywelyn. Dafydd and Owen fled to England, where they were maintained in Edward's court and allowed the opportunity to drip their discontent into the king's willing ear. That King Edward was sheltering men who'd tried to kill him was a primary reason Llywelyn subsequently refused to pay homage to Edward. And it was that refusal that had given Edward the excuse to go to war.

Back then, Owen's confession to the bishop indicated he'd felt guilt and regret. He would not have confessed the sin if he believed himself to have done nothing wrong. He had been only seventeen at the time, and some thought he should be forgiven for being led astray by the much older Dafydd, who at thirty-six was the leader of the conspiracy.

It was impossible to be sure of anything now. Llywelyn had been assassinated anyway; Dafydd had been hanged, drawn and quartered by King Edward in Shrewsbury; Gruffydd, Owen's father, was in his dotage and couldn't remember what he had for breakfast, much less any order of events; and neither Bishop Anian nor Owen had ever said another word about it.

But still, it had happened. A man who'd contemplated murder once could do it again.

With the sheet pooling at his feet, Owen plopped down on the box beside the body. His lips were bloodless, a match to his complexion, to the point that Math was genuinely afraid he might faint.

Math himself had taken a long look at Moriddig before driving away from the festival grounds. The marks on his neck were no less obvious than they had been when Math had first seen him. From what he'd learned from Rhys, they would remain visible, even as the body went through rigor.

Until Math's association with Rhys, he himself hadn't had cause to examine dead bodies, other than to make sure a man who'd fallen on the battlefield actually *was* dead. Math reminded himself that not all men, even Norman lords (or maybe especially Norman lords?), had even that much experience with the dead. While Owen had conspired with Dafydd, Owen's own role hadn't been to do the murdering himself. Math didn't recall that Owen had ever fought in a battle either. He'd been standing beside the king for the invasion of Wales, but that didn't mean he'd ever pulled his sword from its sheath.

Owen finally spoke, his voice small and distant. "He was strangled."

"So we concluded, my lord."

Then Simon, who'd come up a few of the steps, said, "Did you speak with him this morning?"

"This morning?" Owen looked towards Simon, his expression blank, before shaking his head. "No. We talked last night after the dinner held in the king's honor. He played exceptionally well, and I told him so. He replied that the presence of the king had inspired him. He'd sung for the king before, of course, years ago. We are all so honored that Overton was selected as the site of the festival and that the king has chosen to reside in this very castle."

Owen said these words without conscious attention, almost like he wasn't listening to himself. Sycophantic phrases were standard for him. It was as if he couldn't help tacking praise of the king onto every idea he conveyed, giving Math new insight into the man Owen had become. This older Owen no longer saw himself as a sinner. He was the king's man, far more completely than Math himself, even as it was Math who daily wore the king's colors and guarded him with his life.

After a few more breaths, Owen allowed Math to lay the sheet once again over Moriddig's body, and they both returned to the back of the wagon. Crouching down, Owen put his chin in his hand, his attention once again on Simon's face. "So, who murdered him?"

"We don't know. We are pledged to find out," Simon said.

"You mean your man Reese will be finding out." He spoke without emphasis, pronouncing Rhys's name the Norman way.

"Yes, my lord," Simon said.

"And you." Owen turned his attention to Math. "Who are you exactly?"

"My apologies, my lord." He put a hand on his chest. "My name is Mathonwy ap Cynan."

"Ah." Owen almost smiled. "Your brother is the traitor."

"I would beg to differ, my lord."

Simon intervened, which was just as well, since Math was contemplating shoving Owen off the back of the wagon. "The king has accepted Math's obeisance, and he has become a valued member of the king's personal guard."

"Such is the way of war. Who am I to disagree? I am at your disposal if you need anything from me besides the use of a room in which to put the body. As I recall, that is why you brought him here?"

"Reese needs a place to examine it further, yes," Simon said.

"Why would that be?" Owen said. "The man was strangled, that's clear to see."

"It is possible the murderer left something more of himself behind," Simon said. "We won't know until we look."

"The murderer will be a rival bard, of course." Owen started down the steps. "Perhaps that Gruffydd from Gwynedd."

Interestingly, both these names came out in perfect Welsh. At times it seemed as if Owen forgot that he was playing at being a Norman lord. To one degree or another, everyone who served in the royal court wore masks, behind which nobody was allowed to see, while the king moved his men like puppets on a string. Math knew, however, that their feet were still tucked up inside their gowns. Each could run, if he had to. And every one was prepared to do so—if he had to. Including Math himself.

Now Owen made a face. "And if not him, how many more does that leave you to consider?"

Simon cleared his throat. "Nearly a thousand."

"How am I to keep my people safe? The king is sleeping here! My wife is pregnant!"

"My apologies, my lord, I cannot tell you anything other than what the king has decreed: the festival will continue." Simon gave a little bow. "And we will investigate."

Owen let out something of a snort. "Well, you can start with the fact that the murderer wore a ring on his right hand. You can see the bruise it left."

"Thank you, my lord. As you say, it's a start." Simon looked at Math, who shrugged. He hadn't seen it, but then, Rhys hadn't examined the body yet.

Owen nodded. "Then you'd best get to it. Tell Reese that my castle and my men are at his disposal. Anything for the king's quaestor."

14

Day One
Simon

As Owen's men maneuvered the body out of the wagon, the lord himself didn't leave like Simon had hoped, instead surveying their efforts with his hands on his hips. Now that the initial shock of Moriddig's death had passed, he was practically glowering at the body. "What is the world coming to when a bard is murdered in his own wagon? Can you believe it?"

His tone was familiar, but Simon didn't make the mistake of replying in kind. "It is unsettling, my lord."

Before today, Simon had always felt a little envious of the bards for having wagons to sleep in while they were on the road. As a member of the king's guard, Simon traveled with him everywhere he went, as he had done for Prince Edmund since they'd returned from the Holy Land. Thus, he lay his head in the same place for only a few days or a week at a time.

He considered it a blessing they were going to be in Overton-on-Dee for a full two weeks because it meant his wife and children could join him in his tent at the festival grounds. The king was sleeping at the castle, and his guard rotated duty throughout the day and night. But when not on duty, they were not high-ranking enough to actually *sleep* here. For his part, Simon had been overjoyed to be reunited with Elizabeth. They'd known each other since childhood, and theirs was a love match. That fact made their separations harder, rather than easier, to bear.

Owen let out a breath. "It is just too bad the son is not half the bard his father was, not yet leastwise. Likely, not ever."

Coupled with his comment about how well Moriddig had performed the previous evening, Owen seemed to be feeling more sorry for himself about losing his entertainment than mourning his dead bard.

"Perhaps you will find a viable replacement at the festival," Simon suggested. "We do have nearly a thousand bards from whom to choose."

Owen snapped his fingers. "Perhaps one of them will even unseat the odious Gruffydd. I would be the first to make an offer to such a man." He bobbed a nod in Simon's direction. "I appreciate the reminder."

"Certainly, my lord." Out of the corner of his eye, Simon saw Math's expression contort for a mere heartbeat before smoothing back to a polite façade.

Math and Rhys, as the two Welshmen among the king's guards, were allowed their resentments as long as they kept them to themselves. Simon was actually glad to see the degree to which the two had grown closer over these last few weeks. Math had been the first person to whom Rhys had turned when confronted with another investigation. The more connections with others Rhys acquired, the more tightly he would be bound to his service to the king. And to Simon himself, if he was being honest.

He appreciated the pain these Welshmen felt at losing their lord, but he also had to suppress an impatience at the way Llywelyn kept invading their thoughts. The man had been dead nearly two years! It was time to accept the change that had come to Wales and move on.

For some reason, the Welsh mostly didn't think that way. It was a source of endless puzzlement, not only to Simon but to everyone in Edward's court. The political calm the king brought, the clarity of purpose, and the civil structure were all benefits of being part of England that the Welsh somehow didn't appreciate. They hung onto the past in a way Simon viewed as, quite frankly, destructive.

But then, Norman children were taught from the cradle that change was inevitable, that their greatest asset was adaptability, and that their job was to be on the right side of any change when it happened. Families maneuvered constantly in a struggle for land, power, and the wealth that came with it—and were very flexible about their allies and enemies. In fact, if the circumstances were right, enemies could become friends overnight. Thus, the king had forgiven Rhys and Math for their prior allegiance and for fighting against him, and had accepted them into his service. All they'd had to do was bend the knee.

Rhys and Math had done exactly that, but grudgingly, even though the king himself held no grudge against them.

Owen, by contrast, had so taken on his mother's Norman identity that he was almost more Norman than Simon. It made some of his peers wary, but not Simon. Owen had more to prove, and thus more to lose. That made him predictable. With Owen, one actually knew where one stood.

Simon set himself half a step to the left and behind Owen as he followed Moriddig's body into the laying-out room. Math kept pace an additional two or three steps behind Simon, such that the three of them arrived into the relative darkness of the laying-out room one after the other. Math filled the doorway briefly, and then stepped off to one side so as not to block the light. The two men Owen had found to move the body set it on a table in the center of the room and departed in response to a wave of Owen's hand.

That left the three of them alone, staring down at Moriddig. To see the man so vulnerable and exposed, as he had strived never to be in life, felt irreverent. "Sir Reese should be along shortly. Would you like me to stay with the body until then?" Simon asked Owen.

"Not at all. He isn't going anywhere." Owen then added, almost as an afterthought, "Perhaps a cup of wine wouldn't go amiss?"

Simon swallowed down his surprise. "Thank you, my lord."

Leaving Math to wait for Rhys, Simon followed Owen out of the laying-out room, across the bailey, and into the great hall.

They passed several servants along the way, all of whom bent their heads out of respect to Owen, but he spoke to none of them and behaved as if he hadn't seen them. Arriving in a receiving room off the back of the hall, Owen went straight to the fire and began poking at it. He waved a hand towards Simon, who'd been left hesitating a few paces into the room. "Pour the wine, will you?"

"Of course, my lord." Simon did as he was bid, and by the time he turned around, Owen was relaxed in a chair by the fire. He then gestured to Simon that he should take another opposite. This chair wasn't as cushioned, but it still had a back.

Simon handed Owen the warm wine before sitting. They both sipped. By now, Simon had figured out that Owen wasn't just wanting company while he drank. He had brought Simon here for a specific reason, and it wasn't to discuss Moriddig. It would be impolite to prompt him, however, so he drank his own wine and waited him out.

After another sip, Owen said, "How goes it with your brother?"

That was a question Simon definitely didn't want to answer in any meaningful way. The Boydells and the Poles were not friends. If family was what Owen wanted to talk about, Simon was going to have to tread very carefully. Thus, he responded with a platitude. "He has been honored by the queen beyond any expectation."

"That he has." Owen nodded his head in agreement. "He is hoping for a good match for his daughter."

"For Emma. Yes." Simon took another sip of wine, trying not to swallow hard or maybe even breathe.

Owen then leaned forward, his forearms on his thighs, dangling the cup between his knees. "You will have noted that the queen has designs on all of Maelor Saesneg."

Simon would have fled if he could. Instead, he forced himself not to shift in his seat. Owen had spoken definitively, telling Simon a fact, not a supposition. He felt he could half-agree. "It is clear she loves her new manor."

"Of which your brother has been given charge." Owen nodded. "My sources tell me she has mentioned to the king her fondness for the beauty of the River Dee. I begin to think that the king's largesse in granting Overton a market fair five years ago was a mere preamble to what will come next."

Given Owen's frankness, Simon thought it was safe to risk stating another obvious fact. "What came next was the queen took Robert's manor for herself."

"It will not stop there. Your brother would be wise to think about his own estates. One can never refuse to negotiate with the Queen of England, but if one is prepared in advance, one has a possibility of retaining wealth and royal favor in the process. It is the unprepared who find themselves in far worse straits." Owen was being shockingly frank—and also observant. Simon hadn't ever had a real conversation with the man. Until now, he'd assumed everyone was right that Owen was a bit of a fool. Simon wasn't so sure now that he was even naïve.

The truth was, Simon had already warned Osborn of the exact same thing Owen was telling him. Osborn had replied in no uncertain terms that Simon needed to keep his concerns to himself. This week, Osborn had no thought for anything but the main chance in front of him. He aspired to the same heights as any Norman—a lordship; an earldom; the throne. Just because he had little chance of reaching these heights himself did not mean he wouldn't do every-thing in his power to position his family in such a way that a descendant might achieve what he couldn't. Emma's wedding was a first step, and he would not begin by alienating the queen in any way.

He certainly wasn't going to question her commitment to Overton-on-Dee. He would not countenance Simon doing so either. Neither of them, of course, had any control over Owen. If the half-Norman lord wanted to risk what he had and the king's favor by maneuvering against the queen in advance of her maneuvering against him, Simon wasn't going to stop him.

While he had not thought Owen this insightful, it should have been obvious to anyone that the queen wanted the whole of the region for herself. Past experience indicated she was likely to get her way. Thus, he opted to speak the truth too, as far as he could. "Osborn does not believe it is in his interests to look beyond this fortnight."

Owen leaned back in his chair. "No, he wouldn't." He took another sip of wine, his eyes on the fire now. "I don't want to be caught unawares by new developments."

"Nor would my brother, I imagine."

"Then we are agreed." Owen nodded sharply.

After a moment, with Owen's gaze still drawn by the flames, Simon realized he was dismissed. He rose to his feet, bowed briefly, and set his half-drunk cup of wine on the side table. As he left the room, reviewing the conversation, he knew in himself that he had admitted to nothing and agreed to nothing.

And yet, somehow, it felt as if he might have just committed treason.

15

Day One

Math

After Simon and Owen departed the laying-out room, Math stood uncertainly beside the body. He didn't know whether Rhys would prefer him to simply keep vigil or if he was meant to begin examining Moriddig himself. He didn't think Rhys would mind if he had a closer look; nor would he view doing so as usurping his role. Math hadn't actually seen a man strangled before and thus wasn't sure he would have known the murderer had worn a ring.

He did wonder how many strangled men Owen had examined to have realized what he was seeing. What Owen had not mentioned were the implications if he was correct. Before she had left with Hywel to find Gruffydd, Catrin had conveyed the news that Moriddig's own ring was missing. After a few more moments of dithering, Math decided he needed to see for himself and pulled the sheet off the body. Instead of tossing it aside as Owen had done, he folded it neatly and set it on a nearby table.

The body was looking no better than it had in the wagon—worse, really, once Math lit the two lanterns that hung from the ceiling. It was even easier now to make out Moriddig's bulging eyes. They hadn't seemed quite so prominent when he'd been on the floor of the wagon. It also looked as if Moriddig had bitten his lower lip hard as he was dying because there were traces of blood on his teeth. Math felt a sudden pang of sympathy that the man had died in agony.

He was hesitating, ashamed both to look at him and to look away, when Rhys stepped into the room. "You don't have to stay."

Math didn't know how long he'd been there, observing from the doorway. "I feel like a coward." He felt the need to apologize. "He looks dreadful."

"This is my job, not yours. Why do you think I'm having Catrin go through the wagon for clues? She doesn't need to see this." He gave a shake of his head. "I regret that I do. Sadly, it does get easier."

"How did you know what I was feeling?"

"Because it's hard for me too. I can look at the body impartially, but staring at his face feels like we're dishonoring him. Moriddig loved being the center of attention in life. He would hate it now in death."

As he spoke, Rhys lifted Moriddig's wrist. Since Math had already done the same thing, he knew the body was stiffer than when they'd discovered it. Rigor would be setting in more completely as every subsequent hour passed.

"Has anything happened since we last talked that I need to know?" Rhys said. "Did you get anything more out of Patrick and Adam? Where did they go?"

"They're drinking." Math didn't mention Owen's observation about the ring yet. If Rhys didn't see it himself, he would tell him before they left the room.

"Well, he's still dead." Rhys bent to look at Moriddig's hands. "I don't see an indication he fought back. There's no blood or skin under his nails or bruises on his knuckles." He walked around the body to the other side. "You can see the paler skin around his finger where the ring is missing. Maybe Catrin will find it or it's somewhere in his clothes. We should strip him now, before full rigor sets in. We think we know how he died, but we need to make sure he has no other wounds."

They set to work, the whole process suddenly becoming easier for Math now that he wasn't alone. They worked in silence at first, with occasional grunts of effort. As Math folded Moriddig's clothing and put them next to the sheet that had covered him, Rhys stood looking down at Moriddig's neck. Then he stuck out a finger and rubbed the spot Owen had noted.

"Does it look like a bruise to you?"

"Lord Owen pointed that out and said we should be looking for someone who wears a ring on his right hand."

Rhys barked a laugh. "Did Owen have any suggestions as to that person's identity?"

"He mentioned Gruffydd ab yr Ynad Coch."

"He doesn't wear any rings, or at least he wasn't wearing any today; I've just come from speaking to him." Rhys fit his own hands around Moriddig's neck and then asked Math to do the same, the better to imagine how it might have been. Math's fingers didn't quite match up. The killer had larger hands. Math also wore no rings at all, having sold or melted down every one he'd inherited during his years of wandering, just to survive.

Rhys stepped back. "I would not have guessed Owen had an eye for such detail."

Math gave a little cough. "I wondered at the time at his surety or if he knew something he wasn't telling us. Owen wears two rings on his left hand, and one more on his right."

"You are wondering if he murdered his own bard?" Rhys gave a little shrug. "Wouldn't that wrap things up nicely? But I know for a fact that he was in the king's tent for most of the morning and only left shortly before Hywel arrived with the news of Moriddig's death. If we are to believe Adam about Moriddig's movements, Owen isn't even a suspect."

"He has plotted murder before," Math couldn't help saying, aware that Rhys would know exactly what he was talking about. But then, at Rhys's raised eyebrow, he hastily added, "Have you thought as far as who stands to gain from this death?"

"So we're speculating now?" Rhys opened his eyes wider in feigned surprise.

Math waggled his head. "I'm just curious as to what you think."

"I have no opinion at all, as of yet. I sense, however, that you do."

"Since Nefyn, and especially since Vale Royal Abbey, I've been thinking about why men murder other men. Before working with you, I hadn't given much thought to the difference between killing in battle at the behest of one's lord and killing for one's own benefit. For that's what this is all about, isn't it? Someone wanted something, and Moriddig stood in the way of it. That's why Dafydd and Owen plotted against Llywelyn all those years ago."

"While true, your point also makes clear how the idea of *wanting* should be seen broadly," Rhys said. "Sometimes the killer wants what another has. That could be a material thing, like silver or a manor—or the throne of Wales. It could also be a person, like a wife or lover. Alternatively, he could want to be free *of* something. Maybe the dead man was a bully. That makes the killer also a victim and the murder a product of desperation. When wives murder husbands, that's almost always the situation. While murder can arise out of simple greed, it can come from love, hate, or fear. Or even all three at the same time."

"Strangling strikes me as a very personal way to murder someone." Math found himself studying Moriddig's body with a detachment he hadn't felt before Rhys and he had started talking. "What did the murderer gain from killing you?"

16

Day One
Catrin

Even with Catrin's curiosity at its height, she was not immediately comfortable entering Moriddig's wagon, much less going through his personal items. He would have hated to have her poking around in his things when he was alive. She wasn't entirely sure he would have wanted her here even to catch his murderer.

That said, Catrin was by nature a nosy person. It wasn't that she gossiped herself. Quite the opposite. She never told anyone but Rhys what she learned, and sometimes not even him. It wasn't that she enjoyed seeing people falter either. It was more that, ever since she was a little girl, she wanted to know what was happening with the people around her. Given the fraught waters in which she swam, the acquisition of information could mean the difference between surviving and not.

When she was younger, she had endeavored to make herself invisible in order to eavesdrop. At times, she'd been too successful and overheard things she wished she hadn't. These days, she tried to be more straightforward in her approach. To emphasize the degree to which she wasn't doing anything wrong, she hooked the canvas door of Moriddig's wagon open. Still, as she started in on Moriddig's things, she prepared a little speech to give to Adam and/or Patrick if they came by, in order to explain her presence.

She had poked her nose into the castle kitchen before she started, just to check on their whereabouts. They had both looked well into their cups. At some point, they might leave off their drinking long enough to remember that Moriddig's wagon (and thus, Patrick's inheritance) was standing unattended in the bailey of the castle. Although the two men seemed in accord right now, Catrin wasn't necessarily convinced that had always been the case. Adam had implied, at the very least, that there had been some friction between Moriddig and Patrick. She could believe there had been some between the two brothers as well.

These were questions that would need to be asked, but maybe not right now.

She went through every box; every basket; every drawer, working more slowly as time went on as she found nothing of note and she became less concerned about someone objecting. The more she worked, the more necessary she knew her activity to be. Bards were clever men for the most part, inventive too, always willing to try new sounds and new instruments. Moriddig had dozens of whistles, large and small, stringed instruments of all sizes, and multiple drums for keeping the beat. He was also literate so, like Gruffydd, he kept papers and ledgers filled with music and lyrics, some that he'd written himself, most that were part of the bardic tradition in Wales.

Unlike Gruffydd, Moriddig had liked his things ordered, so she made sure to put everything back where she'd found it, which wasn't hard since she found nothing out of the ordinary.

Until she did.

She was just turning to leave when two unexpected events happened simultaneously. The first was that her foot touched the bottom of one of his trunks, and a drawer popped out. It was perhaps two inches high at most. But for her glancing touch, she would never have known it was there. And then, a young woman appeared at the back of the wagon and said in Welsh, "Excuse me!"

Catrin turned abruptly, plastering a smile onto her face, while at the same time pushing the drawer almost all the way closed. "May I help you?"

Every fiber of Catrin's being wanted to know what was in that drawer, but it had to wait. The very fact that Moriddig had a secret drawer meant he had something he wanted kept hidden. She certainly wasn't going to expose him to a stranger.

The woman was perhaps thirty years old, her hair wrapped in a white cap, a few blond tendrils hanging artfully down, and a sweet smile that might have been equally artful. "Is Moriddig really dead?"

Catrin suspected her own smile had suddenly become glassy. She forced a touch of sympathy into her voice. "Yes, I'm afraid he is."

The woman's face fell. "He was just so good with my Thomas." She took a step to her right to reveal a boy of eight, who'd been hidden in her skirts.

"Hello, Thomas." Catrin took another few steps herself, until she was at the end of the wagon, and then crouched down so she wasn't looming over him. "Can you sing?"

The woman's face lit as she answered for her son. "Like an angel. Moriddig said he was going to be a great bard one day."

Catrin shook her head regretfully. "I don't know what to tell you."

"I had such hopes for my boy."

"Perhaps Patrick could teach him. I've heard he's good."

The woman wrinkled her nose at the suggestion. "But not great."

"We do have nearly a thousand bards here this week," Catrin said even more gently. "You could look to one of them."

The woman blinked. "I hadn't thought of that!" All of a sudden, her demeanor transformed to one of determination. She turned away, herding her son ahead of her. Now that she had a new direction, she could dispense with Catrin.

"One more thing, if you will." As much as Catrin would have liked to return to the drawer, she wouldn't be doing her duty as an investigator if she did just yet. "When did you last encounter Moriddig?"

The woman turned back. "I saw him this morning." Then she put a hand to her mouth, gasping around it. "Was that not long before he died?"

Catrin restrained herself from leaping at the woman. "Did you speak to him?"

"I wanted to, but didn't dare approach." Although the woman had been ready to leave, now she preened a bit to be able to relate her special knowledge. "I had hoped to bring Thomas for a lesson, since Moriddig had left the castle before we could speak about it. I went to his wagon where it was parked at the festival grounds. He and another person, a woman, were arguing inside. I overheard the woman say, *How could you do this?* Her voice was quite loud, louder than Moriddig's reply, which I didn't hear properly. Then she said, *Who do you think you are?* and *You have no right!*"

"Did you recognize her voice? Did she speak in French, English, or Welsh?"

"French. I may be exaggerating how loud she was, though. I could make out what she was saying, but her actual voice was a bit muffled." She had the grace to look a little sheepish. "I left because I decided it would be better not to interrupt. Moriddig had already told me he would resume the lessons after the festival. I had just been hoping for sooner. It makes such a difference to know that he might have made Thomas an apprentice once his son was inducted as a full bard. That was to happen within the next year. To tell the truth, I was concerned that Moriddig would encounter a more promising candidate at the festival, one who was older and already established." The woman's shoulders fell. "And now it no longer matters."

"I wish you the best. I am sorry for your loss."

Despondent again, the woman turned away, her hand on her son's head. He hadn't spoken a word throughout, and Catrin had no idea if the mother's notion about his potential was accurate or not. She appeared ambitious enough for Catrin to believe she could make her son a bard by sheer force of will. Catrin also believed what she'd said about the argument. She stood to gain nothing from the story, and thus had no reason to lie, even for a bit of attention.

Unfortunately, that Moriddig and a woman had conversed in French wasn't immediately helpful. Many people here spoke multiple languages. Catrin had heard all three—French, English, and Welsh— in the castle since she arrived. It was also rare for a woman to murder, and even rarer for her to do it by a means as personal and physical as strangling. Although Moriddig was a small man, he still wouldn't have been easy for a woman to overpower, and the bruises around his neck indicated largish hands.

Then Catrin remembered the drawer, which had slid out a few inches again, once she'd stopped holding it closed. Pulling it out all the way revealed another collection of papers, stacked in two piles and written in a neat hand Catrin had come to recognize as Moriddig's. Beside these piles was a bag of silver coins.

Each, in its own way, represented a small fortune.

Sitting on the floor with a stack of papers in her lap, Catrin read poem after poem lamenting the loss of Wales and expressing a hatred of the English that might actually exceed Catrin's own. One ballad even expressed disdain for Owen, Moriddig's lord.

These writings were objectively more flammable than Gruffydd's poem, both in content and in quantity.

When Gruffydd had told her about Moriddig's true self, she hadn't necessarily believed him. But just as he had promised, Moriddig had been a secret *combrogi* all along.

17

Day One

Rhys

Rhys and Catrin were back at the festival grounds for the opening ceremony, which King Edward had made clear was not to be put off for even an hour, not to say a day, because of Moriddig's death. Although the event did open with the usual prayer, even that wasn't directed at the loss of their comrade. It was business as usual ... as usual.

With Gruffydd in the lead, holding the staff of office, the company of bards, mighty as it was, paraded past the viewing stand. Truly, they looked like an army, albeit with *crwths* and flutes rather than swords and spears. By now, it was clear an army was exactly what King Edward saw. If only he knew that the bard who led the company was a commander worthy of the name. From the looks, Gruffydd had assumed the mantle of leadership with aplomb, not that he had much in the way of choice in the matter.

Rhys and Catrin had found a spot from which to watch the festivities near where Catrin had interviewed Gruffydd earlier in the day. Rhys had cleared it with Simon to be relieved of his duties guarding the king until the issue of Moriddig's murder was resolved. Catrin had been given leave by the queen to investigate as well. In fact, the queen's exact words were, "Why are you still standing in front of me? Get out there and find who murdered him and then come back and tell me all about it!" Truly, all four of them, if such a grouping could be conceived, had come a long way since Caernarfon.

Over the last hours as he'd questioned one bard after another, Rhys had picked up on a significant amount of unrest just below the surface. The bards as a whole had already been made upset by Trahaearn's flight. Now, some were wondering if the king hadn't had a hand in Moriddig's death. Rhys had been fighting a rearguard action since Llywelyn's death, much of the time thinking he was alone in the fight. With the revelations about Moriddig and Gruffydd, he was realizing that he and Catrin were not the only ones living a double life, hiding their resentments in order to survive. Others were standing with them. It was in his mind that many of these bards might have been feeling as alone as he, right up until King Edward had gathered them all together.

He'd overheard one bard say to another, not really even in an undertone, "If the king wants names of disloyal men, we can supply them."

When the other bard asked what he meant, the first had replied that they had to fight back with the weapons they had. Really, Gruffydd's poem was a kind of weapon too. With it they had flint, tinder, and spark that could set off a conflagration the likes of which they hadn't seen since before Llywelyn's death.

For now, however, the bards were quiescent, listening to the speeches of their Norman masters without protest. John Boydell, as one of the prominent local lords, spoke first from the stage, followed by Owen de la Pole. Then, to Rhys's great surprise, because he hadn't known he was coming, none other than Humphrey de Bohun moved to the center of the stage. Everyone obediently bent their heads in acknowledgment of his greatness.

Humphrey de Bohun was the Earl of Hereford as well as the Lord High Constable of England. He was also currently embroiled in a dispute with another Marcher lord, John Giffard, over land in Carmarthenshire. Humphrey could have come to Overton less because he cared about music than to plead his case before the king. Up until now, the king, who had given Giffard the land as spoils of war, had taken Giffard's side.

So, if Humphrey was here, that meant ...

In the same instant Rhys had the thought, Miles de Bohun's voice came low in his ear. "Did you miss me?"

Rhys scoffed. "How can I miss you when you keep turning up like a bad penny?"

Miles chuckled low in his chest. "Well, I certainly missed you."

But then he couldn't say anything more because Humphrey's purpose in taking the stage had been to direct everyone's attention to the king himself, who rose desultorily from his seat and stepped to the front of the viewing stand, set at an angle from the stage. All the bards in the grassy square now turned to the left to face him instead of Humphrey.

Spreading his arms wide, King Edward said in a resonant voice, "It is long since such a number of bards have come together. Not since the days of Arthur has there been such a host. Welcome to this great gathering! May the best man win, and may the contest … begin!"

King Edward nodded graciously at the applause and retook his seat.

Then Hugh appeared in the grass in front of the viewing stand, on the same level as the contestants, talking to the bards rather than the audience as a whole.

Catrin wasn't able to make out his words, but since they weren't meant for her, she turned back to Miles, who spoke again. "Rumor has it you have already embroiled yourselves in another murder."

"It isn't a rumor." Catrin's tone was both wry and affectionate. She hadn't known Miles well before Windsor, but the events there couldn't help but bond them all together.

"Am I correct in thinking it is one of the bards? Owen de la Pole's man, Morrydig?" Miles said Moriddig's name the best a Norman could.

"You are well-informed," Rhys said. "You can't have been here for more than an hour."

"It was an hour well-spent." Suddenly, Miles had an unexpected intensity to his tone that made Rhys unsure what they were really talking about.

"Is there some reason you are particularly interested in the issue?" Catrin must have noted it too.

"You mean you don't know? He's been dead for most of the day!"

"Obviously not." Catrin was all patience.

Miles tsked through his teeth. "Morrydig was going to come to Brecon."

Rhys blinked. "And serve your nephew?"

"Of course serve my nephew. Why else would he come to Brecon?" Miles looked for a moment as pleased as a cat who'd just eaten a bowl of cream. "Nobody told you, did they?"

"No." Rhys thought back through all the conversations they'd had so far. "When was it to be announced?"

"After the festival, to avoid causing any disruption or embarrassment to the Poles."

"How long have you been negotiating this?" Catrin leaned forward slightly so she could see Miles's face better.

"He came to me a month ago."

"Do you know why he wanted to leave?"

Miles looked at them quizzically, as if again surprised at the information they didn't have. "He hated the Poles. Did you not know that either?"

"We were learning it," Rhys said slowly. "The inner man was different from the outer."

"Did he actually tell you he hated them?" Catrin asked.

Fortunately, this conversation was being held outside the margins of the crowd. In addition, the bards were readying themselves for their performance to open the festival. In a tournament, they might have started with a joust or a sword fight, but at an *eisteddfod*, it would be with song.

"I pressed him hard as to why he would leave them after all this time. In the end, he told me what sounded like the truth."

Then a thousand bards launched into the first verses of *The Song of Roland*:

> *Carle our most noble Emperor and King,*
> *Hath tarried now full seven years in Spain,*
> *Conqu'ring the highland regions to the sea;*
> *No fortress stands before him unsubdued,*
> *Nor wall, nor city left, to be destroyed,*
> *Save Sarraguce, high on a mountain set.*
> *There rules the King Marsile who loves not God,*
> *Apollo worships and Mohammed serves;*
> *Nor can he from his evil doom escape.*
> *Aoi.*

Distracted, Miles gazed towards the performing bards with a frown. "Are they aware that was Alfonso's favorite?"

"I don't know." Rhys found himself concerned. "I wasn't present for any consultation with the king about the program."

All three of them looked towards King Edward, but he was smiling and tapping his finger on the arm of his throne to keep time. Maybe he had requested this song specifically, in honor of Alfonso.

Regardless, to sing it today was surely a diplomatic choice. If the bards had called up one of the ancient songs about Arthur, even as King Edward had just invoked his name and liked to place himself in his lineage, it might have been perceived as having a double meaning. Arthur had been Welsh. The bards, and everyone else by now, knew if they knew anything, that they were not to sing of the ancient heroes of Wales without explicit permission.

For his part, Rhys was just glad King Edward hadn't opened the festival by building a gallows on the stage and hanging Trahaearn from it.

Turning back to Miles, he blocked out the music in favor of murder. "Moriddig hated the Poles, but he didn't hate your nephew?"

"Oh, he hated him too, but in the same way you do. It was a casual thing for him, without real urgency. My nephew, or the king, for that matter, didn't betray Wales. They simply conquered it. The Poles, on the other hand, were once Welsh, and they turned their backs on their heritage and their people. He could no longer stomach the betrayal." Miles recited what Rhys and Catrin knew by heart but might not have expected to hear from a Norman, even one as insightful as Miles. "A motive for murder, perhaps?"

"But for whom?" Catrin said in a low voice. "A Welshman would celebrate this change of heart."

Rhys eyed Miles. "I assume you were going to pay him well?"

"As if you need to ask. Better than he had been. Plus additional compensation to his brother and son who were, of course, welcome in Brecon too. You must be thinking one of them might be the killer, but they stood to lose more by Morrydig's death than his life."

"We actually don't have any suspects yet," Rhys said. "With this news, I'm wondering if you do? Any more secrets we should know?"

"Not that I can share." Miles gave an elaborate shrug. The singing was ongoing, so their conversation was ending up as a bit of a pantomime anyway. It was clear he was having fun answering their questions—and giving them more questions than answers. "That's your job isn't it? Finding out the who and the why? I'm just the messenger."

18

Day Two

Rhys

The day after Moriddig's murder, Rhys arrived in the pavilion where breakfast was being prepared for the king's servants, of which he was one, to find none other than Prince Edmund waving at him from a table on the far side.

Rhys was within a hair's-breadth from putting his hand to his chest and asking, "Me?"

He refrained, because he knew that Edmund did mean him, and they'd put off the upcoming conversation for too long as it was. In truth, Rhys had been actively avoiding it. With his duties to the king, it hadn't been difficult to ensure he wasn't in the same place as the prince at a time when they could have a moment alone.

He hadn't intended for Prince Edmund to come all the way down here to find him, but it was clear that was exactly what had happened. The moment he took the seat Edmund indicated, his guards and advisors moved out of earshot, though still forming a protective ring around him.

"How are you, Reese?"

That was a fraught question if Rhys had ever heard one. "I am well, my lord."

Edmund raised his eyebrows. "Shouldn't you have said, *as well as can be expected*?"

Rhys knew what Edmund meant, even if his first impulse was to deny that anything was amiss. "You're not wrong. I continue to find the aftermath of the investigation in Windsor difficult to navigate."

"And yet, I hear you have navigated it exceptionally well, despite my brother's initial rejection of your explanation and of you yourself."

"If you say so, my lord." Rhys wasn't being smarmy. He genuinely didn't agree.

Edmund's lips twitched. "Here you are, in the king's good graces, embroiled in another murder. In other words, right where you belong."

Rhys could have again said *if you say so*, but that really would have been disrespectful. Instead, he bent his head in acknowledgment of Edmund's words.

"That said, my brother has made a point to question me at length regarding the situation in Windsor. So far, I seem to have satisfied him, but I need to make sure that the story upon which we agreed is the story you told."

"In every particular, my lord." Of that, Rhys could be sure. He knew better than most about the tendency of liars to embellish the lies they were telling. Ultimately, they couldn't remember what they'd said in the past and tripped themselves up.

"Now, about this Morrydig," Edmund said, pronouncing it the same way as Miles and every other Norman Rhys had so far encountered, many of whom actually went out of their way not to say his name at all. "He was strangled, I hear, by a man wearing a ring on his right hand."

"That is so, my lord, or so we think." Rhys did have to swallow hard this time. "May I ask whence came your information?"

"From Owen de la Pole, who speaks very highly of your skills, by the way, and did so not only in my presence but in the king's." Edmund peered at him. "I am aware that you don't like him, but he is well-favored, and you would do well to treat him with respect."

"I make sure of it, my lord, most particularly."

Edmund might have scoffed again, but he held up his right hand instead. "I wear a ring like Owen described." Then he held up his left hand. "And on this hand too. Of the men sitting around the king's table last night, every one wore at least two rings and some three or four, though I find such displays excessive. I also find that nobles of lesser rank are more likely than those of a higher station to wear multiple rings."

Rhys tipped his head. "So you're saying that a man who wears only one ring—"

Edmund was ready to finish Rhys's sentence. "—is a man who is either an earl and has no need to display his wealth or is wealthy enough to possess just one ring. I'm leaning towards the latter. You're looking for a very minor nobleman or perhaps someone of the merchant class, though they are inclined to wear their wealth ostentatiously on their fingers too."

Rhys put out both his hands. He wore a ring on his left hand, given to him by the king when he joined his service, as a mark of trust. He owned one other, passed down from his father, which he had given as a sign of their union to Catrin to wear around her neck (since it was too large for her much smaller hands). Before they'd met, he'd worn that ring around his own neck, when he wore it at all. A ring worn on the right hand could impede his grip on his sword. One worn on the left could catch unexpectedly on armor or gear. Many warriors wore no rings at all for that reason.

"I would have preferred Owen had not spoken of it," Rhys said. "He shouldn't be telling just anyone."

"Am I *just anyone*?"

Rhys bent his head. "Of course not, my lord. If it weren't impolitic, I would caution him about speaking of this too much. Then again, if our killer thinks I am looking for a man wearing a ring on his right hand, he might remove it or switch it to his left."

"How would that aid you?" But even as he asked the question, Edmund removed one of his rings to gaze at the line of untanned skin on his hand. Moriddig had the same pale indentation around the base of his finger, confirming that he'd worn a ring there that was now missing. "I see."

"Either with the ring or without it, he would reveal himself."

"I will say nothing to Owen, then. He has never met a secret he could keep anyway." A smile quirked the corner of Edmund's mouth. "If, at some point, you need to plant a rumor, as I know you have done in the past, come to me again. All we'll need to do is share it with Owen."

19

Day Two

Catrin

Catrin awoke alone in their tent, Rhys having departed at some earlier point. She had been startled awake, and now she lay in the bed, the covers pulled up to her chin. In the back of her mind, it had been a sound that had awakened her. She looked to her right and saw a man-sized shadow just outside the flap of the door.

Her mouth dry, she called out. "Who's there?"

No reply came, and then between one heartbeat and the next, the shadow was gone.

Her heart racing, she couldn't get out of bed and dressed fast enough. Flinging open the flap, she stood in the doorway. The firepit at which they'd sat last night was burning low, indicating Rhys had tended it before he'd left. With Trahaearn gone, the closest tent a dozen yards away belonged to one of the king's guards, Edgar. His servant, Cedric, came out of the entrance to the tent and smiled at her. He had no Welsh, which had really been a saving grace for Trahaearn yesterday.

"Did you see anyone about just now?" Catrin asked him in English, his native tongue.

Cedric shook his head. "No, my lady, but I have been making the bed these last moments. My apologies. Is something wrong?" He took a few steps towards her.

She put up a hand. "No, nothing. All is well."

All was very much not well. Instead of dismissing the idea that someone had been outside her tent, Catrin accepted the possibility that the murderer had come for her or for evidence they were keeping in their possession. If true, that was bad. But what had her hurrying across the encampment was a sudden fear she wasn't his only target. Someone had murdered Moriddig yesterday and implicated Gruffydd. With the latter effort having failed, Gruffydd could be in danger too. She was ashamed the thought hadn't occurred to her earlier.

Catrin found Rhiannon tending a pot simmering on the fire. She was a small woman, hardly five feet tall, slim at the waist with a long rope of dark hair and one incredible streak of gray starting at the temple. "Is Gruffydd here?"

"He is warming up with Rory." Rhiannon smiled in greeting.

Catrin subsided a little. At least he wasn't alone.

"Would you like a warm cup this morning?"

"Thank you. I would love one." Catrin waited as Rhiannon poured her out a measure and then sipped tentatively. The taste was calming and encouraged her to catch her breath after her headlong rush out of her tent. "May I ask what's in it?"

Rhiannon waved a hand. "Mint leaves mostly, with a few other herbs to soothe the throat. And a touch of honey. It's Gruffydd's favorite, and this week I'll have it always available for him."

"Is that a way of telling me your husband is somewhat demanding?" Catrin took another sip. She agreed with Gruffydd that it soothed her throat. Maybe, if her conversation with Rhiannon went well, Catrin could ask for the full recipe.

Rhiannon laughed. "Not at all, except, of course, when he is."

Catrin laughed too, because she knew exactly what Rhiannon meant. "Is this also true of his work?"

"I know what you're asking. Gruffydd told me everything that happened yesterday, so do not feel the need to tread lightly." Looking around cautiously, Rhiannon added in an undertone. "You saw his song."

"Yes. I await the day he plays it for others to hear."

"You lied for him."

"We did."

Rhiannon bit her lip. "Even to the king?"

Catrin nodded. "Especially to the king."

"Gruffydd told me but I hardly dared believe it. I fear every moment for his life. I won't let him go anywhere alone."

It was the opening for which Catrin had been waiting. "I came here with that very thought and not just because of his song. Whoever put that poem in Moriddig's mouth meant to implicate him, if not for murder then for treason. He might be coming after Gruffydd next."

"The idea occurred to me as well, but I don't know what to do about it."

"Did you speak to Gruffydd about your fears?"

"I tried." Rhiannon let out something of a wry laugh. "He promised not to wander off by himself."

Catrin was liking Rhiannon more and more. The woman had a level head on her shoulders. It was becoming obvious, between Moriddig, Gruffydd, and the thousand other bards here, that being married to a bard wasn't easy. She and Gruffydd had made it work for many years.

Now Rhiannon rolled her eyes. "Not that I can trust him. How do you think the killer found the poem? Gruffydd might leave his head on the floor if it wasn't attached to his body." Then she put her hand over her mouth. "I shouldn't say such things. It's too close to the truth we fear."

"I should ask Rhys if someone can keep an eye on him."

"One of the king's men? We wouldn't thank you for that."

Rhiannon's instant denial had Catrin looking at her anew. "Who are you, besides Gruffydd's wife?"

"Don't you know? Hasn't that been gossiped about enough already?"

Catrin set down her cup. "My apologies for bringing up what is obviously a sore subject, but I don't know what you're talking about."

Rhiannon gave a little scoff. "You've been gone a while, so I suppose you weren't here when Gruffydd and I married. You're going to think it has something to do with Moriddig's murder. I really don't think it does. But you'll find out anyway the moment you start asking questions." The smile was back, with even more wryness than before. "I am an unacknowledged daughter of Gruffydd ap Gwenwynwyn. Owen de la Pole is my half-brother."

Catrin didn't bother to hide her astonishment. "Owen knows who you are?"

"He knows." The corner of Rhiannon's mouth quirked. "My father has always wanted the favor of the Normans, and he taught Owen to seek the same. Maintaining a semblance of propriety was more important than having yet another daughter. Really, from what I understand, his wife was furious to discover my existence, less because he strayed from her bed than because my mother was a nobody. He had sullied himself with a common girl. I still could have provided a means of alliance for him to a lord in Wales, since Normans don't want to marry illegitimate daughters, even when sired by the *Baron de la Pole*." She said her father's title with a snooty French accent.

Catrin tipped her head. "You're saying everyone knows who you are. Except for me, I suppose."

Rhiannon gave a genuine laugh. "There are no secrets in Wales. You know that."

"I'm sorry for prying."

"Don't be. My mother's family took us in. I was a nobleman's daughter raised far from the halls of power. I think that's one reason

Gruffydd found me so interesting, since he, like you, was raised within them."

Rhiannon could have been resentful of her fate, but Catrin recognized that she was just speaking the truth as she saw it. She certainly wasn't wrong. Catrin's family had been stewards to the rulers of Gwynedd since the time of Llywelyn's grandfather. Rhiannon had married into another family so honored, since Gruffydd's father had served Llywelyn as a magistrate. It had been his job to travel throughout Gwynedd, hearing cases and complaints when Llywelyn couldn't go himself.

"May I ask one more thing about this?"

"Surely."

"When was the last time you spoke to your brother?"

"A few days ago. We are cordial. At first he was afraid that I would want something from him, but since I don't, he will greet me on the rare occasions we encounter one another."

"Like this week."

For the first time, Rhiannon didn't answer easily, though she did say, very carefully, "Yes."

If Rhiannon's intent was to gain Catrin's attention, she had it. "Was there something untoward about your conversation?"

"Not that he shared with me, but I could tell he was worried about something. We are not close enough for me to press him."

"When exactly was this?"

"I'm almost afraid to say," Rhiannon wet her lower lip, "but it was the night before Moriddig died."

20

Day Two

Rhys

Rhys had risen early, with the mission of seeking out Adam and Patrick. He had been waylaid at breakfast by Prince Edmund and then by everyone else, from contestants to merchants to a woman he thought might be a prostitute. They all wanted to know if he'd found the murderer yet, if they themselves were safe, and if Rhys could share any information with them. Sadly, he could give them no assurances, only that he was doing his best. Having to confess his failure repeatedly was humbling.

By the time he'd extricated himself from the last questioner, the day's events had started. He wasted another precious hour traipsing about the festival grounds looking for Adam and Patrick. Last night, they'd both been too drunk to converse coherently. Inebriated people were sometimes uninhibited, but the pair had been morose and weepy, which made it impossible for Rhys to get a coherent word out of either of them, other than their endless regret that Moriddig was dead.

Finally, he tracked them down in the bards' pavilion, where contestants waited to be called to the various stages where the competitions were being held. Rhys hadn't looked there earlier because he hadn't expected Patrick to continue his participation in the festival. Once he found them, Adam refused to let Rhys speak to Patrick before he sang and wouldn't countenance any questions while he was in earshot. To Rhys's eyes, Adam had pivoted seamlessly from stewarding for Moriddig to watching over Patrick. To be fair, Adam appeared to have been doing that to one degree or another for some time before Moriddig's death.

Patrick had been falling down drunk last night. This morning he was on his feet and walking in a straight line to where he needed to go, in preparation for his first appearance in the competition.

Adam stopped behind a rope, urging Patrick on with a word of encouragement to continue towards one of the smaller stages set up in the fields around the main stage. With so many contests and contestants, it would be impossible for everyone to participate from just one stage. There were going to be at least three competitions occurring at the same time in different parts of the festival grounds.

Since this wasn't the main stage, it didn't have a viewing stand, just a large space in front for people to gather on the grass to hear the performers.

As Patrick set off, Rhys asked Adam, "How good is he, really?"

"You'll see in a moment."

"You sound a little grim."

Adam allowed himself a small sigh. "Patrick has his father's voice, no question, as well as his ability to control an audience from the stage. He revels in being the center of attention and knows how to perform. He has his father's intelligence too. But the plain truth is that he doesn't have Moriddig's attention to detail and willingness to commit the entirety of his being to the endeavor. A singing voice could be enough, but not if Patrick wants to fill his father's shoes." He glanced at Rhys. "At least, it wouldn't have been enough in the old days."

"Meaning prior to Llywelyn's death."

"It's been longer ago than that for us."

"You surprise me." Rhys found himself respecting Adam's honesty.

"Why? For speaking plainly? You think I can't see what is right in front of me?"

"And what is right in front of you?"

Now Adam smiled a little sadly. "Owen and his father turned to King Edward years ago. These new rules that everyone is so shocked about have been our way of life for a decade."

"Owen and his father turned to King Edward because Owen plotted with Dafydd to murder Llywelyn." Rhys couldn't contain his outrage, even as he told himself this was no way to interrogate a suspect.

Adam put up both hands. "I-I-I didn't mean to imply—"

"Allow me to apologize." Rhys took Adam's arm and moved him away from the other onlookers, a few of whom had glanced in their direction when Rhys's voice had risen. "As I'm sure you can imagine, Llywelyn's death remains a sore point for me."

Adam bent his head briefly. "I do realize that, and I was trying to speak obliquely without casting blame. Please forgive me as well. I know you are here to talk of Moriddig. What can I tell you that you don't already know?"

"Well, first—"

Before Rhys could finish his sentence, he was interrupted by a glorious tenor. Patrick's voice was pure in a way that only a young man's could be, before it darkened with age and time.

"I see now what you mean," he said softly.

At first, Adam's expression became almost wistful as he listened to his nephew. Then he grew more intent—and more critical. "This isn't a song he has written, but one that is well known to many. His voice is magical, up until you realize he has flubbed the words again."

"Has he?"

"Twice now." Adam wrinkled his nose. "That he knows the song perfectly according to the written text matters only when he is being judged. Certainly a lord wouldn't care. *Nobody* cares if the words of any one ballad conform exactly to the way he was taught. But it will matter to the judges here, and if he isn't ranked highly at the end, it might be difficult for Owen to keep him on. Or any other lord to hire him."

"He's hardly twenty. Was he ever going to win, really?"

"Moriddig won an *eisteddfod* when he was twenty. So did Gruffydd."

As Adam had pointed out, those were in by-gone days, when large musical festivals were an annual event. "But surely placing high or, dare I say, *winning* the voice category could be enough?"

Rhys's query seemed to settle Adam a bit. "It could be, though I would prefer he actually learned the lyrics. To be honest, it was going to be touch and go whether Moriddig could have ordained Patrick a bard this year. There is so much to memorize, and he just doesn't seem to understand how much work it is going to take. To tell you the truth, half the time when he should have been working on his music, he was running errands for Hugh. He can read and write, so copying out writs for Hugh was far easier than memorizing songs for his father. I warned him that he was neglecting his studies, but he repeatedly brushed me off."

"Young men often have trouble being told what to do, especially by their fathers—or uncles."

Adam heaved a sigh. "You're not wrong about that. Maybe if Patrick had been Hugh's son, he would have gone running for instruction to Moriddig!"

Rhys put a hand on his shoulder. "It really might not matter. After this week, the order of Welsh bards is never going to be the same. The system of apprenticeship might not survive the festival."

Adam left off his concentrating stare in Patrick's direction long enough to really look at Rhys. "You think it will come to that?"

"I am quite sure it already has."

Adam looked as if he didn't believe him, or at least he didn't indicate he was overly concerned about the possibility. Instead, he focused once more on his nephew.

The song ended and Patrick bowed, to enthusiastic applause from the audience. When he came back to Adam, his color was high, as were his emotions. His father's death was momentarily forgotten, or at least put to the side, and he was feeling joy. Rhys could see it in his whole being.

Adam gripped his shoulder. "Well done, boy."

"I missed a few words, but—"

"It will not matter. Your voice is enough." Adam spoke sincerely, without even a glance at Rhys or an arch look. He was supportive of his nephew and accepted the futility in this moment of being critical.

Their interaction reminded Rhys of his own years of training to become a warrior. As a small child, he'd learned his trade through wrestling and play with wooden swords or bows and arrows. As a youth in Llywelyn's court, he fought against boys of a similar age. And then he'd been included on missions, with the real possibility of battle.

All that time, he'd had older men to follow. Some were dismissive or brutal, seemingly taking pleasure in his failures. Others, the ones he returned to even when he was a member of Llywelyn's *teulu* in his own right, behaved as Adam had done just now. The moments after a fight, successful or not, weren't the time for recriminations or instruction. That came later, on the practice field, with cooler heads. Much of the time, like Patrick, Rhys had already been aware of what he'd done wrong. Creating an environment for a student to identify his own mistakes was a mark of a good teacher.

So while Patrick's mistakes might matter in the end, there was little point in telling Patrick so in this moment. It was done. Adam wasn't a musician himself, but that didn't mean he wasn't a good instructor—and a good uncle to his orphaned nephew.

"If you could bear with me for a moment longer." Rhys made a motion to stop the men's departure. "I need to ask you about yesterday morning." And then, before they could reply in any meaningful way, he followed with, "Where were each of you in the hours before the start of the rehearsal?"

Patrick was still blinking away his performance, so it was Adam who answered first. "With the castle so full of the king's men, I had my own tent in the encampment and met Moriddig for breakfast. Patrick joined us. And then we were called to the rehearsal."

Patrick put out a hand to his uncle at this conclusion. "Actually, Uncle, if I may say so, *you* joined *me* for breakfast. Father had already left. I never saw him at all yesterday." For a moment, he blinked back what might have been tears.

Adam smiled at his nephew. "Of course, you are right. I'm misremembering."

Although a sweet moment between Adam and Patrick, the correction made Rhys wary. Adam had described his day to Catrin in the same terms as he'd just related it to Rhys. But if Patrick was right, Adam's remembrance had been incorrect both times. "To clarify, Adam, if I am understanding correctly, you ate breakfast with Moriddig, departed with him, and then returned to eat again with Patrick?"

"No, that's not right." Adam shook his head. "I shared a meal with my brother, but he left on his own. Then I had a second breakfast with Patrick, after which I—" He hesitated and, for some reason, his face flushed.

Patrick rolled his eyes. "You have to tell him, uncle."

If he'd been someone else, Rhys might have suspected Adam had been with a woman.

When Adam still didn't say anything, Patrick laughed. "He *saw to his needs*, as he sometimes says. My uncle is very particular about his bowels. They must be evacuated every day after breakfast without fail or he thinks he's dying." He shoved at his uncle's shoulder. "You know it's true."

Rhys waved away any further explanation. The small amount Patrick had said was already more than he wanted to know about the workings of Adam's innards. "My apologies. No need to say more."

By now, however, Adam was ready to laugh with his nephew. "It's the truth. I can't deny it." But then he sobered, all joviality leaving him. "That was the last time I saw my brother."

21

Day Two

Catrin

Catrin had known that sensing a stranger near her tent was going to concern her husband. For once, she shared Rhys's opinion that she needed an escort. In fact, she thought every one of them needed an escort and said so.

Her intent had been to enlist her brother for that duty, if he was willing. But when she finally tracked down Rhys to tell him her concerns, he was talking to Miles de Bohun. Somehow, one thing led to another, and it was now Miles himself who was escorting her around the festival grounds. They ended up near the main viewing stand, a few feet from where Math was standing guard.

At his own request, he was back on regular duty, guarding the king. Since they remained completely in the dark as to the identity of the murderer, it was Math's thought that one of them needed to keep an eye on proceedings in the king's court. It also kept Math in his fellow guards' good graces. Rhys was universally acknowledged to be special. As the newest member of the king's guard, Math was still the lowest man in the hierarchy.

On the whole, she wasn't unhappy with the choice of company. As one of the Windsor conspirators, she trusted Miles with the investigation, maybe even more than her own brother. She did hope, however, that she wouldn't trip herself up with all the secrets she was keeping.

"So how does the scoring work?" Miles had been full of questions, which she thought were sincere but which he might be employing as a way to distract her from her worries.

"It's similar to a joust," she said, putting the festival in terms she thought Miles would understand, "except with songs instead of blows. That's what the judges are for. Contestants get points for every event. Over the course of the festival, the bard who accumulates the most points wins."

Math spoke from a few feet away. "One might wonder, then, why Cadwgan is getting such low scores?"

"Who?" Miles turned to him.

Catrin intervened. "Miles, this is Math, of whom we have spoken. Math, this is Miles de Bohun."

Math bent his head. "My lord."

"I know who you are." Miles waved a hand. "Enough of that. Tell me what you're thinking." Though quite different in age and upbringing, they both had been born men of rank. Even if Math was Welsh, Miles appeared happy to recognize a fellow friend of Rhys.

"That last bard." Math made a motion with his head to indicate the man who'd just left the stage.

Math was right that Cadwgan had given an incredible performance, singing a long ballad about the sea in French, to uproarious applause from all parts, even the king and queen. The royal couple hadn't attended every session, but they'd been sitting together for the last hour to watch this event.

Miles nodded. "He was very accomplished. Even I, with no music in my blood, could tell that. Why do you say his scores are low?"

"Because they are," Math said, and then added what seemed at first to be a *non sequitur*. "Have you been watching the bards' faces when they arrive to perform?"

As each bard had taken the center position, he would bow first to the king and then to the judges, and then he'd settle himself to face the crowd for his performance. Because of the way Catrin and Miles had positioned themselves, they had been able to see the face of every contestant when he crossed the stage.

Miles did his best to answer. "Some look nervous; others tense; others grim; a few determined."

"And some are almost knowing, as if amused by the proceedings," Math said. "Sometimes these looks continue after their performances, regardless of how well they did."

Catrin tipped her head. "Cadwgan was one of the contestants who looked particularly grim before he started."

"And he looks grim now," Math said. "I think it's because he knew what his score was going to be before he started singing."

Catrin looked towards the judges. They had their heads together at their table. Hugh stood off to one side, writing in his ledger.

Miles pursed his lips. "Is it in your mind that something untoward is going on? Are you wondering how fair this competition actually is?"

"It's possible Moriddig's murder was about eliminating competition," Math said. "If someone is willing to murder to win, what else might he be willing to do?"

"Cheat." Miles said.

Math made a motion with his head. "Why not?"

King Edward was just rising from his chair, his hand out to the queen. The session was adjourning for a mid-afternoon meal. The judges began rising from their table too, moving towards Hugh who had signaled that they should gather around him. Math bowed briefly to Miles again and, with a smile at Catrin, followed the king and queen, as was required.

Miles gave Catrin a nudge. "Go talk to Hugh. You're Welsh. He'll object less to you looking over his shoulder than to me."

Catrin wasn't entirely sure that was true. He might not like her inquiring about the judging. She didn't even know how each of the judges had been chosen. Up until Miles and Math had started talking, she hadn't cared. She *had* overheard some of them speaking French amongst themselves. That meant they were less likely to be from the heart of Gwynedd. No surprise there.

She did as Miles bid her anyway, gliding up behind the judges and listening to the tail end of Hugh's speech, which, tellingly, was in French. It was about not discussing the results until they were finalized in order to maintain their integrity, after which he dismissed them until the evening program.

When a moment later he spied Catrin, his face fell. "My dear, I have been meaning to find you. I am so sorry to have involved you in such horrible circumstances yesterday. Can you ever forgive me?"

"Of course, I can. It wasn't your fault. I am so sorry for the loss of your friend."

Hugh shook his head. "Awful. Just awful."

Catrin already knew Hugh could not be the killer, since he'd been in full view of hundreds during the time of the murder. Now, she did a quick canter around her conscience and lied. "It has been suggested that I take a look at the current standings."

Hugh's lips formed a shape that might have been about to ask *who suggested you do this?* but then thought better of his question and simply gestured her closer. He didn't give her the book, but he did allow her to read down the lists of contestants, the categories in which they were being evaluated, and their current score. With a thousand bards present, the names took up many pages. In addition, only half the bards had participated today, and Gruffydd had not been among them. Cadwgan's position in the rankings was easy to spot. His total put him in the top ten, but not the top five.

Catrin silently agreed with Math that this was odd.

"Is everything satisfactory?" Hugh's tone was a bit tremulous. "Please assure the queen that I am doing my best."

"Doing your best to do what?" She tried to keep her tone level and unsurprised.

"Keep the contest fair, of course." Hugh's voice steadied. "She was very concerned that no hint of favoritism mar the festival."

Catrin decided to take the bull by the horns. "Cadwgan's score is very low for him. Is that the opposite of favoritism? I wouldn't be the only one thinking he was the best of this last set."

"He was, wasn't he?" Hugh frowned as he turned the book more towards himself. "That is odd. His score should be higher. I'll have to go back through each of the judge's score sheets to make sure the accounting is correct." He let out a disgusted sigh. "Must I do everything?"

"The queen was concerned about favoritism." Catrin repeated Hugh's own words as if the queen had said them to her as well. "How easy would it be for a contestant to bribe one or more of the judges?"

Hugh's mouth worked, making Catrin think his instinct was to deny the possibility. But then he said, "Easy enough. However, I specifically invited only the most reputable men. I am confident in the integrity of the judging at this festival." His jaw tightened. "Besides, we let it be known that the punishment for taking a bribe would be worse than for a bard who sings a forbidden song."

"Worse than losing a tongue?"

"Oh yes. The queen was very clear. This is her land and her festival. A judge found tampering with the rankings will be hanged by the neck until dead."

22

Day Two
Simon

"I don't see many tears," Elizabeth said in a low voice from their position against the wall of the graveyard. "In truth, I don't see any tears!"

Earlier, a crowd of people had packed into St. Mary's Church for Moriddig's funeral and then processed out to witness the burial itself. They were fitting the funeral in between the end of the afternoon sessions and the start of the evening program. Simon knew for a fact that three more funerals were planned for tomorrow. As far as he knew, those deaths had been natural ones. With this many people come to the festival, they had become a small city. Deaths were inevitable.

"With the rain, how can we even tell?" Between entering the church an hour ago and now, it had turned into a wild and windy day. High above them, the branches of the yew trees that surrounded the church moved this way and that with a swishing sound. Some of the trees were so old they'd split. Simon didn't know when they'd been planted, but the legend of Overton said it was before the coming of the Romans.

Simon and Rhys had been hoping that by attending the service and burial they might gain some insight into the identity of the murderer. But with most of the mourners huddled in their cloaks against the rain, there was little to see. Elizabeth had come with him, more out of curiosity than because she knew anything about investigating, praise be, or because she mourned Moriddig more than she would any other stranger. Truly, Elizabeth was right that it made her no different from anyone else.

It was on the tip of his tongue to make a jest about how *someone* better be crying at his funeral, but he swallowed it down. He and Elizabeth were separated too often because of his service to the king, and he had spent too much time in mortal danger, for such a remark to be amusing.

Instead he squeezed her hand and said, "His wife died, and he had only the one son and a brother. I would have thought he would have had friends among the bards, but from what we've learned since his death, he could be a prickly fellow. You're right that most people have come out of duty or because they are spectating."

"Not them." Elizabeth gestured behind them to where Gruffydd and his wife, Rhiannon, were standing. "They're the only ones who seem the slightest bit sad."

While their hoods were up, they weren't clutching their cloaks around their chests but taking the rain as it came. They were also holding hands. Sometimes Simon envied the way the Welsh were allowed to be expressive.

"Apparently, and against all expectation, they were friends."

"Catrin implied as much," Elizabeth said. "Now look past them and tell me what's going on there."

She was looking behind Gruffydd and Rhiannon, nearer to the church gate. There, Adam and Joan, Owen de la Pole's wife, were glaring at each other, their faces a handspan apart.

Given that Adam and Joan were not married and, in fact, were the opposite of married, their closeness would have been deemed improper under almost any circumstance. Fortunately for them, except for Simon and Elizabeth, everyone else was facing Moriddig's grave.

Then the pair separated, Joan leaving the graveyard through the gate, and Adam moving through the crowd to the gravesite where he should have been all along and where Patrick was standing over his father's body.

Just as he passed Simon, a particularly large gust of wind blew Adam's blue hood off his head. He turned to grab it, but Simon had already plucked it out of the air, preventing it from hitting the ground. He gave it back to Adam, who offered a word of thanks, before continuing on.

The graveside service didn't last nearly as long as the mass that had preceded it, which was a blessing, given the weather. Still, Simon found it ironic that no bard sang, though the combined force of the bards present might have been enough to power a windmill. The priest gave the benediction, the pallbearers lowered Moriddig into the ground, and the gravediggers began throwing dirt on the body. At that point, most of the congregation departed for warmer and drier locales.

Simon and Elizabeth paused under one of the larger yew trees, where they were joined a moment later by Rhys and Catrin, wanting to be the last out of the churchyard.

"I didn't see you earlier," Simon said to Rhys.

"That's because we were in the lychgate, inadvertently eavesdropping on an argument Adam was having with Joan," Catrin said.

"Inadvertently?" Elizabeth asked with a smile.

Catrin grinned. Simon had been more pleased than he could say that the two women had hit it off immediately upon meeting. It hadn't been required, but it had definitely been something to hope for. "We were last out of the church, and the lychgate is sheltered, so we paused there, and it just so happened we were right behind the pair of them when they started arguing. Adam was furious."

"Not something we've seen until now," Rhys added.

Simon was struck by a horrible thought. "Could there have been a relationship between Joan and—"

"And Adam?" Elizabeth interrupted his thought with a laugh. "Or Morrydig? Are you wondering if the child she carries is Owen's? You can never tell with young women, but both men are twice her age, and they are—" She cleared her throat. "How do I say this? Not attractive."

Her gaze went to Catrin who confirmed her assessment. "We didn't hear the whole argument, but it was definitely about money."

"On the surface, that is only sensible," Rhys said, "since Adam managed Moriddig's finances. If we understood correctly, Adam was angry at Owen and Joan for reneging on his last payment. With Moriddig dead, they don't think they should have to pay what they owe."

Elizabeth looked at Simon. "Are Owen's finances in that poor a state?"

"I wouldn't know. I would not have said so." Though it might explain Owen's attempt to befriend Simon yesterday over a cup of wine.

"Isn't Patrick going to be taking his father's place?" Elizabeth then asked Rhys and Catrin. "That's the tradition, isn't it?"

Rhys turned one hand palm up. "If so, we have not heard of it. Owen did not imply as much when we spoke to him, and there is some question as to Patrick's readiness."

"Even if Owen did hire Patrick," Catrin said, "his rate would be much lower than his father's."

Rhys glanced at his wife. "At the same time, if Owen and Joan are stretched for coin, they might hire Patrick because they don't have the resources to replace Moriddig with a more accomplished bard."

"I wouldn't have thought the best way of going about that was to alienate Adam," Simon said.

"Or, they could be saving their money *for* that bard," Elizabeth pointed out.

"Either way, Adam was irate," Catrin said. "I have hardly ever seen him without a smile on his face."

"He lost his brother and his livelihood in one go," Simon said. "Two such large losses could bring down any man."

Elizabeth was looking pensive. "What I don't see is what their argument has to do with the investigation. With Morrydig's death, Adam lost everything. And while Joan and Owen might have wanted to get rid of him as their bard, there are easier ways than murder!"

"If I'm going to find the culprit, I'm going to have to dig more into their lives." Rhys sighed. "They're not going to like it."

Simon put a hand on his friend's shoulder, more glad than he could say that they were in this together. He had been worried with this festival, and then the murder, if Rhys's loyalty to the king would be put to the test again. For now, it seemed to be holding. "That may be, but it is also not your problem. Don't be deceived by the king's desire to continue with the festival. While he hates having his plans disrupted, he likes murder even less."

23

Day Two

Catrin

"I have missed you dreadfully, and so has baby Edward." Eleanor was unusually petulant as Catrin entered her pavilion. Although the queen was sleeping at her manor house adjacent to the festival grounds, she had set up a pavilion in the field near her husband's to which she could easily retreat during the day.

There was only one response Catrin could make. "Please accept my sincerest apologies, my lady. This is a murder not easily solved."

"So I've heard." Now her tone was dry, and without ceremony she dumped the baby into Catrin's arms.

Baby Edward was approaching five months old and consequently not yet sitting up or moving about for himself. While Eleanor had been terrifyingly attentive to him throughout his first few months of life, fearful he would not survive, Catrin could see her growing bored with his needs with each day that passed.

Honestly, Catrin had been surprised to see her holding him at all. Eleanor had stopped nursing him herself in the weeks surrounding Alfonso's death. His cradle was no longer even in an adjacent room to hers. Catrin thought her desire to sleep alone and away from him was half the reason she was sleeping at the manor rather than sharing the pavilion with him, his carers, and her ladies.

Because she was holding the baby, Catrin thought she was allowed a chair and sat in order to bounce the boy on her knee. "My lady, may I ask you a question about the festival?"

"What is it, my dear?" The queen had settled herself next to a cup of wine and a plate of food, which she proceeded to place on her lap.

"Did you speak to Hugh about the fairness of the judging? He told me earlier today that if any judge is found to have taken a bribe, he will be hanged!"

"Well, of course. That goes without saying. The judging will be fair or not at all."

Catrin supposed she shouldn't have expected anything less from the queen. She wanted things a certain way and shaped those around her to ensure it.

"Now, tell me what you have discovered about that dead bard." Eleanor was almost gleeful as she munched on a carrot. "He played well enough the other night, but I have long thought his voice was not really to my taste."

"I wasn't aware you had heard him play before."

Baby Edward found the tie of Catrin's coif and pulled on it. She let him untie the strings and tug the whole thing off her head. Anything to keep him happy while her conversation with the queen turned into an interview.

Eleanor waved a hand in the air. "It was a long time ago. I can't even remember when. We were passing through this region and happened to spend an evening with Griffith, Owen's father. Morrydig was younger then, as was I." She seemed lost in thought for a moment, remembering those bygone days, and then she added, "I have to wonder now if he might still be alive had I interrupted that argument he was having before the festival began."

She said this as if Catrin should have any idea what she was talking about. Catrin had already heard about an argument between Moriddig and another woman the morning he died. She'd just witnessed an argument between Joan and Adam. She couldn't wait to hear all about a third.

"My lady, perhaps I wasn't as attentive as I should have been yesterday. To what argument are you referring?"

"It was the other night. Margaret heard him too." She lifted her chin. "Margaret! Where are you?"

Margaret hurried through the back entrance to the tent, her face pink. Eleanor wasn't looking at her so didn't notice, but Catrin met her eyes, and she blushed even more. In a flash of understanding, Catrin realized she'd been with a man. And then she saw, through the half-open doorway to the pavilion, male legs walking away. There was some gossip here she'd missed.

"There you are." Eleanor remained too interested in telling her story to take in the flustered appearance of her lady-in-waiting. "Tell Catrin about the argument we overheard Morrydig having."

Margaret managed to get her expression in order. "It must have been a week ago now, shortly after we arrived in Overton, when the queen and I were walking from the pavilion towards the manor."

"Was it just the two of you?" Catrin said.

"I had my guards with us, of course," Eleanor said. "I suppose you can ask them what they remember. Off towards the river, we heard shouting. A male voice said, *They won't get away with this! Not again!*"

"This was followed by a great deal of profanity." Margaret's nose went into the air. She was one of the few people in the entire world who could embellish a story the queen was telling. They were cousins and had been friends practically since birth.

"Quite inventive profanity," Eleanor said.

"They were speaking in French?" Catrin asked.

"Some of the time. That first bit was in French, and then there were incomprehensible bits in Welsh." This was typical Margaret. It wasn't only that she didn't understand Welsh. In her view, the language itself made no sense.

Catrin put aside that twist of resentment as unimportant. "How did you know it was Moriddig speaking?"

"He came striding out from the trees," Eleanor said. "He practically ran us over before he realized we were there and who we were."

"He was very contrite, but there was no doubt it was Morrydig," Margaret said. "He made his apologies."

"Which I accepted," Eleanor said.

"I think he would have run from us as quickly as he was able if our queen hadn't asked what he was doing." Margaret's mouth twisted into a satisfied smile at the memory. "He didn't want to say."

"Of course he didn't want to say. But I asked him a direct question, and he couldn't get out of answering." Eleanor seemed pleased with herself for having the ability to force a confession. "He apologized again and said it had just been a meeting of old friends."

Margaret nodded towards the queen. "Even then, my lady didn't let it go. She said that it was the people we have known the longest who can be the most difficult. I'm quite sure she was referring to me! Morrydig laughed and said he'd known this friend since childhood."

"I gave him leave to depart after that," Eleanor said.

"So he didn't tell you the identity of the other man?" Catrin was astonished after all this that she wasn't finding more of an answer.

"He did not," Margaret said.

"I would have told you about this eventually, but you didn't come back." Contrary to her earlier petulance, Eleanor had a hint of a smile around her lips. "I was hoping to hear what you'd learned."

"Again, I can only apologize," Catrin said. "I'm here now."

"And you'll want to be leaving again, I'm sure." Eleanor motioned to Baby Edward's wetnurse, who'd been sitting quietly in the corner this whole time, to take the baby from Catrin. "Your husband will want to hear this story."

"Thank you, my lady." While Catrin rose to her feet, she paused before leaving. "If you were to hear the second voice again, would you recognize it?"

Eleanor frowned in thought before speaking slowly, "You know, I think I may already have."

"When?" Margaret and Catrin asked together.

"He sang last of all at the session this afternoon. One of the older bards. Cadigan, I think his name was. His French was perfect. He made me weep to hear his song about the sea."

24

Day Two

Rhys

To have Catrin speak to him twice about the same bard sent Rhys striding through the encampment, on a quest to find Cadwgan. Bards kept late hours, and even with darkness having fallen, he assumed he would find him awake.

As it turned out, Cadwgan was not only awake, he wasn't alone, holding court around a fire circle amongst a dozen bards, most of whom were younger and from South Wales. Some of these lands, like Gwent and Morgannwg, had been conquered by the Normans two hundred years ago. It had been generations since bards there had free rein to sing what they liked, which perhaps was the reason Cadwgan, as their *de facto* leader, had produced such a lovely song. It had fit the king's (and queen's) requirements perfectly.

Rhys hesitated on the edge of the firelight, not wanting this first conversation to be public.

Cadwgan saw him and lifted his cup. "It's the crusader who serves the king." He poked at the young man sitting next to him, telling him to move. "Have a seat."

Internally stifling a sigh at the way he'd been introduced, Rhys took the low stool the young man vacated, apparently without resentment. He simply moved around the fire circle in order to sit next to Moriddig's son, Patrick, on a horizontal log. "It had been my thought to speak to you in private."

Cadwgan motioned with his cup again. "I have nothing to hide."

Rhys wanted to sigh again, but instead he chose to call Cadwgan's bluff, if that's what it was. "You were overheard having an argument with Moriddig."

There had been some side conversations going on around the circle, even after Rhys's arrival, but now they stopped abruptly, like an axe chopping through a thin branch. Cadwgan had said he didn't care if he had an audience. Well now, for certain, he did.

Cadwgan, however, laughed. "If I was really overheard, as you say, you would know what we argued about and thus know that it—and I—had nothing to do with Moriddig's death."

"The listeners had no Welsh." Rhys respected Cadwgan's spirited response, but he didn't back down. "What did you argue about? You were heard to say that someone wouldn't be getting away with something again."

Now, Cadwgan scoffed. He had been speaking in Welsh to Rhys, and it did seem that the men around him understood enough to follow the conversation, or they were putting on a good show of it.

"I wasn't actually arguing with Moriddig. I was disturbed by the order of the proceedings, and the fact that he had all but been crowned winner before the contest even started."

"That is a motive for murder, if I ever heard one."

Cadwgan seemed to think that was funny too. "You might think so, but killing Moriddig still wouldn't mean I'd win the chair."

"Why not? Your voice is incredible, as you well know. You brought the queen to tears today. You might be her favorite so far."

Cadwgan sat up a little straighter at that, even as he said, "Fat lot of good it did me. My score was lower than it should have been. If it was low today, it will continue to be low. I'll never catch up, and there is nothing I can do about it, especially now that Moriddig is dead."

"Especially now?" Rhys looked at him a bit sideways. "I would have thought Moriddig's death would help your chances. That's what you were shouting about."

Another scoff. "No, you have it exactly wrong. Moriddig also thought it was unfair. He was going to speak to Hugh on my behalf." Cadwgan gestured broadly to encompass the men before him. "On the behalf of all of us. He promised."

"Did he follow through?"

"Given my score, apparently not."

Rhys contemplated how much he was willing to share and decided a little more might help Cadwgan trust him. "I can tell you that Hugh noted your low score today and promised to do an accounting."

"You believed him?" Cadwgan burst out laughing. "Hugh is not known for his honesty."

Rhys was definitely missing something, or maybe a great deal. "Are you saying it's Hugh himself putting his finger on the scale?"

Mocking laughter arose from several more men around the fire, telling Rhys what they believed to be the answer before Cadwgan actually replied. "He has always taken bribes. How can you not know that?"

Rhys spread his hands wide. "I am not a bard, and nobody has ever said. Is this scheme with the knowledge and approval of Owen de la Pole? Does the king know?"

The laughter, Cadwgan's included, stopped abruptly, in a manner similar to earlier. In a more thoughtful tone, he said, "I always assumed the old man, Gruffydd, knew and looked the other way. I'm not sure about his son." He glanced at Patrick. "If your father were here, what would he say?"

Everyone looked at Patrick, who swallowed hard. "Hugh hasn't been taking bribes at this festival."

A general chorus of mockery rose up again from those around him, but Patrick held firm. "Hugh did take bribes in the past. We all know it. But not this time. Some of you think my father won his place by buying it. It isn't true." Patrick's chin stuck out at these last words. "He earned everything he ever achieved. As will I."

25

Day Three

Rhys

"We have to start inquiring about Hugh," Catrin said from beside Rhys. The two of them, plus Math, were seated at a table in the meal pavilion, having something of a hurried breakfast. "We have no choice."

"We do have a choice." Yesterday, Rhys had met Prince Edmund here. With another day gone and no arrests, he could feel the eyes of every other person present, judging him for his lack of progress. "Moriddig's murder has to be our first priority. The king may see any questions about Hugh as outside my purview. And that isn't to even mention what Queen Eleanor or Owen de la Pole might say. Perhaps the bards were lying to me last night."

"Did they sound like they were lying?" Math asked.

"How can we believe Gruffydd but not Cadwgan?" Catrin said. "*Someone* is lying to us, clearly, but I doubt it is ten people all at once. Besides, Patrick admitted Hugh used to take bribes, and many of the men believe Moriddig gained his position by giving one, even if Patrick denied that too. We need to know if money is changing hands this week. We have to follow where the investigation leads us."

Rhys found himself shaking his head. "We are wading into deep water."

"I can swim just fine," Math said.

"Can you? You are more confident than I." Rhys looked at the pair of them, both practically glaring back. Then he gave way. "In truth, I don't even disagree with you. I just want you to think about what we may be getting involved in. Imagine if Owen has condoned Hugh's activities? Or the king knows about it and wants to ensure the identity of a winner?"

"The queen was adamant that no corruption occur," Catrin said. "She's going to hang anyone found cheating."

"The fact that she told that to Hugh—and to you—is what's keeping me moving forward right now," Rhys said. "Murder investigations reveal secrets that would otherwise have been kept hidden. We'll start by confirming the story I was told last night. We need to know if bribery is actually happening *before* we speak to Hugh, Owen or, ultimately, the king and queen."

It was time for Math to return to duty, so Rhys and Catrin set out alone. They decided to start with bards from Gwynedd, figuring they were more likely to be sympathetic to their questions. It was helpful that most of them had settled on the periphery of the festival grounds. As Rhys had witnessed last night, bards from the same kingdom tended to flock together.

As it turned out, no subtlety was needed, since the first bard they approached practically spit out his initial response. "You're asking me that *now*?"

Rhys looked at him warily. "If not now, when?"

The man, whose name was Dafydd, threw up his hands in frustration. "Years ago would have been helpful."

"I am sorry not to have done that, but I remain ignorant as to what might have transpired in the past."

They had come upon Dafydd outside his wagon, preparing for the day by tuning his *crwth*. This was not the same Dafydd, or *Dai* as he'd named himself when he'd admitted his heritage, who'd sung in Windsor. Catrin's son, Justin, had identified him as a fellow Welshman, a fact which the bard had begged Justin not to reveal. It seemed he was still passing as an Englishman, because he hadn't answered the king's summons. It was a hard life, living a lie like that. Rhys honestly wished him well and didn't judge.

"Surely there was talk in the royal court before the event!"

"I assure you there wasn't. Nor was I involved in any of the planning for the festival."

"You're the king's quaestor!" Dafydd was still irate.

"If you think that means King Edward confides in me, you would be wholly mistaken," Rhys said. "Even so, I assure you that I was not party to any gossip from anyone who sits closer to the king than I about bribery at the festival. We heard about this for the first time last night from other bards."

Dafydd gave a grunt, obviously finding this very hard to believe.

"I can only apologize again," Rhys said. "It has been years since I attended a festival like this."

"Four years, actually," Dafydd said. "Admittedly, that one was smaller, and included only bards from Gwynedd."

Rhys bent his head. "I do remember."

When his head came up, he met Dafydd's eyes. It was as if the bard had been waiting for the moment. Instead of the recriminations for which Rhys was bracing himself, there was an outpouring of sympathy—from Dafydd to Rhys and Rhys to Dafydd. They both knew what they had lost. He could find irony in how much they had lamented at the time about the reduction of Llywelyn's land and authority to west of the River Conwy. In retrospect, those had been idyllic days.

More in accord, Dafydd said, "I have heard from others that the first time Hugh asked for a bribe was as long ago as three decades, before Llywelyn was acknowledged ruler of all Wales. At that time, irregularities at an *eisteddfod* would not have risen to his concern. That event didn't even take place in Gwynedd, else Hugh would not have been in charge. You were young then too, and soon went on crusade. No man can look askance at you for that, especially because you came home afterwards. Once Llywelyn lost the first war to England, we in Gwynedd held only that one festival. To tell the truth, I barely believed until I arrived that we were having one now."

Rhys would have preferred they weren't having one now, but he didn't say so. This was the man's livelihood, after all.

"Tell us how it started," Catrin said, "for you, anyway."

Dafydd was no longer angry, or even resigned. Just matter-of-fact, since someone was listening. "Years before I was a bard in my own right, my father came home one day cursing. Hugh had asked for what he called his *fee,* implying that without it my father would find himself farther down the rankings. My father gave him the new cloak off his back. He won the festival, which I can't say I was sorry about because his victory gave me a boost as well. I was his apprentice in those days."

"How long ago was this?" Catrin asked.

"Fifteen years? That would have been shortly after King Henry recognized Llywelyn as the *princeps* of Wales." He raised his eyebrows at Rhys. "And shortly before you left for the Holy Land."

"I was oblivious to anything but my own concerns," Rhys said.

"Again, not your fault. This was also in Powys, not far from here but very far from Gwynedd."

"Did your father tell anyone else?"

"Whom would he tell? Besides, once the fee was accepted and he'd won the contest, he was complicit."

"What about the men who gave Hugh fees and didn't win?" Catrin said.

"Now that is a question," Dafydd said, "and I think it's the reason Hugh has got away with his activity for so long. He is too smart to have anyone going away unhappy. He promises different rewards to different men. My father never paid him quite as significant a fee again, but he would speak well of him, or buy him a drink of an evening. Like it was a gift. And because of my father's victory, he never lacked for a patron. I never did either, before the war."

"What about Moriddig?" Rhys said. "It is my understanding he was aware of the situation."

"And that we all thought he achieved his place because he paid Hugh to arrange for it all those years ago?" Dafydd snorted. "As much as he denied it, he wasn't an accomplished enough bard for us to ever believe him."

"He wasn't accomplished enough?" Catrin wrinkled her nose, herself disbelieving.

Both she and Rhys had been present when Moriddig had sung for the king the night before his death. He'd been magnificent. Rhys could believe Moriddig had won his place that first time through a fee to Hugh, but thirty years of service indicated he deserved it.

"Oh, he was a fine bard, but not the finest. Not like Gruffydd." Dafydd put out a hand. "I know what you're thinking. I'm from Gwynedd so my assessment has to be taken with a grain of salt. But if you think so, you'd be wrong. Moriddig had an impressive voice, it's true. It was his compositions that were lacking."

Again, that was a matter of perspective and judgment, which was why festivals needed judges. A musical competition wasn't the same as two men jousting, where one physically knocked the other off his horse. The finest bard in the land could only ever be a matter of opinion. Very rarely was the man who sat in the chair put there by genuine acclaim. Taliesin must have been such a man, in his day, and Aneirin in his. But even then, Rhys suspected they'd had rivals whose names were lost to the mists of time.

"How many of the men here have been subject to Hugh's requests for payment?" Catrin said.

"I couldn't say." Dafydd chewed on his lower lip. "May I ask who told you about the scheme?"

Rhys and Catrin exchanged a glance before Rhys said, "I'd prefer not to say."

"If you were so concerned about it, why didn't you say something earlier yourself?" Catrin said. "Why was it Rhys's responsibility to ask?"

Dafydd continued to look a bit rueful. "It wasn't. Please accept my apologies. Hugh's requests have been an open secret among the bards, and we forget that nobody else would know about them unless we were to tell them. Hugh's schemes should have been exposed long ago."

"Were you ever asked to pay a fee?" Rhys said.

To his credit, Dafydd didn't equivocate. "Yes. Once. And, as with my father, it was worth it."

Rhys had one more question, possibly the most important of all: "Who paid Hugh to win this week?"

"Moriddig." Dafydd said the name with a bit of a sneer, and then his expression turned contrite. "My apologies again. The man is dead, after all."

"Do you know this for certain?" Rhys asked.

"No."

"Would this fee be reason enough to murder him?" Catrin said.

"His death is what I thought you'd come to talk to me about." Dafydd let out a breath. "If you think winning this contest is worth killing over, you'd be wrong. No bard from Gwynedd wants the crown, that's for certain. Maybe some of those from the south would like the honor. The rest of us are just trying to keep our heads down and get through this."

"Even Gruffydd?" Rhys said.

Dafydd tsked. "Especially Gruffydd."

"And why is that?" Catrin said.

Dafydd looked at her one more time as if he couldn't believe she didn't already know the answer. "Because the last thing any of us want is to come to the attention of the king. Gruffydd led the parade at the beginning of the festival only because he couldn't get out of it. He is the last person who would ever have wanted Moriddig dead." He made a motion with his hand. "Again, maybe some of the bards from the south feel differently. They've been scrabbling amongst the rushes for scraps for a long time. They are well-trained. They probably would even see a victory here as an honor. If you're looking for Moriddig's murderer—and the one Hugh will crown in his stead—simply look to them."

Catrin and Rhys said their goodbyes and then trekked back and forth across the festival grounds several more times, marshaling their evidence against Hugh. What exactly the steward's desire for payment had to do with Moriddig's death they didn't know. Maybe nothing.

It was especially confusing that, while every bard to whom they spoke over the course of the morning knew about the *fees* Hugh had demanded throughout the years, none admitted to giving him one this week. None knew from whom he might have taken a bribe. None knew which of the judges were involved because, if such a scheme were to work, at least one of them had to be. They'd have to confront that man eventually too.

In other words, it was a frustrating morning.

And that was before the screaming started.

26

Day Three
Catrin

It was a woman, screaming long, loud, and terrified. The sound came from a barn-like structure on the edge of the woods above the River Dee. Rhys and Catrin had been walking along a nearby path, taking a moment away from the festival and its participants to consider in private what they'd learned and how next to proceed.

Fortunately, they had come far from the festival grounds, and only she and Rhys were close enough to hear above the sound of the rushing river below them. It was another bit of luck, like their proximity to Trahaearn had been, though they didn't know that until later.

Catrin lifted her skirts to run, but Rhys still out-sped her, leaping a low wall that demarcated the edge of the field, while she had to clamber over it. Once reached, the barn looked as if it had been part of a prosperous estate, but was long abandoned and derelict. With the meander of the river undermining the bank year after year, a real danger had developed that the sheep and cattle that grazed in the field might inadvertently fall down the steep embankment into the river.

For today, the barn was in no danger of collapse. It was what was happening inside the barn that was at issue. Rhys reached for the door, only to have it flung open by none other than Simon's niece, Emma, who barreled straight into him.

As Rhys caught her arms, the abruptness of his arrival cut off the noise coming out of her mouth in mid-scream.

In the time it took for her to catch her breath, he asked, "What has happened?"

"A-a-a-man. Inside." She twisted in his arms to point through the now-open door. "I think he's dead!"

By this time, Catrin had caught up, and Rhys practically tossed Emma into her arms before entering the barn. Catrin and Emma stood in the doorway, Emma's face pressed into Catrin's shoulder. The roof was half-collapsed, allowing the afternoon light to shine down on the man lying spread-eagled in the middle of the packed-dirt floor with a large pool of blood around him. He had been stabbed through the midsection.

And it wasn't just any man. It was Hugh, whom they'd spent the morning investigating.

Emma continued to sob, wetting Catrin's dress with her tears. Catrin didn't give in to impatience, reminding herself that Emma was all of seventeen, even if in appearance she could have passed for a woman of twenty-five. Her experience in life was limited. Certainly she had never encountered a murdered man before. Besides, anyone coming upon such a gruesome scene would have screamed.

And then Emma impressed her by pushing back and wiping at her tears. "I'm all right." She looked towards Rhys. "Did you note all the coins, too?"

"They're hard to miss." Bending, Rhys came up with a silver penny, which he showed to Catrin and Emma. "There's many more."

Emma nodded. "It was the coins I saw first. It's like they make a trail to his body!" She sucked in a breath, making an obvious effort not to collapse into hysterics again. "There's so much blood."

The killer had also poured what looked like an entire bag of coins over Hugh's belly, scattering them all around and even in the wound.

Catrin didn't see a purse, so perhaps the murderer had taken it away with him. "This was staged, no less than the opening of the festival."

"Or the murder in Caernarfon." Rhys crouched to Hugh's side, making sure to keep the toes of his boots well away from the pool of blood. "This death is as cold-blooded as that one. Whoever ran Hugh through left him to bleed his life out in an abandoned barn."

Emma had a hand to her face, looking at the body through her fingers. "It really is Steward Hugh, isn't it?"

"It really is," Catrin said. "What I'm interested in learning at this moment is how you came to find the body. Were you here to meet him?"

"Of course not!" Emma recoiled at the very idea.

"But you were meeting someone," Rhys said, not as a question.

"Just a friend." Though, as Emma spoke, she averted her eyes.

Rhys looked at Catrin, who nodded back at him. She knew what to do.

For starters, they had to get Emma out of here before anyone else saw her. She might not be fully aware of how her world had changed this week, but she was not just any girl now. She had met the king, and her father was working to get him to take a personal interest in the man she would marry. She should not, under any circumstances, have been in this barn by herself, waiting for her as-yet-unnamed friend.

Before Catrin departed, she said to Rhys in Welsh, assuming Emma wouldn't understand, "We already knew Hugh had a habit of asking for payment from participants. Maybe he asked the wrong person this time."

Rhys nodded, his eyes on the body. "And they objected, very strongly, to paying."

27

Day Three
Simon

Simon was trying very hard not to yell at his niece. "Tell me again how on earth you thought it was a good idea to meet a man by yourself *anywhere*?"

As Catrin had sought him out before the girl's father, he was guessing he'd been something of a compromise. From Emma's tear-streaked face and the somewhat stubborn set to Catrin's chin when they'd arrived, hiding what she'd done had to have been Emma's first choice, while going straight to Emma's father was Catrin's. Since then, Catrin's description of Hugh's death, and the arrangement of the scene, had gone a long way towards subduing the girl.

Emma appeared genuinely sorry she'd found the body. He wasn't sure she understood that finding the body was of lesser importance than the fact she'd arranged for an illicit meeting in the barn, something for which she wasn't sorry at all. "He loves me, Uncle Simon! He wants me to marry him!"

"Of course, he would say that," Simon said repressively.

"I did try to convey the difficulties," Catrin said in an undertone.

Emma wasn't listening. To either of them. He was quite sure that nothing he (or apparently anyone else) could say would dissuade her of the young man's affections. Simon tried again anyway. "Can you not see that meeting him in a derelict barn was a poor way to show your love for him—and completely the wrong way for him to show how he feels about you! He should never have asked it of you."

"It was my idea!" Emma shot back.

"Now that, I believe," Simon said dryly.

"Young love is not to be denied," Catrin said, "until it is, of course, by people far more powerful and influential than we are."

Emma kept talking, begging really. "You married Aunt Elizabeth, Uncle Simon, whom I know you have loved your whole life. Why is it so strange for me to want a love match too?"

Simon didn't dare meet Catrin's eyes. A moment ago, he had seen a flicker of amusement in them, but Emma wasn't her niece. Girls were different from boys. Catrin and Rhys might be blessed with a daughter one day, but for now they had one son between them, Justin, the child of Catrin's first marriage. Simon struggled to discipline his own daughters and had always been wrapped around Emma's little finger.

That still didn't mean he could give her what she wanted this time. "There is nothing strange about it. I could not be happier for you. But even were this a match made in heaven—" he put up a hand to stop her next protest, "—and I'm not saying it isn't, meeting with

Stephen FitzJohn, a nephew of the Earl of Warwick, in an abandoned barn was always a terrible idea. And that was before you found a dead man in it."

In truth, he was underplaying what, from top to bottom, was a disaster.

Emma finally hung her head. "I know; Stephen didn't want to, but I begged him to come."

"Why?" The word came out a wail. He couldn't help it.

"I wanted to talk to him without everyone around all the time. We are always being watched. It has been unbearable."

"How is it you have been able to speak to him before now at all?" Simon was genuinely curious. If nothing else, he would store away her explanation for the future when he had his own almost-grown daughter to deal with.

"We have managed to sit next to each other at most meals, particularly breakfast, which is so much less formal." Emma smiled beatifically at the memory.

If possible, Simon was even more concerned, not so much at the pair of them eating breakfast together, which was really kind of sweet, but at how much was going on behind her parents' backs. "Your father has allowed that?"

"I rise earlier than he does. I'm not sure he knows."

"And your mother?"

"She is so busy with the little ones, she has sent a servant with me to the pavilion in the mornings. I have to eat, after all! Besides, how could anyone object to the nephew of the Earl of Warwick as a suitor for me? I thought the entire point of this venture was to find someone of a higher station for me to marry?"

She had a point, but Simon didn't want to concede it.

"Just yesterday the earl was happy to speak to my father at length about his circumstances and his estate. Apparently, the queen has been exceptionally pleased with my father's stewardship." She laid out her noble connections as if Simon didn't know them. He had the sense she was working up her arguments in preparation for speaking to Osborn.

"But Stephen never came." Catrin cut through Emma's certainty.

"He wasn't late! I was early. He probably is there now and thinks that I don't want to be with him." She burst into tears. Again.

Catrin met Simon's eyes. "She says she entered the barn, saw the body on the floor, and screamed. There wasn't time for anything else before Rhys and I arrived."

Emma was still sobbing. "And now he's gone forever."

Simon endeavored not to raise his eyes to the heavens in a plea for divine intervention. Instead, he took his niece into his arms. "I cannot say what will become of your love for Stephen and his for you. Your father is hoping for an advantageous match, and allying you with Stephen and his family would fulfill that goal. At the same time, I do not know how Stephen's uncle will feel about it. We are minor nobles, by comparison."

It wasn't that Simon's brother would object to being allied with such a high nobleman. It was just that it could be aiming a little *too* high. For starters, the Earl of Warwick might not want his nephew marrying so far beneath him. While Simon and his brother—and their cousin—knew they were as worthy as anyone, they had not achieved the wealth and land of the Beauchamps. In addition, some of the lesser lords might be jealous of the suddenly closer position to the king the Boydells would achieve with such an alliance. And that wasn't even to mention all the other fathers with daughters who aspired to a similar match.

Emma would concede none of this. He doubted she even saw these matters as issues. "We are Boydells! And Stephen told me his father's sisters married above their station. Yes, his grandfather was the Justiciar of Ireland, and Stephen himself will inherit lands in Ireland and England, but one aunt married the Earl of Warwick, as you know. Another married the Earl of Ulster!"

Emma had neatly summarized her sense of herself and her family, a sense Simon himself shared. Their ancestors had come with the Conqueror, same as Stephen's, even if the latter's were generally more noble. Every single Norman now living was jumped up above their station, beginning with William himself, the bastard son of the Duke of Normandy. William had made himself King of England by sheer force of will. Emma was cut from the same cloth. Her weapons were just different.

Still, Simon looked at Catrin with something of a pleading expression. She bent her head to him. "Come, Emma. I'll take you home. If you are so determined to love Stephen, and he you, then your father should know of it."

"He will be so angry."

"Maybe so." And then Catrin's tone softened even further. They were walking away, but Simon could still hear her words. "I am fortunate enough to have married the love of my life, but only after a twenty-year first marriage. Robert was a good man—"

"—but Reese is different." Emma interrupted. "That's what I want for me."

"I want it for you too—"

Then they were out of earshot.

28

Day Three
Simon

Simon had been in the king's pavilion when Catrin had found him, the king having taken a break from the performances in order to work on a few matters of state. When Simon reentered the pavilion, Edward was in close conversation with his chancellor, Robert Burnell.

"The first French armies have advanced into Roussillon," Robert was saying. "The pope has declared the Aragon war a crusade."

"I have dreamt of another crusade," the king said, "but this is not the crusade I would have chosen."

"No, my lord. Sicily isn't Jerusalem and Pope Martin is a puppet of the House of Anjou." Robert was similar in age to Edward and they had been friends since before Edward had become king. It had been Robert who'd stayed behind in London during the last crusade to secure Edward's interests, and it had also been Robert who'd acted as regent until Edward could return after his father's death.

Robert was so trusted that the chancery was now seated permanently in London, with Robert given the authority to sort the petitions that came and show only the most important to the king. When he'd heard how the people of Vale Royal Abbey had brought their petition straight to the king instead of going through proper channels, he'd been quite put out.

Given that Robert and his clerks were allowed to profit from the fees charged for sealing patents, charters, and writs, there might also have been a bit of self-service in his outrage.

"You will get no argument from me," King Edward said, "but it is still a crusade, and France is embroiled in it. It may be that we will be pulled in too."

"I will put all my efforts towards avoiding it, my king." Robert looked up as he finished speaking to see Simon standing a respectful distance away. They did not know each other well, since Robert had not been on crusade with the king, and Simon had mostly served in Prince Edmund's household. So far, they'd had no difficulties either.

King Edward eyed him. "You have more bad news; I can tell."

"Yes, my lord. I have just received word of another murder. This time it is Hugh, Owen de la Pole's steward. He was stabbed and left for dead."

Robert looked askance. "Isn't he in charge of the whole festival?"

"Yes, my lord, he is."

Trust Robert to get to the heart of the matter, if that matter was keeping to the king's agenda. "If you in any way need the assistance of me or my people, please do not hesitate to ask."

"Of course, my lord." Simon bent his head. It was also just like Robert to assume he would be capable of contributing to, or even taking charge of, something he knew nothing about. He was an excellent organizer, there was no question, but he didn't know the Welsh, didn't know music, and would undoubtedly rub everyone he worked with the wrong way. "So we go on?"

"We do. Keep me apprised."

"Yes, my lord."

As Simon strode away from the king's pavilion, he found himself both suspicious of every face he encountered, and at the same time crossing suspects off his list, dozens at a time, simply by the fact that they could not have walked to the barn, murdered Hugh, and returned to their respective locations without anyone noticing. And the vast majority of those here would certainly not have left a purseful of coins behind.

Once at the barn, he pulled open the door a little too roughly and practically ripped it off its hinges. It sagged as it swung back behind him, and Simon cooled his temper by carefully adjusting the door so it settled into an open position.

Rhys had watched the display without comment, crouched as he was over Hugh's body. He was accompanied by a young man, the very Stephen FitzJohn about whom Simon's niece had just been lamenting.

Simon could have been furious again. He might have had an impulse to stride up to Stephen and backhand him across the face. The young man's foolishness could have ruined Emma.

But instead, all of a sudden, Simon found himself quite cheerful.

Not about the body, because certainly another dead man at the festival, and one of such standing, was not good news. But because the young man was *here*. He had come to the barn, as he'd promised Emma, and that meant there might be hope for his niece and this Stephen after all.

29

Day Three

Rhys

Stephen FitzJohn straightened from where he had been explaining himself to Rhys. His eyes went for a moment to Simon, whose identity he, of course, knew, and then returned to Rhys. "My father told me I was to make my own choice, that life was too short to live it with someone I didn't love. I have made that choice."

"Emma Boydell." Rhys glanced past Stephen to Simon too.

"Yes." Now Stephen turned to face Simon fully and gave him a respectful nod. "I truly do love her and intend to marry her. I hope that I can do so with your blessing."

"It is not mine to give, son." Simon knew, as Rhys did, that Stephen's wishes, his father's, or even his uncle's, despite being steward to the king, would matter little if the king himself did not approve of the match. The gauntlet appeared to have been thrown down, however, and Stephen was looking to be as stubborn a young person as Rhys's short acquaintance with Emma had shown her to be.

Stephen certainly hadn't been much dismayed by the dead man in the barn, other than the fact that Emma had seen him too. Once Rhys had explained that he'd sent her off in the care of Catrin, Stephen had settled on his heels, studying the body with the eyes of a scholar. "May I ask what you make of this?"

Rhys had glanced at him. "You see what I see."

"A man stabbed through the belly. Though," he gave a shake of his head, "not just any man. Hugh, steward to Owen de la Pole. The coins are an interesting touch." His voice was light, observing but not judging, and his eyes were on the pile of pennies, farthings, and half-farthings that had mixed with the blood around and on top of Hugh's body.

"Interesting is one word for it."

"What blade was used? Not a sword I'm thinking."

"Not a sword. The blade appears to have been narrower, possibly tapered to a sharp point and had a clean edge." Pointing, Rhys embellished on the topic. "It was driven into Hugh's body below his ribs and upwards to his heart. And then he was stabbed again through the middle of his belly for good measure."

"With significant force, I'd guess," Stephen said, "indicating a measure of hate."

By that time, the young man's detachment had been starting to bother Rhys a bit, where before he'd been impressed. "Have you ever seen a murdered man before? You encompassed the sight of him with more equanimity than most."

"Is that a mark against me or for me, to your mind?" Stephen gave a low laugh that indicated no pleasure. "I was at Landelo Vower two years ago." He meant Llandeilo Fawr, a place in south Wales. "I saw men slaughtered there. It isn't that I am inured to it, but I learned to see without seeing." He paused. "I was also at the Menai."

That news rocked Rhys back a bit. Stephen had just named two battles during the war that the Welsh had won decisively. Stephen been in both, and survived them both, which meant he'd seen his share of carnage. Simon hadn't been at either battle, a fact for which Rhys was grateful, even if Simon was not. At both, Norman knights had died in large numbers.

"How did you survive?"

It was a reasonable question. The Welsh victory at the Menai Strait had precipitated the Mortimer brothers' decision to end the war by assassinating Llywelyn. By then, it had been the only way to achieve an English victory.

At that time, the Archbishop of Canterbury, John Peckham, had been at Llywelyn's palace at Aber, negotiating for an end to the war. Earlier, King Edward had sent an army, led by a man named Tany, to Anglesey. Tany was tasked with building a bridge of boats across the Menai Strait west of Aber, near Catrin's family's estate at Penrhyn. Meanwhile, the king sat at Rhuddlan Castle, preparing to force the River Conwy at Caerhun. Before the archbishop had intervened, the plan had been for Edward to invade Gwynedd from the east and Tany from the north in order to catch Llywelyn in a pincer movement.

Tany, for reasons that nobody would ever know, since he died on the day, decided not to wait for either Peckham or Edward. On the sixth of November 1282, he started his men across his bridge.

Rhys had been among those posted on the beach, waiting for them. Tany had meant to surprise them. Instead, the Welsh had met the English army with overwhelming force. When word had got out they were coming, *combrogi* had come running from miles around. It was bad enough that the English had taken the Anglesey harvest, they weren't going to take the heart of Gwynedd too.

In the time it took Tany's army to arrive on the Gwynedd beach, fight the Welsh forces, and flee in desperate defeat, the tide had turned. Literally. The currents in the Menai Strait were treacherous at any time of day, with the only relatively safe time during the hour of slack water before the turn of the tide.

Once the tide turned, however, the water was at its most dangerous. Caught between the Welsh forces on the one hand and the Menai Strait on the other, the English army chose to recross their bridge. Straining under the weight of so many men and horses, the bridge broke, dumping nearly the whole of the English army into the sea. While the Welsh suffered a handful of casualties, Edward lost over four hundred men that day, including knights, squires, and Tany himself.

But not Stephen FitzJohn.

Stephen met Rhys's eyes. "I can swim, and I knew better than to fight the current. I was fortunate enough to end up on the Anglesey shore alongside Otto de Grandison. Rumor had it there were no survivors on the mainland side because you killed everyone, even those who surrendered."

"You should know better than to believe everything you hear." Rhys himself knew better than to become angry at the slander. It was typical of the English to make up a story that the Welsh had killed their prisoners because the real truth was even more tragic: every Englishman who'd made the beach had chosen the water over surrender. None of that was Llywelyn's fault.

Stephen grunted his acknowledgment. "We are all members of the same court now. But my experience in battle is why the sight of Hugh did not send me outside to vomit." He paused his speech, frowning a bit. Then he leaned forward over the body in order to reach in, despite the blood, and come up with a gem the size of a pea. Once the blood was rubbed away, it proved to be a garnet.

Showing it to Rhys, he said, "What say you?"

Rhys took the stone. "I say it could have come from a hilt or sheath. The murderer got close, and that means Hugh knew him. I'm guessing he was meeting someone here today too. Heaven knows why."

"Like Emma and I intended to do?" Stephen was horrified at the thought. "If Emma had arrived even a quarter of an hour earlier, she might have witnessed the murder—or been killed too!"

"A lesson to you, perhaps?" It was the most censorious Rhys had been. Emma wasn't his niece, and this wasn't his fight.

At that point, Simon arrived.

Now, Stephen bent his head to Simon again. "I will speak to her father immediately."

"Good luck to you," Rhys said to Stephen's retreating back. Then, once the young man was out the door and on his way, he added softly, under his breath, for Simon's ears alone, "You're going to need it!"

Simon watched him go too before bending to pick up one of the coins a few feet from the body. "Oh, I don't know about that, Rhys. My niece is a determined young lady, and it looks to me as if she has truly met her match."

30

Day Three
Catrin

Murder had a way of complicating pretty much every-thing. By the time Catrin had escorted Emma home, explained the situation to her father (accompanied by a renewed flood of tears from Emma), and made her way back to the abandoned barn, Rhys and Simon had arranged for a wagon to remove Hugh's body to the castle.

She had just missed crossing paths with Stephen himself. Catrin wished him well. The sooner he threw himself at Osborn's feet, the better.

While two of the king's servants prepared the body for transport, Rhys, Catrin, and Simon retired to wait outside the barn doorway. It was refreshing to be in the breeze, without the scent of blood.

Simon looked at Rhys. "I should head to the castle now. This is going to be a nasty surprise for Owen, and I want to arrive well before the wagon."

"It will be a surprise only if Owen himself isn't the killer," Rhys said. "Sadly, I doubt this is his doing. We've had hints he's short of money. If nothing else, he would not have left a pile of coins on top of Hugh."

"That is a curious issue," Catrin said. "Who leaves that amount of money behind—or any amount of money, for that matter?"

Simon, who had already started to walk away, said over his shoulder, "Someone who is very angry, very offended, or both."

Catrin watched him go and then Rhys put an arm around her shoulders to hug her to him. "A barn, a dead man, you, and me."

He was referring again to their first investigation in Caernarfon, where they'd been searching for the killer of a man found dead in a barn. It wasn't entirely true that they'd fallen in love over a dead body, but it wasn't far off.

"I don't see anyone spending the night in this barn, no matter the reason. Which then begs the question as to why Hugh was here." She pushed on the broken door with one hand. "He had to have been meeting someone, but there are so many tracks already, some of which are ours, it's impossible to distinguish one from another."

"Shall we make a start on the rest then, like before?" Without waiting for her assent, Rhys set off around the outside of the barn, walking slowly, his eyes on the ground.

Catrin followed, making a circle a bit wider than his. The main door of the barn faced the field they'd crossed to reach it, but the woods had started encroaching on the rest of the building. By the time they reached the back side, they were hacking through some waist high brush to keep to their intended trajectories.

Catrin was detaching her cloak from a clinging blackberry bramble when Rhys said, "I see a footprint. There's two more." He pointed deeper into the woods.

Having successfully extricated herself, Catrin crouched to the ground, squinting a bit as a sudden ray of sunlight pierced the leaves above her head to reach the forest floor. Then she was able to trace the progress of the tracks with her eyes. "It looks like he came from the north."

She might have been proud of herself for being able to see the footprints at all, except several were clearly evident in the mud at the far corner of the barn. In other places, grass and dead leaves obscured them, but it looked as if water draining off the barn's roof had been funneled to this one spot, into which someone had stepped.

Making sure he didn't mar any of the footprints himself, Rhys took his own foot and hovered it above the print. "I'm not the murderer, but he wears boots similar in size to mine."

"Too bad he doesn't have either huge feet or small ones," Catrin said, now comparing the prints to her own smaller feet. "I'm going to be looking at everyone's boots now as well as their fingers!"

Rhys crouched to study the marks more closely. "He walks on the outside of his feet, judging by the pattern of wear on the heel."

"Like I do," Catrin said. "You walk much more straight and put holes right in the center of the ball of your foot."

The barn was falling down a bit more at this corner, with big chunks taken out of the wattle and daub construction. Peering through one of these gaps, she could see the spot where Hugh had died. Much of his blood had soaked into the ground, but little pools remained that glistened in the sunshine coming through the roof and the barn's open door, which was almost directly opposite from where she was standing. Occasional wisps of straw or hay moved in the air, but otherwise the barn had been cleaned out years ago.

Meanwhile, the men were finally maneuvering Hugh's body onto the bed of the cart. Catrin and Rhys followed the footprints down the side of the barn wall until they reached the front door again, where they became lost amidst many others.

Catrin studied the body for a moment, made thoughtful by what had just occurred to her. "We should take off one of Hugh's boots to compare it to the prints."

Rhys instantly agreed, motioning to one of the servants, who had not understood Catrin's Welsh. "Our apologies. We won't be a moment."

The servants had wrapped Hugh well, but Rhys unfolded the bit of cloth that covered his feet and managed to get one boot off him. Another few hours and the body might have been too stiff to accomplish it without breaking the bones in his foot.

Instantly, it was clear that the boot was of similar size to Rhys's. Moriddig had been a small man, but Hugh was of average height, just an inch or two less than six feet. The boots showed wear on the outside of the heel, enough that it was hardly necessary for Rhys to place the boot in the print.

Catrin grunted to see the perfect fit. "We had it backwards. It was Hugh who followed someone else to the barn."

Rhys looked up at her as he concluded, "And that someone else killed him."

31

Day Three

Simon

Although Simon did not pretend to know as much about investigating as Rhys, he did know politics, God help him. Never mind that he made it his mission in life to avoid embroiling himself in the maneuvering which was the lifeblood of the royal court. While it had turned out that Math had to be the poor soul who'd informed Owen de la Pole of the death of his bard, Simon was determined to take on the responsibility for telling him about this new murder. Moriddig's death was one thing, but to add on the death of Hugh was quite another. There was a double murderer on the loose, and it looked to Simon as if he was getting closer to Owen with every step.

It was raw anger Simon had seen on the floor of that barn. He'd been in too many battles and seen too many angry men let off their leash to be confused about what had gone on. That anger could be expended, but once allowed out in the world, it was never completely sated.

Being the one to break the news would also give Simon a chance, and an excuse, to inquire about Hugh's finances—and thus Owen's. Up until now, Owen's station had made such questions unseemly, and Rhys hadn't wanted to approach him without better evidence than hearsay. Yes, they were investigating the murder of Owen's bard, but Owen remained in high favor with the king. All of them were reluctant to rock that boat.

But if the murder of Moriddig was a summer squall, Hugh's was a winter storm that Owen might not be able to weather.

As a bard, Moriddig held an important place in Owen's court, but Hugh had been Owen's steward. His responsibilities extended beyond this festival. Simon didn't know Owen well enough to have witnessed much in the way of the internal workings of his household, but in most, a steward knew everything about his lord and his doings. Hugh would have been in charge of Owen's accounts, his employees, his alliances, and possibly his very thoughts. His loss would be a severe blow.

Simon entered the castle's receiving room to find Owen speaking with his wife, who was noticeably pregnant with what Simon knew to be their first child. Owen and Joan were a decade younger than Simon, though of course so much higher in station that Simon put his heels together and bowed. "My lord. My lady. I am afraid I have some more bad news."

Owen's lips twisted. "Someone else is dead?"

"I am afraid so." Simon knew it would be best to speak plainly. Having just told all this to the king, he had it in his head how best to do it. "It's Hugh, my lord. He was found dead just now. Murdered too."

Joan's eyes narrowed. "Murdered? How?"

He had been hoping not to have to explain while Joan was in the room but, despite her pregnancy, she had shown herself to be the opposite of a delicate flower. "Stabbed in the belly. We found him in an abandoned barn above the river. The killer appears to have left a trail of coins from the door to the body." This was a detail they might normally have chosen to keep back, but he used it here as a segue into talking about money in Owen's household. "It looks as if he even emptied a bag of coins on top of Hugh after he killed him."

Joan eyed him carefully. "How much money?"

"We have collected it, but haven't counted it," Simon said. "Many of the coins are covered in blood and still inside the wound."

"Where is the body now?" Owen continued to evidence more dismay than his wife. "Don't tell me you're bringing him here too!"

"Yes, I'm afraid so, my lord. The body should arrive momentarily. This was Hugh's home, and Reese has informed me that you have adequate space for the dead in the place Morrydig lay before his burial."

"I'll see to it," Joan said in an undertone to Owen, though loud enough for Simon to hear. "I'll speak to Adam, too, about stepping for a time into Hugh's shoes. It's a good thing Hugh was so organized. From here on, the festival can practically run itself."

Owen nodded, and his wife departed.

Simon had never really seen the pair of them interact before, outside of formal events. From even this brief exchange, he would have said they had something of a compatible marriage. He didn't know why he hadn't expected it. Perhaps it was seeing Joan in the churchyard with Adam. Or just that Rhys despised Owen so profoundly, it was hard to imagine a woman making a life with him.

Now alone with Owen, Simon told himself he couldn't get away with looking elsewhere above Owen's head. He had to act as if he had no concerns about the last time they'd talked, that strange exchange after Moriddig's death. For his part, Owen seemed at ease, throwing himself into his regal chair and once again waving a hand towards the sideboard. "Pour us some wine, will you?"

Simon again moved to obey. "I am sorry to have brought such bad news."

"Unless you murdered him yourself, none of this is your fault." Owen nodded his thanks as Simon handed him a cup.

If two days hadn't passed since their last conversation, Simon might have wondered if he was reliving previous events. "My lord, I'm afraid I have an even more fraught issue to discuss with you, one related to Hugh's death. It might even be directly relevant as it is in regards to money."

"You mean the coins poured onto the body?"

"Perhaps." It was time to get to the crux of the matter. "We know that Hugh had a history of taking bribes, what he called *fees*—from contestants when he oversaw a music festival."

The expression on Owen's face could not have been more astonished. "That never happened. He couldn't have. You've been lied to."

"We have multiple testimonies to that fact, my lord. What we don't know is how, or even if, his actions had anything to do with his death. We don't know from whom he might have taken a bribe this week."

Owen managed a laugh. "And yet, you say his body was covered in coins. Who would do that? Why kill him if the hope was to pay him for services rendered."

"I don't know, my lord. All I know is that Hugh is dead." Simon hesitated, fearing to be more forthright, but also thinking it was necessary. "We may have to consider the idea that Hugh could have been selling more than just a victory at this festival."

Owen frowned at him, genuinely confused. "What more are you talking about?"

"Your secrets, my lord. Hugh could have gone to the barn thinking he was about to get paid ... and was killed instead for what he knew."

32

Day Three
Catrin

“I should seek out Mary and Jane.” Catrin said to Rhys. She was referring to Hugh's wife and daughter. “Last I saw, they were watching one of the contests. They might already be wondering where he might have got to. How much can I tell them?”

“Start with enough to get them out of the festival grounds and back to the castle. You don't want them to cause a scene that disrupts the festival. The king is still adamant about that.”

Catrin promised to do her best, which was how she found herself a quarter of an hour later edging her way through the onlookers to where Mary and Jane were standing. Speaking to the family of someone who'd died unexpectedly was never easy, made far worse by the fact that the deceased had been murdered. Catrin had managed to wade through Adam's grief. She could endure the grief of Hugh's wife and daughter too.

Hugh and Moriddig were connected in several ways, but the two most important appeared to be, firstly, that they both served in the household of Owen de la Pole; and secondly, that Moriddig had achieved his position because he had given Hugh a *fee*. Or so rumor had it, even if roundly denied by Moriddig's son.

Similar in age to Moriddig, Hugh had served Owen's father before Owen's maturity. Once it was clear Gruffydd was no longer capable of managing his own estates and needed a different set of retainers, Owen inherited Hugh along with the responsibilities of lordship. Up until now, Catrin had only ever viewed Hugh as respectable, responsible, and trusted. The way he died would have called into question everything they thought they knew about him even if they hadn't already heard about his bribery scheme.

Catrin fetched up beside Jane, Hugh's fifteen-year-old daughter, while at the same time reaching out a hand to Mary's sleeve to gain her attention. "Mary, Jane, I was hoping you could come with me."

At first, Mary was too focused on the singing to look away, but when Catrin tugged on her arm again, she glanced over long enough to take in Catrin's expression. Her face fell at the sight of it. "What's wrong?"

"I need to tell you away from here." Catrin had been trying to make her expression mild and unassuming—and had clearly failed. At the same time, any instance where the wife of the king's quaestor asked a person to come with her, trouble had to be the reason.

Without waiting to make sure the other women were following, Catrin turned with some abruptness and headed back the way she'd come. By the time she looked over her shoulder, Mary and Jane were five steps behind.

She didn't manage to extricate them from the crowd of festival goers until they reached the entrance to the festival grounds. At that point, Catrin set off towards the town. It was a good quarter-of-an-hour's walk, and for the first half of the journey she was moving too fast for either Mary or Jane to find the breath to ask questions.

Finally, however, Mary grabbed Catrin's arm, stopping her abruptly in the middle of the street. "What has happened? You must tell me before I take another step."

Catrin looked left and right, seeing a few people but none paying much in the way of attention to them. They were near St. Mary's by now, so Catrin gestured for them to enter the churchyard. With its many ancient yew trees, they could be hidden from prying eyes.

Once under some spreading limbs, not far from Moriddig's grave, Catrin could put off the truth no longer. "It's your husband, Hugh. He is dead."

Jane let out a painful shriek, which was exactly what Catrin had been trying to avoid. In truth, it was unavoidable. There was no good way to tell a wife and daughter that the man upon whom they depended was dead.

Mary wrapped her arms around Jane and stared at Catrin over her daughter's head. "How can this be? He wasn't in ill health. I saw him earlier today, and he was well!"

Catrin didn't answer immediately, instead taking Mary's elbow and guiding her and Jane towards the church itself. Jane continued to sob in her mother's arms, but Catrin managed to get them inside and settled on a bench against a wall. Only then did Catrin lay out the full explanation of what they knew, without getting into any of their speculation as to who might have killed him or why.

When Catrin finished, Mary bent her head and breathed slowly in and out for a time. Catrin had sat herself on the bench beside her and now took her free hand, the one that wasn't holding onto Jane. "I am so very sorry."

"I can't believe he's dead." Mary's voice sounded like it came from very far away. "You're sure it's Hugh?"

"Yes."

"I don't understand the bit about the coins. He promised me he wasn't accepting payments anymore."

Catrin's heart thumped to hear her speak so plainly. "You knew about those?"

"Of course I knew." Mary sniffed. "For years, I told him what he was doing was bad for him and for the men from whom he took these *fees*." The word came out with a bit of a sneer. "He had finally listened. He had changed! Or so I thought."

Catrin wanted to comfort her, even if she thought it unlikely, given the circumstances of Hugh's death, that he had changed. "Maybe he did stop. Maybe this was about something else, or a grievance from the past."

"That would be some comfort." Mary let go of Catrin's hand in order to wrap both arms around her daughter, who continued to sob. "Were the coins from *his* purse, do you know?"

"We didn't find a purse on him."

Mary's face was so pale Catrin was afraid she might faint. "He owned a leather purse, embossed with his initials, H and C. He was never without it." At Catrin's regretful shake of her head, Mary continued, "Money can be poisonous to relationships. It soured ours for a long time. Hugh cared too much about accumulating wealth and having fine things. He did everything he could to ingratiate himself with these Normans. Like Owen, he changed his name and insisted we do the same. I was born Marared and Jane was christened Geneth. He said those days were over, and if we wanted to survive, we would have to adapt. I did as he asked. And then, one day, he did as I asked, which was to stop taking payments. I told him so many times it would catch up to him. To us." At last, her face screwed up, and the tears began to fall. "I thought things were better. We were doing so much better."

Tears pricking her own eyes at seeing their grief, Catrin remained with her arms around both Mary and Jane until they quieted. She was sure now that Mary's surprise at her husband's death was genuine. She hadn't murdered Hugh. Truly, Catrin should have known that already, since she'd seen Mary at the festival grounds at some point during her treks across the various fields with Rhys before Emma had screamed.

And yet, it had been vaguely possible that she could have killed him and then rejoined her daughter without anyone noticing. Maybe that could have been true of Jane too, if the idea that Jane killed her own father with a stab to the heart wasn't wholly laughable. It did occur to Catrin that if Emma and Stephen had agreed to meet in the barn, Jane could have too. Catrin could imagine a scenario where Hugh had spied on Jane and her lover. Then, after Jane left, he tried to bribe the man to go away—and been killed for his pains.

That wasn't a topic to broach in this moment, but she filed it away for later consideration.

Eventually, Catrin was able to ask a few gentle questions again. "Can you tell me what you meant when you said things were *better*?"

Jane had laid her head in her mother's lap and appeared to be almost dozing. Maybe that was just as well, given the conversation.

Mary rubbed her eyes with her fingers. "I have to go back a ways for you to truly understand."

"Take your time; I am happy to listen."

"Hugh's father had been steward to the Lord Gruffydd, Owen's father. Unfortunately, he—Hugh's father, not old Gruffydd—had fallen to gambling and drinking in his later years. For a while, his vices put the whole family in a precarious position. They were in danger of losing everything for which he'd spent a lifetime working. Even though Hugh was young, he managed to convince Lord Gruffydd, who saw what was happening, to take him on instead of his father. Hugh was only twenty, but anyone could see how competent he was."

She gave a shake of her head. "His father died not long after; Hugh and I married after that, and, after some more years, I had Jane." She rubbed her daughter's shoulder again. "From the start, Hugh was haunted by his father's fall from grace and became obsessed with shoring up his own position. By the time we married, he justified what he was doing by saying he was only making sure that if anything happened to him, Jane and I would be protected. And he did protect us. Even with his death, we have a home of our own and enough wealth to maintain us—Jane until she marries, and me for as long as I live."

"That is quite a gift."

Mary ducked her head. "He was paid well by the Poles, but he felt it wasn't enough. That's why he supplemented his income." She stopped.

"Did these fees really amount to that much?"

"It wasn't just payments given to him at an *eisteddfod*." Mary allowed herself a low laugh. "As the Poles' steward, Hugh was in a position to extract similar fees from a whole host of supplicants. Did a man need to see the lord today rather than tomorrow? A small fee would ensure it. Or did that man want to win a dispute against his neighbor? If so, that would require a bigger payment." Her laugh became mocking. "How is the king's chancellor any different with his fees? How is a sheriff any different, collecting money when a man dies?"

Catrin found herself swallowing down a rebuttal she didn't actually believe in. "Did Hugh keep records?"

"I suspect you won't be surprised to learn that he did. I will get the ledger to you."

"Did anyone ever pay him a fee and then *not* get what they paid for?"

Mary gave a quick shake of her head. "He worked very hard to ensure that was never the case."

"Never?"

"If he couldn't fulfill what he promised, he returned the money."

Catrin wanted to believe her, for her sake more than Hugh's, for whom it no longer mattered. "Did Owen know?"

She held her breath as she waited for the answer, but it came quickly and surely. "He did not."

Catrin endeavored not to look as skeptical as she felt. "Really?"

"Owen took over the full reins of the estate only in the last year. I think it was that event, more than anything I said, that convinced Hugh it was time to take a step back. He even returned money he'd taken from the most recent supplicants. He was trying to make amends!"

"But he still had enough money for you to live comfortably."

Mary's head shaking was very expressive. "He set a certain sum aside, money he wouldn't touch, for me and for the running of his estate. We have people who depend on us. He knew he had done wrong, but he didn't want me to pay for his mistakes."

"Did you notice anything strange with him recently? Did he express concern or fear about someone from the past coming back to haunt him?" *Or hunt him?* Catrin didn't say the last thought out loud, but she was picturing Hugh hiding outside the barn, watching what was happening within.

Mary looked at Catrin curiously. "You ask all the right questions. Yes, he was very concerned about his role in this *eisteddfod* because of the people from whom he'd taken money in the past. In truth, he couldn't just pay them all back, and most had been satisfied with the arrangements they'd made anyway. Look at Moriddig—" She broke off. "Well, maybe don't look at him."

"He took money from Moriddig?"

"Once, years and years ago."

It was nice to have that suspicion confirmed. "Is that what ties the two of them together, besides their employment by the Poles?"

"Is it? I don't know. They weren't at odds, and neither seemed concerned about the other. I don't know why they're both dead." Mary frowned. "I can tell you about something strange that happened, even though I can't see how it's related. Hugh went to fetch his horse from where he left it in the corral at the festival grounds, and it was gone."

Catrin sat up straighter. "That is something." A horse was a valuable asset and theft a major offense. "What did the boys keeping watch say?"

"I don't know; Hugh just told me that the horse was gone."

"Those were his exact words?"

Mary nodded. "Before he could say more, he was called away by another matter. I never found a moment to ask about it again."

"When did you last speak to him?"

"Last night he came to bed after me. He kissed my forehead and told me he loved me." Mary's tears began to fall again. "He had left our bed by the time I awoke this morning."

Grief often manifested when a person thought about life with the deceased and realized they'd never be able to be with that person again. From this day forth, Mary was going to bed alone, as perhaps she had often done. But never again would Hugh come to kiss her awake in the middle of the night and tell her he loved her, as he had done last night. Those words were from what from now on would be her former life and would be buried with him.

33

Day Three
Simon

"Are you implying that Hugh's death has anything to do with me?" Owen surged to his feet, almost spilling his cup of wine as he did so. He contained his ire long enough to lick the slop from his finger and then drained the cup in a single breath.

That seemed to settle him enough that he was able to hear Simon's reply. "Two of your men are dead, my lord. Not only that, they were both murdered. Questions are going to be asked, and not just by us."

"So now you think *I* killed them?" His outrage was palpable—and understandable, if he didn't do it.

Still, even through the glaring, Simon sensed an odor of duty about him, as if Owen was outraged because that's how he thought he was supposed to feel. For the first time, Simon wondered how much of Owen's sycophancy and pomposity was because he had observed such behavior in other men in the king's service, and he was mimicking them, not because he believed in it fully himself.

Not that this was relevant in the moment, so Simon felt safe answering, "No, my lord. Nobody is wondering if you killed them."

"Really? Because it looks to me as if that's the first thing on your mind. I told you where I was when Morrydig died, and I have been either within the castle or with the king today. There must be a hundred witnesses who can testify to that fact. I didn't kill my steward!" Then he snorted. "I feel almost insulted that you would think I would be foolish enough to murder Hugh or Morrydig so publicly. I can assure you there are better ways, ones that would not prompt an investigation."

As Simon had already thought of that, he didn't argue. "As I said, you are not under any suspicion. But we must still address the fees we have learned were being paid to Hugh."

"This is what you were talking about earlier—Hugh accepting payments from contestants at this music festival?"

"Yes."

"I still don't believe it."

"We have—"

"How many of your witnesses paid him this week? None, didn't you say?"

Simon was forced to concede the point. "That's right. None would admit to it or knew who might have done so. None could say for whom the festival is rigged, particularly now that Morrydig is dead. Nonetheless, they believe absolutely that it is."

"I can't help what they believe. Nor could Hugh." Owen shook his head. "And now he is dead, and you think this is the reason."

"Let's just say it's a question we are asking. Even if mere rumor, we must look into it."

"Everyone will assume I'm involved." Owen made a broad gesture with both hands. "You know how hard it is to find men you can trust. I trusted Hugh. Why wouldn't I, given his long service to my father?"

"No reason." It was a rhetorical question, but Simon answered anyway.

"The king knows this too." Now it sounded as if Owen was trying to convince himself. "He has the same problem, which is why he surrounds himself with crusaders, including you and Reese. My loyalty to the king is absolute, as is yours, as was Reese's to Lewelen. He would have died for him. From what I hear, he thought he had. The king employs him because he knows Reese is capable of holding his ground to the bitter end. It is a rare quality in men."

All of a sudden, Simon was glad Rhys wasn't here. This was a conversation Owen might not have been able to have with the Welshman. His point was also well taken. Rhys *had* been willing to die for his lord. Simon knew for a fact that at times he'd wished he had. Simon also hadn't ever thought about the king's willingness to employ Rhys as resulting directly from what happened at Cilmeri rather than in spite of it.

Owen was back to thinking about himself. "Hugh's loyalty to me was of that quality. I would swear to it. If he was accepting payments from contestants, I did not know about it. If he was selling my secrets, I didn't know about that either. Does that make me a fool? Many will think so, but I submit that greater men than I have been betrayed by those they thought loyal."

Owen had that right too, but to say so didn't entirely let him off the hook. "But you are personally having money issues, are you not? Your wife was overheard arguing with Adam about the last payment to Morrydig. We understand you have declined to fulfill his contract."

"The man is dead. Of course I wasn't going to pay him." Owen let out a sound of disgust. "I regret that now, since Joan has gone to ask him for help. We'll have to make amends."

"Even for the work Morrydig did that went unpaid?"

"Yes. Yes. It's all different now with Hugh dead." Owen flung himself into his chair. "With bards, no contract is ever signed. They know they can be dismissed without prejudice at any time. It's a lord's prerogative. I had, in fact, dismissed Morrydig the day before his death. That's the reason I wasn't going to pay him once he was dead."

Trying to keep his eyes from crossing in confusion, Simon put up a hand. "My lord, did you just say you had dismissed Morrydig?"

"I did say that, and yes, I had dismissed him." Owen was projecting defiance, his arms folded across his chest. "It was time for a change, and what better opportunity to find a new bard for my household than this festival?"

"Did anyone else know of this?"

"I didn't shout it from the rooftops, if that's what you mean. My wife knew. Adam knew because he was there when I gave Morrydig the news. I did say they could keep their quarters until after the festival. I wasn't angry with him, and I understand it's easier to find a new patron when you still have your old one."

"Do you know if he'd found a patron?" Simon asked as mildly as he could muster. Rhys had told him about the Bohun offer of employment to Moriddig, but this was a new twist on the whole issue. Owen also had conveyed none of this two days ago when he'd been asked about his bard.

"I have no idea. I didn't inquire. In case you were wondering, that's the reason Morrydig was sleeping in his wagon." Owen shivered. "In that sense, perhaps it is my fault he's dead."

"Did Morrydig's son, Patrick, know?"

"I did not tell him."

"What were your plans for the boy with Morrydig gone?"

"I hadn't decided."

Simon genuinely didn't know what to make of this tale. Because this was the first he'd heard of it, Owen could have concocted it on the spot as justification for not paying Adam. Given that the Bohuns had kept their offer a secret, it was impossible to interrogate Owen about the issue. Adam, however, could be questioned.

Such was the way with investigations. While it would be nice to have an infallible method to sift truth from lies, a large part of the job involved accumulating so much evidence that no conclusion was reliant on the word of a single man.

"Did Hugh know about all this?" Simon said.

"Of course, he did. As I have explained, he knew everything about my household."

"Do you know if Hugh told anyone else?"

"I do not." Owen let out something of a moan. "I was going to suggest you ask him, but you can't. Nobody can. Nobody will, ever again."

"Is there anything else you can tell me about Hugh's activities that could have resulted in his death?"

"I can't imagine. I don't really have any secrets worth selling." Then Owen's face paled. "Was he tortured before he was killed?"

Simon took a sip of the wine before answering. He didn't believe Owen had no secrets, not when he'd just trotted out the secret he'd kept about Moriddig's employment, or lack thereof. "Reese has not yet fully examined the body, so we cannot say. If he was tortured, those wounds aren't obvious. I can say that he does still have all his fingernails, for example."

Owen shuddered at the description, reminding Simon once again how young he was and how little experience he had with a brutal world Simon took for granted.

And who was to say which way was better?

"What was the money for then?" Owen asked a bit plaintively. "For services rendered? But to whom? And if this was about money, why leave even one coin behind?"

34

Day Three
Rhys

Maybe Rhys should have followed the wagon back to the castle straight away, but right now he felt that examining the body further was of lesser priority than the acquisition of other kinds of information. The body was still going to be there in an hour, and he didn't know how much more he was going to learn from it. He was pretty sure he knew how Hugh had died.

It was *why* he had died that was of paramount importance. The only way he was going to get at that answer was by asking, preferably before it was common knowledge that Hugh was dead. Someone had killed him; someone had dumped a purseful of coins onto his bloody wound. In their pursuit of answers about Hugh's *fees* at the *eisteddfod,* they had neglected the second half of the arrangements, which had to be passing some portion of said fee onto a judge.

Rhys had been asked to act as a judge only once, at an archery tournament. That had been during the time he'd served Llywelyn, and he'd done it only when the original adjudicator had gone down with a stomach ailment. Rhys had felt comfortable as an emergency replacement, since he knew how to shoot and didn't feel he had a great deal more to learn, up until the moment he'd become responsible for the fate of the contestants.

At that point, he'd never felt more uneducated. His saving grace had been the relatively objective nature of archery. Whether or not a man hit the target with an arrow could be ascertained. Things got more complicated when the margins decreased. What really was the center of a target?

And then there was the matter of violations and deductions of points. Was every arrow of equal length and weight? Did a contestant's toe go over the line? The latter issue could become extraordinarily contested. Unlike an arrow, which became fixed in a target, a man's toe could move for a heartbeat when he shot an arrow, and then move back. Then it became a matter of who saw what when and if he could be believed.

Through that experience, Rhys had come to see that the most important decisions a lord made when he decided to hold a tournament (or festival) were in regards to the identities of the chief organizer, which at this festival had been Hugh, and the chief judge, whom Rhys hadn't yet met.

A pavilion had been set aside specifically for the judges. Given the number of events, and the fact that three judges needed to attend each one, Rhys estimated that nearly twenty had been employed for the fortnight. Like bards, judges had a hierarchy, where younger, novice judges were chosen to adjudicate the lesser and earlier events.

As the contestants were winnowed down, only the most experienced judges remained employed.

The sides and flaps of the judges' pavilion were closed, and a soldier had been conscripted to stand guard to prevent anyone from entering who wasn't authorized. Hugh had been thorough in his efforts to ensure the contest was fair.

As Rhys approached, the guard recognized him and straightened to attention. "Sir."

"Hello, John. No need to fuss about me. I'm on the king's business."

"Yes, sir. I know, sir. You may come and go as you please."

Although five men were present in the pavilion as Rhys entered, four were either already on their way out or took one look at him and decided they had better places to be. That left one man alone. He was about Rhys's age, between thirty-five and forty, with a full head of prematurely gray hair and piercing blue eyes.

Rhys had seen him at the start of the festival and recognized him as the senior judge and, in fact, the man he most wanted to talk to. "May we speak? I am Rhys ap Iorwerth, the king's man." He spoke in Welsh.

"I know who you are. I'm Alun. My father was also a Iorwerth." His smile was wry. "I hail from Denbigh."

"It is a pleasure to meet you. I was hoping to talk to you about Hugh."

"Our esteemed commander? What would you like to talk about?" On the surface, he was very accommodating, but his eyes had grown wary at the mention of Hugh's name.

"I must ask first if you have judged any contests today?"

"Of course. I was busy at three different events just this morning."

Rhys decided that instant to dispense with the need to confirm this information. He didn't have time to track down every alibi, so he cut straight to the point. "I need you to tell me who is going to win the *eisteddfod*."

"Excuse me?" Alun frowned, genuinely appearing to be confused.

"We know that over the years Hugh demanded fees from contestants and then paid judges to rank those contestants higher. I want to know who has paid to win this time."

"You're serious." Alun studied him. "Nobody has paid to win."

"How can you be sure?"

"For starters, I know each of the judges here personally. I helped Hugh select them. They are all good men." Alun let out a breath. "Besides, there would be signs."

"What kind of signs?"

He held out one hand palm up. "Obviously superior bards receiving low scores and obviously inferior bards receiving higher ones."

"As happened to Cadwgan yesterday?"

"Yes, yes. Hugh spoke to me about that." Alun waggled his head. "That was an accounting error made worse by illegible handwriting. It has been corrected."

"Did you know that Hugh took bribes in the past?"

Alun settled back on his heels at the question. "I have no interest in speaking ill of Steward Hugh."

"I need you to tell me the truth. This is a murder investigation."

Alun wasn't happy, but Rhys was the king's quaestor, and he couldn't lie. "I did know. He assured me before I agreed to participate in this festival that those days were past. I refused to be tainted by his ill doing."

"Did he ever offer you a bribe?"

Alun didn't like that question either. It took him a bit longer to answer, so when he did, Rhys felt like it might be a relatively complete truth. "Yes, he did, years ago now. I did not take it, but it was a great sum, and I was tempted." He eyed Rhys for a moment. "Integrity can't be bought, and once lost is difficult to reclaim. Hugh has been discovering how true that is."

"Can you elaborate?"

"He has a history, as you said, and many don't believe he has changed his ways. He told me several contestants had offered him a fee to ensure their place in the standings and grew angry when he refused them."

Rhys took a step closer. "Do you know their names?"

"He didn't want to say, and I didn't press him. I don't want my own judging to be biased by the knowledge. They should win or lose on their own merits."

Rhys gave way to the man's honesty. Here was another who was still serving to the best of his ability.

But Alun wasn't done. "He also asked me to tell him if I saw or heard anything untoward this week." His expression shifted to one of concern. "Where is Hugh, by the way? He should be here answering your questions, not me!" And then, when Rhys didn't immediately reassure him, he added, "Has something happened?"

"Yes. Something has happened." There was no sense hiding the truth. Soon everyone was going to know. "Hugh has been murdered."

"Oh, I'm so sorry! Poor Mary. Poor Jane!" Alun put his fist to his mouth. "Did he die like Moriddig?"

"Not exactly like Moriddig, but murdered nonetheless. We have cause to think it had something to do with this scheme of his."

"As I said, Hugh took payments in the past, but that was over."

"What about Moriddig?"

"We all know the rumor. If it's true, he was still a great bard who lost his way one time. I can understand why, with the father he had. The pressure on him to succeed was immense."

"Were you at that festival?"

"Not me." Alun made a qualifying motion with his head. "Moriddig was already well established before I became a judge."

"The other judges in the pavilion beat a hasty retreat when I arrived. Why would they be afraid of me if they have nothing to hide?"

Alun gave him a quizzical look. "You're the king's quaestor."

"I am aware."

Alun genuinely smiled at Rhys's dry tone. "Nobody wants to be anywhere near you, on the off-chance you decide they've done something wrong."

Rhys was more than a little offended, though he tried to keep the outrage from his voice. "I would not arrest someone without cause."

"Many have lived most of their lives under the Norman boot. They don't know you, and they fear anyone wearing the king's colors."

Rhys supposed he should have known that. "You might tell them from me that the more they run away, the more suspicious I become of them. If one of them took a bribe to favor a contestant in this festival, I am going to find out, one way or another."

"I believe you. Though, I have to say, Hugh already said as much to them—not specifically in regards to your investigation, but in general. They would be far better off coming forward now and confessing all than waiting for discovery." He paused. "If they don't, and they're caught, I understand the queen has promised a hanging."

"So I also understand."

"That is only going to make it harder for anyone to come forward. You could promise them grace all the day long, and they won't believe you."

Rhys didn't have to ask why not. The queen was not known for her mercy. "They see fickleness instead of justice. That isn't me. That will never be me."

"That may be so. I believe you. But then, you aren't the one making the decisions, are you?"

35

Day Three
Catrin

"Alun is right, of course," Catrin said. "You aren't the one to decide who lives and who dies. You do what you can and hope the king will listen to you when it comes to justice."

"I have little hope of that, in truth," Rhys said, "and none at all from the queen."

Catrin sighed. "Unfortunately, that means our chances of getting anything useful out of any other judge is so low as to be nonexistent."

"It was never high."

Typically for them, this conversation was being held over Hugh's body. Darkness had fallen, at the end of what felt like another very long day. Math and Simon were going about their duties, and Catrin had promised one more visit to the queen before she retired for the night. Here at the end of a third day of investigating, she felt like she needed to sleep for a week.

"No defensive wounds again." She lifted Hugh's wrist.

"I would say he knew his killer, just like Moriddig."

"That has to narrow the culprits." Her eyes kept going to Hugh's torso and the two slashes in his belly. The first was an up-thrust to the heart, right under the ribs. The second had laid him open. He should have died very quickly from the first blow, but for some reason known only to the murderer, he had cut Hugh again. Out of spite ... or rage?

"But who really does it eliminate?" Rhys moved around the body, looking for other bruises or wounds. Again, they knew how Hugh had died. What they wanted now were indications as to the identity of the killer.

"I think we need to seriously consider the possibility this was done by a woman," Catrin said. "Moriddig was heard arguing with a woman before his death. He was a small man, so a strong woman could have managed it. He would not have known to fear her and could have allowed her to get close. The same is true of Hugh, though he was much taller. A man like him wouldn't have been wary of a woman."

"Who are our suspects, though? Mary, Jane, Rhiannon, Joan, who is six months pregnant? Emma?"

"I admit, the idea seems less credible when you put it that way. But then who do we have amongst the men? Adam and Patrick of course, Gruffydd, Cadwgan, or Owen de la Pole? We are missing too much—" She broke off as she leaned over Hugh's belly, focused on it despite herself. He had been tall but thin, and the bulge in the lower left quadrant of his abdomen was notable now that he was under direct light and lying on his back. "Is this some kind of swelling from the stabbing?"

Rhys leaned in too, eyeing the lump, because they really had to call it that. It was very near the second wound, and after a quick look of approval from Catrin, he expanded the gap further with both hands.

Catrin positioned the lamp so they could see better. "What is it?" Her initial thought had been that the murderer had left more than just coins and the garnet behind and had actually hidden something within the body itself.

But what Rhys exposed was an elongated mass of tissue connected to Hugh's innards, just taking up space in his belly. "That doesn't look like I think it should."

Catrin put her hand to her own abdomen. Neither she nor Rhys had made a personal study of human anatomy themselves, but she had cared for many ill people over the years and had seen drawings in one of the king's physician's Greek texts.

"It definitely isn't right—" She broke off at the sound of hooves on the flagstones in the bailey.

Rhys hastily washed his hands in the bowl provided while Catrin threw a cloth over the body. Stepping outside, they bowed to the king, who had just arrived with his party, which included Math and Simon.

Simon separated himself from the group and came over. "What have you to tell me?"

"He wasn't tortured," Rhys said, "and he does not appear to have fought back against his attacker. I'd say he was taken entirely by surprise."

"As we thought, then. As we feared."

"We think he might have been ill," Catrin said. "He has a lump of odd tissue in his belly. If he knew it, it could better explain his change of heart regarding the bribes, more than just a result of the transition from Lord Gruffydd's stewardship to Owen's." Then she looked past Simon to where the king was talking to Simon's brother, Osborn. "Is all well there?"

Simon turned to see what Catrin was indicating and, in a rare light moment, his face blossomed into a smile. "If one good thing can come out of today, it might be that."

"Osborn has blessed the union of Emma and Stephen?"

"Not only that, but so has the Earl of Warwick—and the king!"

"I don't believe it," Rhys said. "How often does young love win out?"

"Queen Eleanor was thirteen when she and the king married. On the first of November they will mark their thirtieth year together. Apparently, in the lead up to their wedding, today was a special day for them too. If I understood correctly, it was the day they confessed their love for each other."

Catrin had been such a girl once, though sixteen and marrying a lesser lord. She met Robert only a few days before their wedding. Hers had not been a love match, however. Edward and Eleanor had been lucky.

And, it seemed, despite Hugh's death and the horror that accompanied it, Emma and Stephen might be too.

36

Day Four
Math

"When you say that Hugh told his wife his horse was gone, does that mean it was stolen? Horses don't just go wandering off by themselves." Ralph declared this in the voice of a man who knew what he was talking about—as he should. For him, as for all of them, horses were a way of life.

"Not generally, not if they're tame. Still, it is the question Rhys has asked us to pursue today." Math eyed his companion, who appeared brighter-eyed than Math was feeling.

He had woken earlier in the day than he otherwise might have liked, since he would be on duty tonight with the king. Being awake, however, meant that he could help Rhys. If Moriddig had died on day one, this was now day four. The festival was half over. Two men had been murdered. He didn't feel much closer to knowing why than he had that first day.

He and Ralph shared a tent, so Math had kept Ralph up to date with the progress of the investigation. Since Math liked the other man and thought he could be useful, he'd agreed to let Ralph tag along and watch his back. Up until now, Math had been far more concerned with keeping the existence of Gruffydd's lament to Llywelyn a secret than discovering who killed Moriddig. It didn't help their progress (or lack thereof) that all the people who seemed to have a stake in Moriddig's life had alibis for his death.

Math's biggest concern about including Ralph was that this portion of the investigation might lead back to Gruffydd too. That would be unfortunate, to put it mildly. Ralph's uncle was the Justiciar of North Wales. No matter how much he liked Math or Rhys personally, his sympathies could never lie with the Welsh.

"What would be good to know is what Hugh's death has to do with Morrydig's." Like the other Normans, Ralph had removed all Welshness from the name, but Math knew whom he meant. "It's hard to believe the deaths aren't related. And by *hard,* I mean *impossible.*"

"We agree." And then Math modified the thought. "Rhys agrees. We are hoping that by pursuing Hugh's killer, we will find Moriddig's too."

"Hugh could have killed Morrydig, and then someone killed Hugh in retaliation." Ralph wrinkled his nose. "But from what you say and I observed, that would have given Hugh a very busy day. He was organizing the festival. People would have noticed he was absent."

"We might have asked him eventually. Either way, we still have a killer on the loose."

They began their inquiry regarding the whereabouts of Hugh's horse at the corral where he would have left it. When the various stable lads on duty gave them nothing but blank looks and shaken heads, they came ultimately to a last youth sitting by himself in a far corner by some trees. Math had seen him watching them out of the corner of his eye while at the same time whittling a slingshot. As it turned out, this was the only Welsh lad among the horse boys, which at first Math assumed was the reason for his isolation.

Until they started talking.

"I saw him with another man." The lad had answered easily enough, but then he stopped, his eyes on his whittling.

"When was this?"

"The day before he died. He gave away his horse."

"You're sure it was Hugh?" Math felt the need to clarify.

"Yes." The lad twitched his shoulders like he had ants crawling on him. "I know Hugh."

"Can you describe the other man?"

"He was your height but thinner, dark hair, brown eyes, he had a mole on his right cheek by his eye, and he had a funny laugh." The youth's words came rapidly, as if he was reciting them from memory.

"Did you hear what he and Hugh spoke about?"

"They were talking too quietly. But then the man took Hugh's horse, and Hugh let him go."

This entire conversation had been taking place in Welsh. Now Ralph nudged Math. "What is he saying?"

Math explained, after which Ralph pursed his lips. "It's all very odd."

Math wasn't sure if he meant the youth or the situation. Either way, he was correct. Then Ralph added, "Ask him which way he went."

Math had been about to do exactly that when the boy surprised him by answering the question himself in French. Again, he spoke very quickly, as if he couldn't wait to get the words out. "He went south, but he didn't get very far, since I saw him later in the common room at the inn on the high street."

That was news indeed. "Right here in Overton?"

"Yes. He's still there too, or at least the horse is because I saw it the last two mornings in the stables there."

"Do you work at the inn too?"

"No."

By now Math had figured out that the boy would answer a direct question but he wouldn't necessarily elaborate unprompted. "Why were you there?"

"To check on the horses."

Ralph tipped his head, curious and entertained by the boy at the same time. "Why would you do that when they aren't your responsibility?"

The youth's focus returned to his whittling, implying he'd lost interest in the questions. Still, he answered Ralph's anyway. "I check on all the horses in the town every day."

"All of them?" Ralph blinked. "How many are there?"

"Usually there are fourteen at the castle or its outside stables, three at the inn, and eight throughout the town. Today there are twenty-three at the castle, ten at the inn, which is more than those stables should hold, forty-seven in the town, and six hundred and eight in the fields associated with the *eisteddfod*." He paused and motioned towards the entrance to the corral, where a man was just arriving dressed in traveling gear and a merchant's hat. "Six hundred and nine."

Math thought about and discarded a dozen questions before he settled on, "How do you keep track? One horse looks much like another."

"Not to me."

"Will you come with us to point out the horse and the man you saw?" Math asked. "I can clear it with your supervisor."

"That was Hugh. I don't know who it is now." The youth paused for a heartbeat and then added, in reply to Math's previous question, "You just have to pay attention."

As they set off towards the entrance to the corral, Ralph muttered to Math under his breath. "Do you believe this?"

"I don't have to believe it. In a moment, he'll show us whether or not it's true."

"And if it is?"

"Then we will have an invaluable source of information to share with Rhys."

37

Day Four
Catrin

Mary watched Catrin closely as she inspected Hugh's ledger. "I know what you're thinking." She bent her head slightly. "I am ashamed to have been a part of this for so long. I hated what Hugh was doing. But after so many years, I was certainly complicit."

Having conferred with Rhys, Simon, and Math after her last interview with Mary, Catrin had sought out Hugh's wife again this morning, this time at the castle, where she and Jane had their quarters. They had not been evicted to make room for the king's party. Catrin had to spend a mere moment inspecting the ledger Mary gave her to be both grateful and horrified. She was grateful that Mary had mentioned the book at all. She hadn't had to, since it incriminated her husband. And she was horrified to see the long list of names of people who'd paid fees to Hugh.

Catrin wanted to be kind. "You wouldn't be the first person to find herself in a situation out of her control."

Mary gripped Catrin's arm, desperate to be heard. "Hugh was a good husband." She motioned towards the book. "Because of his father, he spent too many years afraid of the worst thing that could happen to a family. Now, that worst thing has happened. But, when it came, it was something he never thought of. He *was* trying to make amends. He *had* changed."

"I believe you, especially after examining him last night. He was ill, wasn't he?"

Mary met her gaze. "You saw it? The lump?"

"We did."

"We consulted with the best physicians, including two of the king's, as well as herbalists. Only one had ever seen anything like it before, and she said there was nothing to be done."

"He didn't seem particularly unwell when I spoke to him."

"He was tiring more easily, and he found it difficult to eat. The herbalist gave us some hope that he could live for years this way. The question was how big that lump would get and how terrible might be his end."

Catrin felt for Mary, but nonetheless held up the book, which was the main reason she'd come. "I will have to share this with my husband."

"I know you will. I knew that when I told you about it. I shared it even knowing that by doing so we might lose everything we have." More tears welled in her eyes, but then she straightened her spine. "It is no more nor less than we deserve."

Catrin shook her head. "Maybe you do deserve to be punished, but judgment is for God, not me, and certainly not my husband. Our task is to find the murderer. Even if this book aids us in finding your husband's killer, we won't necessarily have to share its contents with anyone else."

Mary's face filled with a pathetic hope. "My Jane is only fifteen. She is not yet ready for marriage. I don't care about me, but I wouldn't want her to suffer from something that wasn't her fault."

A sour part of Catrin might have commented that everyone suffered from things that weren't their fault, all the time. And yet, even if Catrin and Rhys had suffered in their own way, Catrin's pain was not Mary's fault either. There was no need to make any person's life unnecessarily worse.

Since Mary appeared to be coping with her husband's loss as well as could be expected, Catrin felt able to ask a few more relevant questions, beginning with: "Did you know that the day before Moriddig died, Lord Owen had discontinued his services?"

Mary's look of surprise appeared genuine. "Are you sure?"

"This is according to Lord Owen, who said Hugh knew, as did Adam, but that everyone agreed not to speak of it until after the festival, to give Moriddig time to arrange a new position for himself." She didn't mention that, according to Miles de Bohun, Moriddig had already done so with the Bohuns.

"Could Lord Owen's decision have had something to do with Moriddig's death? Or my Hugh's?" Mary asked.

"I do not know the answer to that. I'm sorry." Catrin flipped to the front of the book and started going through the names once more. "Moriddig's name isn't here."

"It wouldn't be."

Mary's flat tone caused Catrin to look up.

Mary nodded to see it. "At first, I wondered about that too. Hugh left some names out, ones that he was too ashamed to write down, even in a private book."

"So there are others like Moriddig, men he didn't choose to mention, even to himself?"

"Two others that I know of." Her hand went to her mouth. "Two others that are here in Overton!"

"What? Who?"

"Bari and Einion. They are brothers, born a year apart. They grew up with Moriddig and Hugh. You did know that Moriddig and Hugh have known each other practically since birth?"

"I didn't know that in particular." Catrin could have asked how it was they were on the fourth day of the investigation, looking for a link between their murder victims, and it was only now that anyone had cared to mention their personal history. "But go on."

Mary obliged. "All four of them were wanting to be bards, even Hugh for a time, even if it seems unlikely now. But, of course, only Moriddig had a father who already was one, and only Moriddig, in the end, had the necessary talent and perseverance." She paused. "Or so the others were told."

"Told by whom?"

She made a face. "I always assumed that news was broken to them by Moriddig's father, who was their teacher. All I know is that Hugh became what was expected of him, which was a steward; Moriddig followed in his father's footsteps after he won that first *eisteddfod*; and the two brothers went off to make their fortune elsewhere."

"Do you know where?"

"At some point they joined the English army. I'm sure they went to the Holy Land."

Two Welshmen who'd gone on crusade were definitely something Rhys would want to know about. He might even know them, as the crusader community was relatively small, and the Welsh crusader community smaller still.

Mary continued, "Hugh mentioned their presence in passing in the days before he died. He and Moriddig even met with them one evening to reminisce."

Catrin looked down at the book again, "So where do their fees come in?"

"Moriddig gave money to Hugh to help arrange his victory at that crucial *eisteddfod*. I honestly don't know how much of the money Hugh kept for himself, but Hugh definitely paid at least one of the judges to ensure Moriddig's victory."

"And the others?"

Mary looked truly rueful now. "I think he went to each of his friends separately to offer them the same bargain, to be fair, you see. They paid, but they lost. That was the last time he accepted money from multiple people to achieve the same end."

"Any sense of how good the brothers were?"

Mary shook her head. "I genuinely don't know. It was before our marriage. And, as you can probably imagine, it wasn't something Hugh liked to talk about. It came up only once, at a time when Hugh was well into his cups. He had taken money from friends—money he'd asked for—and had been unable to deliver on his promise. On top of that, he didn't give the money back afterwards. I know he regretted the whole affair ever since. Because of it, he lost them as friends."

"Until this week? You said the four of them met to reminisce."

"So he said." She shrugged. "So it seems?"

Catrin felt like cold water was trickling down her spine. The four men had reunited after many years apart, and now two of them were dead.

Forcing herself to observe the necessary social graces, she thanked Mary for her time and her honesty. Inside, however, she was wondering if Bari and Einion had come back after all these years, still holding onto how they'd been wronged as young men, and took their revenge by murdering the two former best friends who'd wronged them.

38

Day Four
Math

The stable boy's name turned out to be Gwrgenau, a name that made Ralph's eyes cross even more than Moriddig's. Math suggested they call him Gwrgi, but while the boy didn't necessarily take offense, he was insistent: "My name is Gwrgenau."

So Gwrgenau it was.

"Is it hard for you when the horses come and go, like is happening this week?" Math asked as Gwrgenau led them unerringly across the fields to the village and the inn in question, known (appropriately) as *The Mare*, with a sign of a trotting horse for all those who couldn't read.

"I have never minded when new ones come, but I used to get upset when any would leave or die. That was when I was younger. I am better about it now."

This was a small village to have its own inn, but with the proximity of the bridge across the Dee, it was a common stopping point for many. It also marked the border between England and Wales. Overton had become an English town, albeit with many Welsh (like Gwrgenau) in it, making a living as best they could. As they all were.

By now, Math was starting to realize the kind of person Gwrgenau was, and that he'd met men like him before. They were often brilliant in their own way, about their own very specific interests. For Gwrgenau, it was horses.

"That's him," Gwrgenau said in a loud voice and pointed with his whole arm. "That's the man."

Subtle, he was not. But then, he had done as he had promised and had given them more of a lead than anyone else had so far.

The man they had come to see was just getting up from the table where, from the looks, he had enjoyed a splendid repast. His eyes went wide at the sight of the two men in the king's livery looming over him. Ralph put a heavy hand on his shoulder, forcing him back down to his bench. The common room had a dozen other people in it, every single one riveted by the scene before them. Math had never been more aware of the king's crest on his chest.

"What do you want with me?" The man spoke first in a small voice and then, when he too felt the eyes of everyone in the room, with more force. "I didn't do anything. I don't know anything!"

Unimpressed with such a comprehensive denial, Math came around the table to the other side of the bench, boxing him in. "Everyone has done something. What's your name?"

"Roger de Retondeur." This was all happening in French, the same as his name.

"You're a shearman?"

"A draper, as was my father before me. He gave me his name too." He had calmed a little, since they'd asked him questions he could answer easily.

"Let's take this conversation outside, unless you want your business shared with everyone else in the room?"

"I have nothing to hide." It was a protest, but not as loud as before.

Math bent forward. "Is that so? How about that good horse you have suddenly acquired?"

Roger's jaw fell open. Into the momentary pause, Ralph lifted Roger to his feet and urged him towards the door.

On the way, Roger motioned to the room at large. "I have done nothing wrong. This is just a formality. I am a decent man!" As Ralph got him outside, he added, "You have to believe me!"

"We don't, actually," Math strolled out the door after them, "but we are willing to be convinced."

It was definitely easy to think the man was protesting too much. If he hadn't made such a fuss to everyone else in the room, they might have let him stay seated, but he'd turned them into a spectacle. By the time they got him to the stables and in front of the horse Gwrgenau helpfully pointed out as the one that had been Hugh's, Math was feeling more impatient than anything else. "Gwrgenau tells us this is Steward Hugh's horse." He cut through Roger's continuing assertions of innocence.

To salvage whatever was left of his dignity, Roger straightened his tunic as best he could and threw back his shoulders. "It *was* Steward Hugh's horse. He gave it to me of his own free will."

"He *gave* it to you." Math's voice was steady. "Why would he do that?"

"To make amends."

Math studied him, wondering if things might all of a sudden be starting to make a tiny bit of sense.

But Ralph glowered as if he didn't believe him. "Amends for what?"

"For something that happened with my father, years ago."

That sounded like the truth to Math. "What *something*?"

Roger gave his head a shake. "It had to do with needing a good word with the old Lord Gruffydd, and Hugh making him pay for it. It was before I was born."

"Can you tell me more about the dispute?"

"Not really. Steward Hugh didn't want to explain. I thought he was embarrassed, frankly. That's why I took the horse, to make it easier for him."

"Your generosity knows no bounds," Ralph said dryly.

Roger chose to ignore the sarcasm. "He wouldn't take no for an answer. What was I to do? *Not* take it? It's a horse! Of course I was going to take it."

Honestly, Math could appreciate the man's dilemma. "What happened to Hugh after that?"

"How should I know? He went off with a woman, and that was the last I saw of him."

Math turned now to Gwrgenau, who'd been listening to the conversation with an impassive expression, as if he didn't care about its outcome one way or another. Maybe he didn't. Maybe all he really cared about was horses. "Did you see Hugh with a woman?"

"Yes." He spoke as if the answer should have been obvious.

Roger interrupted. "Why don't you just ask Steward Hugh to confirm my story? I am telling you exactly what happened."

That flummoxed Math for a moment. "Steward Hugh was murdered. How could you not know that?"

Roger's mouth fell open again. "When?"

With Hugh's body waiting for burial, Math was truly astounded Roger would still be ignorant of his death. He had assumed knowledge of the murder would be all that was being talked about. "Yesterday. He was stabbed." Math held out his hand. "May I see your blade?"

His face paling, Roger fumbled at his belt to comply. Although an afterthought on Math's part, he thought it might be a good idea to start making a study of belt knives, in the same way he'd started looking at hands for a ring or indication that a person had removed one recently.

This sheath was plain and unadorned, giving no indication any gems had ever been affixed to the leather. Math freed the knife and held it up to the light. "It's been cleaned and oiled recently."

"As it should have been," Roger said. "I don't doubt that you care for your sword nightly."

Ralph still had a grip on Roger's shoulder, and he shook him a little. "Did you kill Hugh?"

"No! Of course not! Why would I do that?"

"For the horse, of course." Math turned from the knife to focus on Roger's face. If Roger had begun with *why would I do that,* thus answering a question with another question, Math would have been immediately more suspicious. But the denial that had preceded it had been unforced.

"I already told you he gave the horse to me. If he were alive, he could have confirmed it. I am far worse off now that he's dead."

Ralph glared at Roger one more time, but then released him. Meanwhile, Math thrust the dagger back into its sheath and returned it. "Do not leave Overton."

Roger blinked. "Such was not my intent. I have a stall at the market fair. Good cloth, if you need any." That he would take a moment at the end of being questioned about a murder to sell his wares only improved his case.

Leaving Roger, who had collapsed against his horse's stall at being released, Math stepped outside the stables and looked once again at Gwrgenau. "Now, about this woman."

39

Day Four
Rhys

With the murder of Hugh, Moriddig's death had briefly been made secondary. A fresh body always had to take precedence. Nonetheless, Rhys hadn't forgotten that he had two deaths to investigate. For that reason, he endeavored to track down Adam, Moriddig's brother, once again. Lord Owen had insisted that he'd dispensed with Moriddig's services. Moriddig had also argued with a woman inside his wagon right before his death. Adam had said nothing about either event. Rhys needed to know what he knew.

"I didn't tell you that my brother was leaving Owen's service because he was dead. What difference did it make?" Adam shook his head sadly.

Rhys thought he once again heard tears behind Adam's words, as well he might, given the magnitude of his loss. "So it is true."

Rhys had found Adam in one of the pavilions, Hugh's *eisteddfod* ledger in hand. Now he snapped it shut and gave Rhys his full attention. "It's true, though—"

Rhys pounced at the hesitation. "But some of the details are wrong?"

Adam appeared to have hesitated because he was uncomfortable with the truth, but under Rhys's steady gaze, he couldn't keep silent. "My brother told Lord Owen he was leaving, and only then did Lord Owen tell him he would dispense with his services."

Somehow, that was exactly what Rhys had suspected had happened.

"When was this?"

"The day before he died."

"But he still performed for the king that night?"

Adam was astonished at Rhys's ignorance. "They were keeping his departure a secret until after the festival! Neither was prepared to announce their separation in front of the king."

"How was Moriddig's mood after that conversation? Was he offended that Owen had let him go?"

"Not at all. He was the one who'd instigated the break. He was as confident as ever, as well he should have been since he'd already found himself a new place with the Bohuns." Adam had been watching Rhys's face, and when Rhys gave no sign of surprise, he nodded. "You knew already. Was this a test of me?"

"I endeavor not to believe anything anyone tells me until I confirm it independently. I had been told of this move. How did it make you feel? Your livelihood depended on him."

"It was fine with me one way or the other. I was my brother's steward. Where he went, I went."

"So you would have gone with him? Left your home and the people you know?"

Adam seemed surprised by the question. He scratched at his scalp under his hood, the same beautiful blue one he always wore. It had been helpful to Rhys in finding him amidst the crowds. "He asked me how I felt about it before he began his negotiations with the Bohuns. I told him I would go, and he proceeded with his plans."

"So you knew from the start?"

"Of course I knew. Even were I not his steward, we were brothers! I know he could be prickly, maybe more with me than with anyone else, but he was honest, and he cared about me as I did for him."

"What about Patrick?"

Adam waggled his head back and forth in a kind of denial. "Moriddig didn't discuss it with him at first."

"Was he upset when he found out?"

"He didn't find out until the day Owen released Moriddig. We hadn't wanted to risk impairing his performance in the festival, but once it was confirmed, Moriddig didn't feel right about keeping the secret any longer."

"You'd feared he'd be unhappy." It wasn't a question.

"We knew he would be! How could he not, young as he is and faced with leaving behind everything he knows? He was mightily relieved we had somewhere to go, however."

"You're saying he was going to come with you?"

Adam spread his hands wide. "I thought so. We didn't really discuss it at length, or at least I didn't. I was there for the initial conversation, but then Moriddig implied I should go and leave Patrick to him. By the next morning he was dead, and it no longer mattered."

"Was there any hope that Lord Owen would hire Patrick to replace his father as a bard?"

"I do not know." His expression turned momentarily eager. "Did he say so?"

"Not to me."

Adam subsided. "So I feared. All the more reason to hope Patrick succeeds at the festival."

That seemed a good way to slide into the next round of questions. "Tell me about that initial bribe."

"That initial what?" Adam looked genuinely confused.

"Decades ago, Moriddig won his first festival because he paid Hugh to bribe the judges."

Adam threw back his head and laughed. "Is that what you heard?" He waved a hand. "He was always going to win. The only reason he bothered to pay Hugh was because he was afraid other men would do the same. He didn't want to be put at a disadvantage."

"Has he ever paid a fee since?"

"Of course not."

"Did you know it was that initial bribe that set Hugh on a path where he took them regularly?"

"I suppose I did know that." He wrinkled his nose. "I couldn't stop him, and he did become rich doing it."

"Did Lord Owen know?"

Adam's scoff gave Rhys the answer before Adam said the words. "He sees only what is right in front of him. Now, the old lord, Gruffydd, was a different matter. He did know."

"And looked the other way?"

"I think he admired Hugh's resourcefulness. He was wily, that one, before his mind went."

"What about more recently? We hear Hugh was trying to make amends."

Adam rubbed his nose. "He was more than trying. He was a changed man."

"Did you know he was ill?"

Adam pressed his lips together. "I did know. It was worrying, but he didn't seem in any immediate danger."

"When we first interviewed you, you said every bard at the festival could have wanted your brother dead. Would you say the same of Hugh?"

"Honestly, I don't know what I was thinking when I told you that. I don't think it true of Moriddig. I certainly don't think it true of Hugh. Unless—" He stopped abruptly, like before, unwilling to finish the thought.

"Unless what?" Rhys shouldn't have had to prompt him, but sometimes voluble witnesses closed up when they realized how much they'd said.

"Unless it was someone from his past who couldn't forgive him?"

40

Day Four
Math

Ralph chose that moment to let out a huge yawn, but Math was feeling more awake than before. They were on the hunt. He had understood for a while that it was this part of the job that kept Rhys interested. Math had experienced a bit of the excitement himself at Vale Royal Abbey, particularly when he'd gone about on his own, poking his nose where some might have said it didn't belong. At first Rhys hadn't liked that, more because Math might have got himself into trouble than because he was usurping Rhys's authority. The fact that he'd given Math this entire assignment all on his own showed the extent of his trust.

Gwrgenau took them into the market, wending his way among the many stalls. The places nearest to the festival were the most desirable, but Gwrgenau continued to stride along, passing stall after stall, until they were almost out of the market, at the far north-eastern end. Once again, Math was made very conscious of his tunic emblazoned with the king's crest. It wouldn't do for anyone to see him amongst these stalls and wonder if his business here was personal.

They were on the margins of polite society. They wouldn't find hair ribbons and soaps here. This area was host to questionable medical remedies, home-brewed alcohol, gambling dens, and, at the very edge, prostitutes.

Ralph hesitated too, prompting Math to wonder how worldly his friend really was. He had traveled. He served the king. His uncle was Justiciar of North Wales. But that didn't mean he'd spent much time in the less savory corners of the earth any more than Math had.

"This woman we are seeking ... she's a *putain*?" Ralph asked. And then, when Gwrgenau nodded, he came to a complete halt. "You can't trust a word any of them say."

Math nudged him forward. "We are the king's men, on a quest for the king. We go where we must."

With each step into this den of iniquity, Ralph's eyes got a little wider. Gwrgenau, meanwhile, was paying their concerns no heed. Women called out to him from every side, and he grinned and waved as if there was nothing strange about him bringing two of the king's men into their midst.

Finally, he stopped at a stall slightly less makeshift than those on either side. Each was basically a single room with curtains all around. Once the financial transaction was made, the prostitute and her latest customer would retire behind a pulled curtain for as long as the man had paid for. Men were coming and going unabashedly. Exchanging money for sex happened in Gwynedd, but just not in as organized a fashion as this, not even in the sea-trading towns of Llanfaes and Nefyn. There wasn't a brothel in the whole of north Wales.

Or rather, there hadn't been during Llywelyn's reign. With so many foreign soldiers permanently stationed throughout the country, maybe there were now, despite King Edward's similar views to Llywelyn's on the matter. There was even talk within the court that the king was going to ban all prostitution from the city of London proper. He might not know this corner of the market existed.

Math decided then and there to leave it to Ralph to tell him, if he needed to be told at all.

"You want to talk to Mina." Gwrgenau brought a dark-haired woman closer. She was past her prime, though that didn't mean she was old. It was a hard life she was living, and she was swaying as if she had started early on the ale or one of the gut-rotting drinks, or maybe hadn't stopped since last night.

That fact honestly made Math more sympathetic to her instead of less. None of these women would be here if they had any other choice of employment. Although his own work was different, and much more respected, he had sold himself to the king to survive. Maybe every single person had to sell themselves in some fashion or another. His soul was still his own, however, or at least that's what he told himself. He feared most of these women had given up on theirs a long time ago.

That he felt for them didn't mean he wanted to stay here any longer than needful. Ralph still looked as if he was about to bolt, so

Math started right in. "Gwrgenau saw you with Steward Hugh before he died. Why were you talking to him?"

Mina simpered at him in a way she might have thought was attractive but turned Math's stomach. "How much are you willing to pay for the answer?"

He didn't want to pay, and he was certain that any answer she gave had an even chance of being a lie. Thus, he turned to Gwrgenau. "How much, Gwrgenau?"

"A farthing," he said immediately, "and another if you think she's told the truth."

Mina pouted. "You're no fun."

"I saw you, Mina. And Steward Hugh is dead. If you don't want them to think you killed him, you should tell them why you talked to him."

Math wouldn't have told her all this so abruptly, but Gwrgenau's words had the desired effect. He had spoken loudly enough that others around them overheard too.

Mina didn't feign ignorance. "I heard about that. I didn't do it."

"Someone did." Math put a farthing into her hand. "What did you talk about?"

"What makes you think we *talked*?" She was back to simpering.

Internally, Math sighed at having to play along. "He wasn't that man."

He said it with such certainty that Mina gave up flirting. "He paid me to fetch him to someone else."

"Another woman?" Ralph asked.

"No. Two men. Brothers. I didn't know them."

"Can you take me to them?"

"I'll lose my trade!"

Math gave her another farthing.

She clenched her fist around it. "I don't have to take you. They've been spending all their time either in the market or at the inn in the village, *The Mare.*"

They'd just come from there. Math wanted to throw up his hands in frustration. "I'll need you to point them out."

"No, you don't." She turned to Gwrgenau. "Tall, both of them, blond. One has a scar on his right cheek."

Gwrgenau brightened. "I saw them. I know the people you're talking about."

"Good boy." She patted his arm. "Gwrgenau knows everyone, you see, not just the horses."

41

Day Four

Rhys

Now that the day was at an end, the inn was packed with customers. Math and Ralph were meant to be on duty shortly so had passed the torch to Rhys. Gwrgenau had subsequently pointed out the two men in question and then left the inn on his own reconnaissance, perhaps to pursue his evening count of the horses.

The boy would be an acquired taste for anyone threatened by his prodigious memory, not seeing it for the useful tool it was. Rhys wasn't sure how easily directed the youth might be in the long run, but they had been happy to have him helping them as long as he had been willing to do so.

For this new undertaking, Rhys had removed his gear and wore what he thought of as traveling clothes. He had also brought reinforcements in the form of Miles de Bohun and Catrin's brother, Hywel. Maybe it was unorthodox to ask his friends to dress like common men, but he knew from experience that Miles could look like anyone he wanted, and Hywel had always been one for adventure. Rhys and Hywel, in fact, had been adventuring together far longer than Rhys and Simon, or Rhys and Miles—since birth, really, having both grown up in Llywelyn's court.

Rhys studied the two brothers for a moment as they sat talking and drinking before making his move. He didn't want to scare them into rabbiting. However, they'd planned for that event too, in that Miles had chosen a spot near the corridor that led to the back entrance to lean casually against the wall, and several of his men kept watch around the outside of the inn. All of them were dressed plainly too.

Hywel and Rhys had acquired cups of mead, to better blend in with the clientele. Rhys was just happy they were close enough to Wales to get the drink easily. It was very watered down to minimize drunkenness (as well as to make the supplies last longer). Cups in hand, they edged their way through the crowd to where the brothers sat on benches near one of the few windows, darkened now against the night sky. Math had figured it was just as well he wasn't coming along, since he and Ralph had removed Roger de Retondeur from this very inn earlier in the day and might be recognized, even without their royal gear.

As promised, the brothers were large and blond, with a white scar marring one brother's cheek. Further examination revealed work-roughened hands, with thick fingers, big feet and broad shoulders. Either one would have had no difficulty with the physical demands of strangling Moriddig or stabbing Hugh.

The nature of their fingers did give Rhys a moment's pause, however. Neither wore a ring, and it would be hard to imagine how a ring could comfortably fit on any of their fingers.

"Have you heard the news?" Rhys spoke in Welsh, approaching from one side, while Hywel slid onto the bench on the other.

With them safely buttressed, Miles was then able to leave his position and sit on the other side of the table. Rhys's initial move had been casual, but there was no hiding the sudden intensity each of them exuded.

The scarred brother looked from one to the other and then correctly determined that Rhys was in charge. "What news would that be?"

His accent was South Walesian. Rhys understood what he was saying, but to his ear, the man's words came out mushy compared to the clear tones of someone from the north.

"Steward Hugh is dead."

The man lifted his cup. "We did hear about that."

The other brother drained his drink and set his cup on the table with a thunk, his manner immediately more combative. "Why would a king's man be speaking of it to us?"

"So you know who I am?" Rhys said.

"Spotted you the moment you came in," he gestured to Hywel and Miles, and seamlessly switched to French, "you and the lords."

Miles replied in the same language. "I was wondering if you'd recognized me. It's been a long time, Einion." He looked at the brother with the scar. "And you, Bari."

"That it has," Bari said, "and that you're looming over us once again must mean you aren't any more pleased with us tonight than you were all those years ago in the Holy Land."

Miles was intent. "That day, you were a hair's-breadth from being hanged."

"We were too good at fighting, and you had too few men who were healthy to disable those that could walk. You had to settle for a night in the stocks. Besides, we did nothing wrong, did we? Just held back when the skirmish was a lost cause. We were far from the only ones."

"You allowed good men to die."

"Better them than us."

Rhys had caught on by now to the incident they were referencing. "These are the men?"

"Indeed." Miles eased back in his seat, the cloud that had figuratively been looming over his head dissipating a bit. "Bari and Einion, after all these years."

Once again, memories of the crusade rose to the fore. Rhys didn't dream of those days nearly as often as he once had. He'd survived. They'd survived. Maybe that really could be an end to it.

Except the crusade kept coming back into Rhys's life, not the least because the king surrounded himself with former crusaders as a matter of course. "We understand the two of you, plus Hugh and Moriddig, spent an evening together last week."

"It wasn't just the four of us that first evening," Bari said. "It was a whole crowd from the old days. I didn't even recognize Moriddig when he first arrived."

"He wept to see us, though." Einion gave a shake of his head. "He said he was working on a song about our friendship."

"Was that in the way of making amends?" Miles asked.

Between one breath and the next, the men's faces turned completely blank. And then Bari said, "What would he have to make amends for?"

"We know about that first *eisteddfod*," Rhys said. "We know that Hugh spent the intervening years taking bribes. It's what drove you apart."

Einion rolled his eyes. "That was a long time ago. It wasn't what drove us apart anyway."

"It was important enough to send you two to the Holy Land," Miles said.

"That was later," Bari said. Given that the two brothers were a good ten years older than Rhys and Miles, the timing made sense. "We were never going to be good enough musicians to become bards, and we knew it. That's why the four of us went our separate ways. We didn't resent Moriddig for his talent and his victory. While it's true he always thought too much of himself, we were too different and our paths would have diverged eventually. It just happened sooner rather than later because he won that *eisteddfod*."

"But you resented Hugh?" That was from Hywel, who was perceptive enough to notice the hitch in Bari's voice when he talked about Hugh as compared to Moriddig.

"He became too good for us, but in a different way," Bari said. "To be fair, he had money, and we didn't, and we didn't like him thinking that made him better than us."

"Did you seek him out when you returned from crusade?" Rhys always wondered at the way he had to prompt his informants. They rarely just spilled out what they knew all in one go. Then again, maybe they didn't think about their lives in an orderly fashion and see how they needed to explain something such that a stranger would understand. To them it was obvious.

"We didn't bother." Bari held up his hands. "We found another calling. Stone masons, both of us."

"That's why we came to Overton, not because of Hugh or Moriddig." Einion looked forlornly into his empty cup. Rhys would have had it filled again for him if the inn's proprietor wasn't currently besieged by requests from customers three-deep around the bar. "We heard the king was hiring."

"So if you had already met Hugh and Moriddig again, why did you pay a trollop to bring Hugh to you the day before he died?" Rhys asked.

"It was Hugh who paid a trollop to find *us*." Bari settled back a bit more in his seat, in a sign that he was sure of his answer and comfortable with it. Rhys had asked the question that way on purpose, just to see if he would agree with Mina. "He wanted to speak to us, not the other way around."

"Why?" Hywel put in.

"Because it was bloody well time!" These words burst from Einion. "We were friends once, and we were going to be again if he hadn't gone and got himself killed!"

"We were friends for nearly a week." Bari consoled his brother. "He wanted to make amends, but he also wanted something from us."

"There was a lad bothering his daughter," Einion took up the story. "The silly girl imagined herself in love with him. Hugh had bought him off with a horse, and he asked us to make sure the promise stuck."

"This is a fellow named Roger?" Rhys said.

Bari blinked. "You already know about him? We saw him dragged out of here earlier today. That was for you?" He didn't wait for Rhys to do more than nod before adding, "Stupid fool. Watching him was dull, but it isn't as if we were going to stop."

"Even with Hugh dead?"

"Especially with Hugh dead! It was Hugh's last request of us, and with him gone, who does his wife and daughter have but us?"

"Since Roger is very much alive and staying at this inn," Hywel said, "maybe he killed Hugh to get to Jane."

Rhys was happy to have the question posed. Emma and Stephen had met at the abandoned barn. Roger and Jane could have met there as well and been spied upon by Hugh. Then, after Jane left, Hugh could have tried to bribe Roger again, this time with coin, and been murdered for his pains. However unlikely, Roger could have dumped the offending coins on his corpse in an act of disdain.

It could have been a viable theory except they already knew Jane had been with her mother the entire day her father died. And now, Einion confirmed that Roger hadn't been at the barn. "I wish it were true, but he can't have. We haven't let him out of our sight since

Hugh asked us to keep an eye on him. We even followed Roger and your men out of here, so we wouldn't lose him if they let him go and he wandered off."

Bari looked balefully at Rhys. "My brother and I are left wondering if it's Hugh's back, rather than Roger's, we should have been watching."

42

Day Four
Miles

Talking to Roger, about why he hadn't told the truth, was the last task of the day. Fortunately, as promised, the brothers had been doing their job, and he'd been sitting on the other side of the common room all along. Miles, Hywel, and Rhys hadn't had to do more than stand and weave their way through the increasingly raucous crowd to his side.

On the way, Miles was blocked by two men arguing in a fashion that implied they knew each other well. "Of course the judging is fair. The king expects it to be fair."

These were two of the judges he'd seen on duty today at one of the contests, albeit not the main one in front of the central viewing stand.

The other man gave his friend a hard look. "Does he?"

The first looked disconcerted. "Doesn't he?"

"The king wants the outcome he wants, which you must realize has nothing to do with who is best, particularly if that bard is someone he finds politically unacceptable."

These were brave words, firmly spoken. This judge probably thought they were safe thoughts to voice in a crowded tavern in French, which most of the people here wouldn't speak. Miles had heard a great deal of Welsh and English, but French was reserved for those who worked for Normans or sold to them. *The Mare* was an inn for common folk. The king's men generally drank somewhere else. Miles was glad he was wearing a workman's clothes, the better to eavesdrop.

The face of the first man to speak fell. "I suppose I did know that. Gruffydd might be the best, but you don't think he's going to win?"

"Again, it depends. Does the king want to favor Llywelyn's former bard? I doubt it. But he might want to appear magnanimous to the people of Gwynedd, who are already suffering under his yoke. In that case, a win by Gruffydd would be like throwing them a bone."

"It would please Lord Tudur."

"But does the king want that?" The second man had a theory about everything. "What I told you earlier about Hugh wasn't the full story. What you don't know is that he had a change of heart this year about giving men like us money and has spent the last year trying to make amends for the previous thirty. Believe me, five years ago, you could have made yourself rich judging a festival for him."

The younger judge looked disconcerted. "Nobody has ever offered me mon—"

Then several other men arrived to interrupt their conversation, and Miles slipped away, arriving at Roger's table after the others.

Rhys wasn't wearing his tunic emblazoned with the king's crest, and none of them wore their swords. But Roger must have recognized either Rhys himself or the look on his face, because as they settled around him he licked his lips and glanced quickly about, looking for an easy exit. If his back had been to the door, he wouldn't have seen them coming, but he also might have had an opportunity to slip away amongst the crowd.

As it was, Rhys sat on a stool opposite, Miles leaned against the wall Roger had chosen to sit against, and this time it was Hywel who dropped onto the bench next to him. Honestly, watching Rhys work was always an education. Even having been involved in the investigation at Windsor, Miles was never sure what idea or thought Rhys was going to come up with next.

In this instance, Roger needed little prompting to start spilling out the truth. All Rhys really had to do was look at him hard. "As I told the other two earlier, I took the horse from Hugh because he gave it to me. I swear it!"

"You lied about why. You were a threat to his daughter, which means the horse wasn't given freely at all. Did you demand it in exchange for staying away from her?"

"No! Nothing like that. I love her."

"And yet, a horse was enough to make you stop loving her?" Rhys said.

Roger replied in something of a sulky voice, "Horses are valuable."

"Why did you lie?" Hywel said. "Why did you think the excuse you gave would be believed?"

"It was believed, wasn't it?" Roger glanced around at the three of them. "Everybody knew what Hugh had been about this last year. Why couldn't I have been a beneficiary too?"

"It's been that public?" Rhys said.

Miles could have told him that it had, given the conversation he'd overheard between the judges. As it was, Roger tilted his hand back and forth. "Maybe *everyone* doesn't know, but it was known among the merchants that Hugh could be bribed for the best spot at the fair. In fact, extra payment was required. And then, when we got here, he refused to take my money. He refused to take anyone's money!"

That answered a question that had passed through Miles's head earlier, that they should be inquiring of the merchants what payments they'd made. There was no question it cost money to have a market stall. It was one of the many ways the festival wasn't entirely a drain on the exchequer. The question was if anyone had been required to pay Hugh personally a little more to get the best spot.

And now they knew they hadn't, at least not to Hugh. So far, they had found no evidence of bribery of any kind at this festival.

Miles bent forward and whispered in Rhys's ear. "Was this the reason Hugh is dead? Had he uncovered a bribery scheme, just one not run by him? I hate to suggest it, but could Osborn, Simon's brother, have seen a way to line his own coffers? After all, the festival is taking place on lands he manages. He, or the queen, must be getting something out of it."

Rhys absorbed these observations for a moment, and then leaned forward to put his elbows on the table. Even as he'd listened to Miles, he'd kept his face expressionless and his eyes on Roger. "So you had money, but nobody to pay it to."

"Who else could I have paid? Everyone is all so ethical."

"What about Osborn, the queen's steward?"

Miles settled his shoulders, pleased Rhys had been listening, even as Hywel's eyes widened at the question.

But Roger merely shook of his head. "I've never even met him. I don't know why you'd ask me that."

"Were you angry?"

"We had a system. There were the public rates and then the private ones. Those of us who got here first and were willing to pay a little more could override what had already been set. But Hugh refused to participate! Maybe I flirted a bit with his daughter to get back at him. It isn't my fault she fell in love with me."

"And you with her?" Miles said dryly.

"Maybe I exaggerated my feelings."

"You got a horse out of it," Rhys said. "Or you did until we learned the truth. You can't keep it."

Roger's chin jutted out. "How is what I did any different from what he did for all those years?"

Hywel was glaring at Roger as if given half the chance he would run him through. "Is there a possibility the girl could fall pregnant?"

Roger finally looked sheepish. "Maybe."

Miles remembered that Hywel had a daughter the same age as Jane. "She either could or she couldn't."

"She could."

Now Miles also wanted to punch Roger in the nose. "And if that were to occur, what would you do then?"

Roger couldn't look Miles in the face, but he wasn't finding a safe haven in Hywel's or Rhys's either. "Provide for the child, of course."

Rhys put a heavy hand on his arm. "You will give back the horse first thing in the morning." When Roger's expression turned sullen, Rhys added, "I assume I don't have to threaten you with consequences if you don't?"

"No, my lord. I will do as you say." The words were right, but Miles saw a wiliness in Roger's eyes he didn't trust. It might be wise to speak to Bari and Einion before they left the inn about making sure Roger kept his word. He didn't appear to have murdered Hugh, but he wasn't a good man.

Then the door to the common room was flung open, and they all turned as a young boy stood in the doorway, red-faced and breathing hard. "Fire! The castle is on fire!"

43

Day Four
Math

A half-hour earlier ...

It had been Math's role to be one of the men standing guard outside the king's door at the point the king retired to bed. He often returned to his chambers early because he liked to wake early, before the first petitioners arrived and the expectations of the day began. It also gave him an opportunity to get started on the endless stacks of paperwork that were required for ruling his kingdom. Probably also, he was looking to have a moment alone in peace.

Tonight, Math had heard movement within the room for some while after the king shut the door. It seemed as if he might be asleep now, but he could also be reading. Math shifted his stance, preparing himself for a long, quiet night.

Then Thomas, one of the Normans among the king's guard, appeared in the stairwell. In a low voice, so as not to disturb the king, he said, "Take a turn around the castle. I'll stand here for a time."

Math couldn't keep the smile from his face. "Is Janet after you again?"

Thomas rolled his eyes. "She isn't allowed up here, but if I'm out in the bailey or patrolling the palisade, she sees me as fair game."

"You can stay here as long as you like tonight." Math pushed off from the wall, pleased to be able to combine being helpful to Thomas with his personal preferences. Standing for so long made his lower back ache. It was much better to move about. He also liked knowing what was happening in the castle instead of being shut away in a tower.

Owen had given King Edward the best room in the castle, located at the top of the keep. He had his own men keeping watch from the tower's battlement and the walls of the castle, but three of the king's own guards were specifically tasked with his personal security. At all times, one of them was posted outside his door; one kept watch outside the main door to the keep; and one was on patrol.

The third member of their group tonight was Fulke, one of three Frenchmen amongst the king's guard. He had bright red hair and a very large physique which appeared to Math to be a throwback to some earlier barbaric ancestry.

"You all right?" Math asked him as he went by.

"A cup of water wouldn't go amiss."

"I'll find someone to bring you a carafe."

They weren't allowed to drink alcohol on duty, but a man who was thirsty was not at the top of his form.

"Not Janet."

Math smirked. "Surely not. Apparently we are protecting Thomas tonight as well as the king."

Fulke grinned back.

The motte was not a particularly high one, so it was a matter of two dozen steps down to the bridge across the dry moat in order to reach the inner gatehouse.

The guards keeping watch there let Math through with a wave, at which point Math said, "How goes it?" He always tried to be friendly. So far, he had felt no animosity from Owen's men. Their lord was loyal to the king; Math was too. He couldn't fault them.

"Well enough. Quiet. Most are asleep by now." This particular guard was half-Welsh and remembered the language. "It's my favorite time of night."

Math surveyed the bailey with him, noting a light in the stables that meant someone was seeing to a horse. A couple of drunk young men, arms around each other, staggered towards the gatehouse. He thought one of them might be Patrick, Moriddig's son, but he couldn't be sure from this distance. Really, he couldn't blame the boy for drowning his grief in ale, although Math could have told him it wouldn't lessen his sorrow. The pain of his father's murder would remain, just now with a sore head.

Otherwise, the bailey was empty. The blacksmith's fire was banked, with just smoldering coals. One of the remaining kitchen workers came to the door, yawning and stretching. It was almost midnight, which meant for about four hours nobody would be in the kitchen either. Then the work would start up again for another day.

All of a sudden, the guard beside Math took one step forward and said, concern in his voice, "Do you smell something?"

The air always smelled of smoke, but Math sniffed with him. "That isn't a wood fire, it's—"

"Oil!" The guard's exclamation had Math hustling towards the center of the bailey, still not sure exactly where the smell was coming from and trying to follow it with his nose. Whatever its source, it had a sharper bite than woodsmoke.

Then, off to his right, the thatch roof of one of the smaller buildings, sandwiched between the stables and the laundry, burst into flames. Hardly three breaths later, the nearby wall of the stables caught fire too and then, before Math could take another step, flames came through the roof.

"Fire! Fire!" The guard took off at a run, not towards the buildings that had just gone up, but towards the main gatehouse where he knew other guards like him would be awake.

Math made a similar assessment of how quickly the fire was spreading and turned to run up the steps of the motte. Fulke met him two paces from the door.

"Stay here. Nobody gets past you. I'll wake the king." Then Math was through the entrance and up the spiraling stairs of the keep to the king's room.

By the time he reached the top, Thomas was alert with his sword bare in his hand. "What is it?"

"You won't need that, at least not yet," Math said as he went by him. "The castle is on fire."

"I heard the shouts." King Edward opened his door before Math could knock. "Do I have time to put on my boots?"

"Yes."

The king held the door wide, implying Math should enter his personal chamber. And, for the first time ever, Math did. Even when the king's valet came hurrying in a moment later, Math didn't leave, helping the other man shovel the king into his mail armor and even buckling on his sword while his servant adjusted his cloak exactly right.

"Come. Let's see what this is about." King Edward led the way to the door and then down the stairs to the entrance to the keep.

Fulke was still there, standing guard. He hadn't even allowed Owen de la Pole, who'd arrived all a-fluster, to enter. Fulke knew, as the whole of the king's guard knew, that the fire could be a distraction for an attempt on the king's life. The concern wasn't necessarily about Owen, but they had a plan for incidents like this, and any deviation from it could be the difference between success and failure—a live king or a dead one.

From their vantage point at the top of the motte, they could see above the castle wall to where a hundred people or more were streaming towards the castle. The main gate was open, and some had already taken their places in a line from the closest water source, a winding brook that was almost small enough to leap across, passing buckets hand-to-hand. Others rescued horses from the stables, having covered the horses' eyes so they wouldn't bolt.

"You are too exposed here, my lord," Math said in an undertone, having kept close to the king's side. "If the fire was set in order to lure you out of the keep, we've played into the assassin's hands."

"And if we don't leave the keep, I could burn along with the rest of the castle," King Edward said. "Owen, I commend the speed at which your people have set to work, but those buildings are a lost cause."

"I fear you are right, my lord, but we will try to save what we can," Owen said. "I will direct some of the folk to turn their attention to the hall and barracks. They aren't on fire yet."

"Shall we take our chances in the bailey ourselves, my lord?" Math asked.

"That would be my preference." The king set off without haste down the steps to the inner gate. Fulke's huge bulk partially blocked any view of the king from those below, and Thomas and Math buttressed him on either side. Owen took up the rear. Math had already decided that if Owen was going to stab the king in the back, literally instead of figuratively, he would have done it by now.

By the time they reached the bailey, Simon had arrived, along with four more of the king's personal guard, all of whom should have been sleeping. They spread out around the king, forming a protective circle.

"We can go through the postern gate." Owen motioned towards a small door on the northern side of the bailey.

"Where does it lead?" Simon asked.

"To a path above the Dee. We can take it towards the eastern fields."

He was referring to where the festival was being held. To the west, behind the motte, was a steep drop to the River Dee.

The king raised his eyebrows, looking to Simon for confirmation, but it was Math who shook his head. "Bad enough we were seen leaving the keep so obviously. If I were waiting for you, hoping to do you harm, I'd be waiting outside the postern gate."

"Math is right, my lord." Simon instantly agreed.

King Edward put a hand on Owen's shoulder. "I appreciate your concern for me, but I won't be whisked out of sight, even to keep me safe."

"Yes, my lord." Owen bent his head, the very epitome of a loyal subject, which by now Math had decided he truly was.

They set off again towards the main gate. Math and Owen somehow had taken the lead, with Fulke guarding the king's back and Simon among those pressed in close to him. The stables were fully engulfed in flames now, as were other buildings along the southern side of the bailey. That included the blacksmith's workshop, which was always a hazard because of the open fire. The guesthouse was on the other side of the stables, and people were streaming out of it now. Others had already started tossing water on the thatch roof, but their buckets were drops compared to the ocean of water they needed to save what remained.

Because of the number of people attempting to enter through the castle gate, Simon had the king step to one side until the way was clear. As they waited, Owen spied Adam, Moriddig's brother, among the lines of people and waved him closer. "Find someone to take your place."

Adam had been helping to direct where to throw the water, while at the same time hefting a few of the buckets himself, one after another. "But, my lord, they need me—"

"Anyone can do what you're doing. I need you in the hall. I have documents to protect, if the fire jumps that far. I want you in charge of saving as many as we can."

"Yes, my lord!" Adam set off at a run as he'd been directed. A moment later, Patrick, Moriddig's son, looking much less drunk than before the fire started, also separated himself from the crowd and went with him.

"At least I still have Adam. Though—" under his breath Owen scoffed to himself, "—there's irony for you. Because of the events of the last few days, he and Patrick moved from their rooms in the castle to festival grounds. *Their* possessions are safe. And yet, here they are, as loyal as ever. Even Patrick can prove his worth, since Moriddig trained him in reading and writing too."

Math listened to this outpouring of regret without comment. Owen had been speaking musingly, and not really to him—or to anyone, for that matter.

The king must have heard something of what he said too, however, because when Owen made to continue amongst his guard, he stopped him. "See to your people. I am well protected."

Owen bowed deeply. "Thank you, my lord. My deepest apologies."

"Unless you set the fire, I can't see how this is your fault." As usual, the king's manner combined a demand for subservience with impatience at its forms. Owen had done nothing wrong, as he'd said.

He didn't need to apologize. The royal temper was well known, but the king wielded it like a weapon, unsheathing it only when needed.

Owen himself went to the line where Adam and Patrick had been working, becoming instantly wet as he accepted his first bucket. On the surface, it didn't make sense to send Adam to do an important job, one that Owen could do himself, while Owen helped put out the fire. But Math saw it for the piece of diplomacy it was. Owen was showing his people that he was willing to work side-by-side with them to save his castle. Math didn't think he was imagining that each person around Owen began to work a little more quickly and diligently.

Then the gate was clear enough to move the king through it. He too received bows and accolades. "God bless you!" One man said in English.

Others nearby took up the chorus.

Edward put up a hand in acknowledgment and replied, also in English, recognizing the need, "Many thanks! Thank you for your service here."

Rhys met them on the road just outside the gate, with Miles and Hywel on either side, and the three of them seamlessly joined the king's party, moving away from the castle in earnest. When Rhys took Owen's place at the front of the company beside Math, he soon voiced Math's ongoing assumption: "Is it our thought that the fire was deliberately set?" He spoke in French, which meant he intended those with them to understand.

"Yes," Math said.

Not a single man broke stride to hear this assessment. The king's guard would always assume that any danger developing in the king's vicinity was a genuine threat to his person. But there was a difference between assuming it because it was their job and knowing it for certain.

Most of the people in the road were still heading the other way, towards the castle. To avoid them, Math and Rhys led their party down a side street that ran parallel to the high street between the church and the castle, with the festival grounds their intended goal. The king could spend what was left of the night in his pavilion.

"Tell me why you think so," King Edward said.

"I saw the first flames, my lord," Math said. "They began in the dead house, the little building where Hugh's body is lying. There was nothing in there to start a fire, not even a lantern."

"Could be I missed something," Rhys said to Math in an undertone.

"Or maybe that's just what the killer wants us to think."

44

Day Five
Catrin

Catrin had been deeply asleep when the call to put out the fire at the castle had come. Having let Rhys, Miles, and Hywel deal with the situation at the inn, which she could see was no place for her in the late evening, she had retired to their tent. At Rhys's request, some of the other guards had moved their tents closer to hers, so she'd felt safe enough without him. Still, she'd lain down in her clothes while she waited for her husband to return, and then fallen asleep without meaning to.

By the time she reached the castle, the word among the onlookers was that the king was safe with his men, although where exactly he'd gone, nobody was sure. Catrin assumed Rhys, though not on duty, would be with him, and was thus safe too.

A woman passed her, hurrying with an empty bucket to join the line of people hauling water. "Of all nights for it not to rain!"

Up ahead, Catrin spotted Owen, his face streaked with ash and his blond hair almost black with soot. Little remained of the buildings on one side of the castle, but nobody was letting up on their efforts. If nothing else, they had a chance to save the great hall and the keep.

Catrin looked around at the other helpers. Unlike murderers, whose goal was generally to put as much distance as possible between themselves and their victims, arsonists were known to watch the aftermath of their work.

The only reason she knew anything about these matters was because there had been a young man in her first husband's following who had been caught setting fires throughout the county. His obsession had begun small, his parents later explained. As a child, he'd loved to watch any fire burn. They'd caught him setting little fires on their property, and he'd once almost burned down their outhouse. They hadn't told anyone of his proclivities until it was too late: he burned down their neighbor's barn with animals left inside. By the time the neighbor woke, the barn was too consumed to save them.

The young man had watched from the shadows, after which he had pretended to arrive to put out the flames. But his parents had known he hadn't been home when it started, and they confessed their suspicions to Catrin's husband. In the end, Robert had forced a confession from the young man and hanged him. Some men, he'd explained, could not be allowed to live.

Tonight, however, there were so many people volunteering to help that it was impossible to distinguish one person's interest from another's. *Everybody* was watching the fire; everyone's eyes followed the sparks as they swirled around the bailey. With no stars or moon tonight, the flames reaching towards the sky were the only light.

Gruffydd had been working shoulder-to-shoulder with Cadwgan, and Catrin took a place next to them. "Are you sure either of you should be here?"

"Where else would we be?" Gruffydd seemed genuinely surprised at the question.

"The cold water can't be good for your hands." Catrin's already hurt, and she'd just joined them.

"You're right about that." Gruffydd clenched one hand into a fist. "But who would we be if we didn't help?"

"We do what we must." Cadwgan swung another bucket towards Catrin, which she took and passed to her neighbor on the other side.

They had been speaking in Welsh, and a few of the people nearby in the line were nodding.

"If I were not a loyal citizen, I might be glad to see such catastrophes come upon Owen." Gruffydd now spoke much more in an undertone. "What worries me, though, is that the culprit is one of our number."

"A bard, you mean?" Catrin asked.

"Welsh."

Gruffydd was right to be concerned. It was one thing to murder two Welshmen, even if both belonged to Owen. It was another to attack Owen directly, as burning this castle had done.

"Even more, whoever burned the castle, if, in fact, the fire was deliberately set, has indirectly attacked the king," Cadwgan said.

"King Edward will be caring far more about this investigation now than he did when he went to bed."

Gruffydd expression was particularly grim. "Get to the bottom of this, Catrin. You and Rhys. None of us will be able to breathe freely until you do."

Catrin might have replied that they were never again going to be able to breathe freely, no matter how the investigation was resolved. Even in Welsh, it was not something she could say in the bailey of Owen's castle, in ruins or not.

Gruffydd and Cadwgan returned to their work, and Catrin might have as well, if only to better eavesdrop on what everyone was saying about the fire, if Hugh's daughter, Jane, hadn't come shooting out of a lane to the west like an arrow from a quiver. Arriving in front of Catrin, she wrapped her arms around Catrin's waist. "We could have been in there! We could have been killed!"

Catrin put one arm around Jane's shoulders and with the other she reached for Jane's mother, Mary, who had followed at a more sedate pace. "Where have you been?"

Jane's face was pressed into Catrin's shoulder, so that left Mary to be the one to answer, as had been usual up until now. "Neither of us could bear to stay in our quarters, so we spent the night in our wagon in the festival grounds."

"You have a wagon too?"

"Of course." Mary looked puzzled that this could be news to Catrin. "We travel the country, same as the bards. It would hardly do for Moriddig to have his own wagon and not us." She gave Catrin a gentle smile. "I sometimes feel sorry for men of higher rank. Sleeping in a wagon is somehow beneath them. It is a home away from home for me and Jane." She sighed. "As it had been for Hugh."

Catrin turned to look at the burning guesthouse. As she watched, the roof, which they had hoped might be saved, collapsed.

"So much destruction." Mary blinked back tears. "We lost everything that was important when Hugh was killed. And now this. I find myself suddenly grateful for what I still have."

45

Day Five
Rhys

Rhys couldn't help but feel a profound sense of failure. If he had caught the murderer, the castle might still be standing. Another day of wandering the festival without a culprit for these crimes might result in Rhys being out of his position as quaestor.

Maybe that would be a good thing. Certainly it would make his life more predictable. But, if he was being honest with himself, he wouldn't want to serve the king without this additional burden. When he feared he'd lost the king's favor at Vale Royal Abbey, he had considered leaving his service. Part of him wanted to run away every single day.

And yet, he couldn't pretend that the world wasn't as it was. In so many places in Wales, his people were exposed and unprotected. Before his death, Llywelyn had written to the Archbishop of Canterbury about the way the king's officers had reduced his people to servitude. Rhys couldn't be everywhere at once, but wherever he was, he could stand between his people and the king. In that way, he was serving Llywelyn once again, carrying on his legacy the best way he knew how.

To do so, he needed to be a trusted member of the king's court, which meant he needed to solve these crimes, the sooner the better.

While he'd been speaking to Roger at the inn, he'd been thinking that he needed something dramatic to happen. He'd wanted to take this investigation by the shoulders and shake it to see what fell out of its pockets. The fire had fulfilled his wish for change, in a most dramatic fashion.

"Tell me again what you saw," Rhys said to Math as they approached the laying-out room. Up until a half-hour ago, Math had been with the king because he had suddenly become a favorite. Rhys would find out later how Math was taking that elevation in station.

Once the fire was out, Rhys had found Catrin sitting on a log, filthy and wet. For once, Rhys had used his husbandly authority, which he employed as rarely as possible, to send her for a bath and to bed.

After hours of fighting the fire, they'd been saved by a rainstorm that blew in as dawn approached. Everything was blackened with ash and wet with rain, including Rhys and Math. In the end they'd saved most of the buildings on the other side of the bailey from the laying out room, including the hall, the kitchen, and the barracks.

"I was standing near the inner gatehouse when one of its guards and I smelled the smoke and then saw flames coming from here."

Rhys hesitated at the entrance to the building, feeling a bit of heat still coming off some of the larger timbers. The roof had been built with sturdy beams that were blackened and charred but had not collapsed. The thatch was totally gone, as were most of the wooden planks that had made up the walls. Then he ducked under the still-intact lintel, absent an actual door, and came to a halt by the remains of Hugh's body.

Hugh was to have been buried at noon today, during a break in the festival proceedings, so the maximum number of people could attend. Now, Rhys honestly didn't know what was going to happen.

The body had been lying on a spindly table, which had effectively vanished. Even Hugh's remains were barely that, burned beyond recognition. Crouching to the floor, for a long moment Rhys couldn't find anything to say. He didn't know that he had ever seen anything this horrible. The fire had burned off Hugh's skin and fatty tissues, exposing the muscles and bones beneath, and the body had deformed until it looked as if Hugh was holding his hands in front of him, ready to defend himself. It was the stuff of nightmares.

Finally, he managed, "He's unrecognizable. He could be anyone."

"Don't we have enough intrigue without you inventing more?" Math said from the doorway.

Rhys was grateful for Math's retreat to the sardonic. "That's a very Simon thing to say."

Math even managed something of a guffaw. "I can think like a Norman when I want to. In this case, all I have to do is think like me. Are you really worried the body isn't Hugh's?"

Rhys's hands were so filthy he didn't hesitate to sift through the ashes around the corpse. He didn't know what he was looking for but also wasn't surprised when he came up with the blade of a knife, still in its charred leather sheath, and a ring, since Mary had wanted Hugh buried with both.

He turned slightly to show them to Math. "Not anymore. But I have to wonder what else might have been on or about the body the killer didn't want us to see."

"Something like the mark on Moriddig's neck?"

Rhys pushed to his feet, now looking directly down at the remains. "Maybe I missed something in my examination. Maybe the fact that I had to pick coins out of the wound distracted me from seeing more clearly."

"If the killer had wanted the coins, he shouldn't have poured them over the body." Math was back to his dark humor. "I could be wrong, too, about the fire being set deliberately."

"It was set deliberately." Simon had arrived, and Math made room for him in the doorway.

Glancing over, Rhys noted neither had entered. "It is unlike you to be squeamish."

"I'm not squeamish," Simon protested. "I just bathed."

"And I am untrustworthy at this point, same as you, Rhys," Math said. When both men turned to look at him, he added more to Simon than to Rhys, "Rhys has been awake longer than I, and I am seeing double. If I took part, I'd likely tread on valuable evidence without knowing it."

Rhys *was* exhausted and had been struggling to push through it. He was also covered in wet soot from head to toe. He hadn't ever looked worse except after battle.

"Do you see anything that will help us find who did this?" Now Owen de la Pole appeared too, though he kept even further back, despite being more soot-covered than Rhys. He'd come with another man whom he introduced after Simon and Math backed out of the doorway. "This is my woodsman, Emyr."

By the name, the man was Welsh, and when he spoke, it was in French with a thick Welsh accent. "I was just delivering a last supply of wood to the kitchen, so they'd have enough to start the morning, when I heard the shout in the bailey. Like everyone else, I ran towards the fire, which had just burst through the roof here." His eyes went to Hugh's corpse. "He was wrapped in linen, wasn't he, in preparation for burial?"

Rhys returned his gaze to the body. "As far as I know. He should have been. Why?"

"If the arsonist soaked the linen in oil and set it alight, it could explain the rest of what I see."

"That was what we smelled first." Math perked up. "An oil fire."

"We haven't found an oil lamp," Rhys said.

"Doesn't mean there wasn't one. Whoever did this could have brought it away with him. Oil would explain the speed at which it spread, even without much fuel in here. Then it jumped to the stables. Let me show you." Emyr made a motion to indicate they should follow him to the narrow alley between the laying-out room and the stables.

The two buildings were a matter of two feet apart, and there was another gap between the back of the buildings and the very damaged palisade that protected the bailey of the castle. The reason for the gap had been to deter a fire from spreading. It hadn't worked.

"See how blackened both walls are, particularly right in the center? They match one another." Emyr stood in the alley and flapped a hand back and forth. "It's a miracle any of the timbers are still standing. We'll have to take them down anyway, but what it tells us is that the fire burned hottest first in the dead room, and then spread to here."

Rhys looked from one wall to the other, both of which were charred and being held up more by habit than actual construction materials. Then he walked past Emyr towards the palisade. The wall was in a similar condition right at the back of the laying-out room, but the farther he moved away from the core of the fire, the less damaged were the walls. Many of the buildings in the bailey had burned, but that was more because the fire had passed from thatch roof to thatch roof, than because the flames had burst through the walls of the buildings.

It was Owen de la Pole who finally stated the obvious. "Someone set fire to my castle. Math was right the first time." Owen pressed his lips together pensively. "Moriddig, Hugh, the castle. Were they killed to get at me? Because of me? Am I next?" His expression filled with horror. "Or Joan?"

"We don't know, my lord. We are doing our best." Simon spoke sincerely, but it was exactly the wrong thing to say.

Owen gave them all a hard look. In this moment, he was Norman through and through. "Do better."

46

Day Five

Catrin

Catrin opened her eyes and almost leapt to her feet in her surprise at seeing Owen de la Pole's wife lying on a pallet next to her.

Then she remembered how Joan had come to be there and subsided.

In the early hours of the morning, having been lovingly shooed away by Rhys, Catrin had gone to the queen's manor in search of a bath. She'd discarded the idea of plunging into any stream or even the River Dee on her own. With the morning rains, the channel was full from bank to bank, and she wasn't that good a swimmer.

On the way, she'd encountered Joan and Owen, arms wrapped around each other, with Joan sobbing into her husband's chest. Catrin had wanted to pass by without comment, but it had been impossible to do so without forcing them to acknowledge that she'd seen them at their weakest.

Or maybe at their strongest, come to think on it.

Either way, Owen took the opportunity to hand Joan off to Catrin, at which point, she had no choice but to take the other woman to the queen's manor.

Catrin had also not forgotten they had questions for Joan about her argument with Adam in the cemetery. However, the early hours of the morning when they were both stretched to the limit was a bad moment to ask them. They'd bathed instead, and Catrin had settled Joan on a pallet next to her own in one of the manor's tiny rooms off the hall. Most nights, it was full of the queen's ladies, but by now all of them had risen. Many had been already going about their day by the time Catrin had lain down.

Settling herself back on her pillow, she met Joan's eyes. "Did you sleep?"

"I must have slept some. I thought I wouldn't."

"You were tired."

"Exhausted, really." She rubbed her pregnant belly. "At least he's happy."

Since Joan was being so accommodating, Catrin didn't waste her moment. "What do you think is going on?"

With a harrumph, Joan suddenly rolled onto her back and flung her arm over her eyes. "I have no idea. I can't begin to think, except it's all I can think about. What did Morrydig, Hugh, and our castle have in common other than the fact that each belonged to Owen?"

"It does seem straightforward when you think about it that way. But maybe we need to stop looking at the situation from a bird's eye view."

Joan turned her head to look at Catrin. "What do you mean by that?"

Catrin pushed herself to a sitting position on her pallet. "We have three distinct events. Maybe we shouldn't look at them as one but take them one at a time."

Joan started ticking items off her fingers before Catrin herself could. "Someone strangled Morrydig; someone stabbed Hugh; someone set fire to the castle. I know we aren't certain of that last point, but let's just say."

"We have inquired at length about Moriddig's movements during the last morning of his life," Catrin said. "He rose, he breakfasted, he practiced, all blameless activities."

"Blameless?" All of a sudden Joan was pushing up from her pallet too. "That was the last thing Morrydig was."

Catrin gaped at her sudden agitation. "What do you mean?"

"He was leaving us, after all these years! Can you believe it?"

Catrin motioned with her hand, trying to calm Joan, who'd spoken quite loudly. They were alone in the room, but the doors and walls were wooden. Anyone stopping outside could overhear. "Owen told us that *he* had relieved *Moriddig* of his duties." They knew the true story already from Adam and Miles, but Joan did not know that they knew.

She gave a low *tsk.* "My husband is at times prideful."

"And then we understand he refused to pay Adam the remainder of Moriddig's salary. You were overheard arguing with Adam about that in the churchyard at Moriddig's funeral."

"We didn't owe him anything." Joan's reply came quickly, almost as if rehearsed.

Catrin raised her eyebrows, unafraid in this moment to convey her doubt.

Joan obliged with a further explanation: "Morrydig did tender his resignation, but he said he would continue to serve us until after the festival. Owen was furious and told him we were finished with him that instant."

Catrin could picture the scene and made a guess. "At which point you intervened and suggested they both keep the secret until after the festival, for propriety's sake."

"That's exactly what I did. Even so, Morrydig removed himself to his wagon. It put him closer to the festival grounds, so he felt sure nobody would notice or comment. Owen didn't object. With Morrydig leaving, he didn't even want to look at him anymore. He also didn't want anyone inside the castle who wasn't loyal to us. Owen was true to his word and didn't tell anyone else. I don't know about Morrydig. To be honest, we were hoping he'd change his mind."

"Do you know if Moriddig had arranged for another position already?" Catrin held her breath to hear the answer.

Joan shook her head. "He didn't say."

"Did he say why he was leaving?"

"He kept repeating *it's time* and wouldn't explain more. That's why I went to see him myself, because I thought maybe I could change his mind if I got him alone."

"When was this?"

"The next morning."

"The morning he died?"

Joan shrugged, which Catrin took to be assent.

If the conversation hadn't already been so surprising, she would have been gaping some more. "What hour was this exactly?"

Joan shrugged again. "Mid-morning, perhaps. He was in his wagon, and I cornered him there." She didn't sound the least bit apologetic about it either.

"Did you end up changing his mind?" It was dawning on Catrin that she'd found the woman with whom Moriddig had argued in his wagon, the one she'd learned about that first day after she'd found his secret stash of forbidden music. They'd asked about the incident, but nobody else had come forward or remembered hearing the argument—or had volunteered that she was the one with whom Moriddig had argued.

"No, I did not."

"My apologies, but I'm afraid I don't understand. Why was it so important that he continued to serve you?"

"Because of how it looked! Owen is disadvantaged because of his birth, compared to some of the other lords. To have such a public defection, right in the middle of the king's festival, would have called into question everything we've been working so hard to build. It would be especially bad if Morrydig went to one of our rivals in the March, having defeated all the other bards at the festival."

Catrin had served in the queen's retinue long enough to understand how important status was amongst the various barons competing for the king's favor. They would use any advantage to place themselves above another. Owen's mother was a Le Strange, and his father's mother a Corbet, both well placed Norman families. His father had been Welsh, however, as had been his grandfather. Now that Wales no longer existed as a political entity, Owen was striving as hard or harder as any Norman to raise himself above (as Joan had said) his disadvantaged (meaning Welsh) birth.

At this point, Catrin didn't want to come across as censorious, but she couldn't restrain herself from saying, "You do realize it would have been of benefit to our investigation to have known about this earlier."

"Why? He was hale when I left him. Morrydig's death had nothing to do with *us*."

"You may have been the last person to see him alive."

Joan was already shaking her head before Catrin finished her sentence. "That would be Adam. He entered the wagon after me."

Catrin had given up on gaping. "You saw him?"

"Of course."

"Are you sure it was him?"

"He was wearing his hood. It's a color blue I particularly admire. I have no doubt it was Adam."

"*When* exactly was this, in relation to the start of the rehearsal?"

Joan frowned in thought. "Within a half-hour, I would say. I was still walking back to the castle when the bell tolled to call the bards to the viewing stand."

"Did Adam see *you*?"

Joan's chin came up. "Well, he wouldn't have, would he? He was in the distance when I came down the steps, with his head down, striding along with purpose. I went the other way so he wouldn't see me." She made a face. "My husband didn't know I was going to see Morrydig, and I was ashamed to have done so, since he'd refused to change his mind. It looked too much like begging. My route took me around the rear of the wagon, but I came out on the path again in time to see the back of Adam entering it." Her brows drew together. "Why don't you just ask him. I'm sure he'll tell you the same."

47

Day Five

Math

It was late afternoon by the time Catrin found Rhys and Math to tell them what she'd learned. To be fair to Joan, she had no knowledge of the chain of evidence so far accumulated that made her observation of Adam directly contradict his description of how his morning had gone.

"Adam lied to us deliberately." By now, the burning sensation behind Math's eyes was reaching a critical point. That was probably why his words were so blunt.

"Repeatedly, from what you've said." Miles spoke out of the corner of his mouth, his eyes on the high table where Owen was sitting beside the king. Given his destroyed castle, Math couldn't begrudge him the honor.

Adam was standing behind Owen, wearing his blue hood, as he always did, even when in line with the water buckets. Since then, he'd been in attendance on his lord in such a fashion that made it impossible to walk up to him and, essentially, accuse him of murder.

"The more I look at him, the more I can see how everything that has happened was his doing," Catrin said.

"All for personal gain?" Rhys said. "It seems so misguided."

"And petty," Math said. "He must have murdered Moriddig to stop the move to Brecon, and then murdered Hugh in order to step into *his* shoes, which Owen obligingly offered him immediately upon Hugh's death. Adam effectively eliminated everyone between him and Owen, and then made himself indispensable to ensure his elevation."

"Somehow, we've all missed the degree to which Adam is deeply and fundamentally angry." Catrin's chin was in her hand. "He hides it well. He's always smiling! I see it now only because I know he murdered his brother. All along that hatred has been simmering beneath the surface."

Math found himself suddenly depressed. Brothers were supposed to love each other, not turn themselves into Cain and Abel. Rather than dwelling on the whereabouts of his own brother, which he still didn't know, he squashed the emotion by rising to his feet. "I see Patrick. Let's ask him where his uncle was last night, just for a last confirmation."

Patrick was looking a bit worse for wear again, though better than his friend, who was staggering drunk and needed an arm around his waist to keep him upright. The friend was waving a cup about, calling for another portion of ale. Math came up on his other side and said, "You've had enough."

"Not nearly enough." This was Dewi, one of the younger bards from Rhuddlan, and his words were slurred. "Never enough."

"If you keep on this way," Patrick said, "you'll ruin your chances in the festival."

"I never had a chance anyway. I'm not good enough."

"Your singing is beautiful," Patrick insisted. "You should not give up."

With Patrick on the other side, Math helped wheel Dewi around and, best they could, head for the troughs of hay that had been placed outside the pavilion for when revelers had imbibed too much.

"Didn't you hear?" Dewi moaned. "The winners are already decided."

Math looked at Patrick, eyebrows raised. "Do we know that for sure?"

"There's talk—" Patrick started to say, but then his friend lurched forward and vomited into the nearest hay trough.

Fortunately, Math saw it coming just in time and stepped back. Patrick came with him, and they both gazed somewhat impassively at Dewi's continuing heaves.

"Why does Dewi think he hasn't a chance?" It might be they weren't quite as done with the investigation as they'd thought.

"Rumors only. He isn't the only one who is worried about it."

"Are you? Worried, that is?"

"No."

"Hugh was known to take bribes in the past."

"Not at this festival; not anymore. I told Sir Rhys that days ago."

"Who does rumor say is going to win?" Math said.

"Not Gruffydd; not Cadwgan. Some bard from the south, I think. Different people are saying different things."

Math's next question was a *non sequitur*, but he hoped Patrick was either too drunk or too distracted to notice. "When we talked the day your father died, you told us your uncle breakfasted with you and then went to the latrine. How long before the rehearsal was that?"

Patrick shrugged. "I don't know exactly. Less than an hour, but still quite some time."

"When did you see him next?"

"At the rehearsal." The answer came easily and matched Joan's assessment of when Adam had arrived at Moriddig's wagon. Unless someone had then gone to the wagon immediately after Adam, there seemed little doubt at this point that it was he who'd killed him.

The vomiting was ongoing, along with mumbled regrets. Patrick called out, "You all right there, Dewi?"

"No." The word came out a moan.

Patrick wrinkled his nose, which seemed the right time for Math to ask a follow-up question: "Weren't you and he this drunk just last night? I thought I saw you leaving the bailey right before the fire started."

"Was that where I was?" Patrick turned to him with widened eyes. "Dewi and I had made it to the latrine in the festival grounds when we heard the call that there was a fire. I honestly wasn't sure where we'd been drinking before that, though it was clear that we had."

"You recovered quickly since you were there when your uncle called for you to come with him."

Patrick shot him a rueful smile. "I'd emptied myself out, much as poor Dewi is doing now. And there's something to be said for having a bucket of cold water thrown over you."

Math finally said what he'd been thinking. "Drink won't bring your father back. Like you said to your friend, it won't help you in the festival either."

"I do know that." Patrick looked at the ground as he answered, digging at the dirt and grass with the toe of his boot. "You won't find me so drunk again. I have a legacy to live up to." Suddenly his head came up. "Lord Owen has even offered me a position!"

"As his bard?"

Patrick made a motion with his head. "Not that; not yet; maybe not ever. But I'll be assistant steward to my uncle. It's a real living!"

"Congratulations." Math looked at him curiously. "You sound happy about it."

"Maybe I am. Maybe I've finally realized that being a bard was always my father's dream for me, not mine."

48

Day Five

Rhys

Catrin was sitting opposite Rhys, so he saw the moment her gaze flicked from him to someone behind him and then back to him again. The second glance encompassed a look of warning. They hadn't been married long, but he'd known her since they were children. Someone was coming she thought meaningful.

With as casual a manner as he could muster, Rhys turned in his seat, located at the end of a long bench, to see a young man he didn't recognize almost upon him. He looked no older than fourteen but could have been the same age as Math. Even though his initial approach had appeared purposeful, he didn't stop to talk. Instead, he brushed past Rhys and used the brief encounter to drop a note into his lap.

Rhys was the king's spymaster as well as his guard and quaestor, so he was not wholly shocked at being on the receiving end of a surreptitious contact. What was different during this festival was to be surrounded by so many literate people. Bards were the educators of the Welsh and the repository of their history. Reading and writing were part of their job.

With his hands under the table, Rhys unfolded the paper and read the few words written there. "Meet me outside."

That was an easy enough request, one with which he had no trouble complying. Math was already outside somewhere with Patrick. Fortunately, this young man had chosen to leave the pavilion in the opposite direction. Rhys rose languidly to his feet, not really feigning fatigue, and followed the young man as if he were heading to the latrine instead of a secret meeting. Once outside, he walked slowly from the entrance, giving the man plenty of time to see him and to come to him.

When he reached the gate that allowed access to the next field, the young man stepped into the path behind him. "You came. I didn't know if you would."

"Of course I came." He turned completely around. "Who are you?"

"Bedwyr ap Geraint." The young man's parents must have rivaled King Edward in their enthusiasm for King Arthur. "I'm one of the judges. I know I look young but this is the third music festival I've judged. My father was a bard from Ceredigion, and I was raised to be a bard. I had an accident when I was sixteen, a fall from a horse. I almost broke my neck, and I haven't been able to sing since." He poured out this stream of information as if he'd rehearsed it, which likely he had.

Rhys didn't object. So often he had to ask question after question of an informant just to elicit the basic level of information that Bedwyr had offered unprompted. "It sounds like you are lucky to be alive. Why are we here? Why not talk to me in the pavilion?"

"I'd prefer none of my fellow judges know we have spoken. They're flustered enough as it is."

"Flustered?"

"These deaths." Bedwyr waved a hand, dismissing any further questions along those lines. "I am often in the latrine for long periods of time, but my friends will miss me eventually. It's the latrine excursions that I've come to speak to you about." He took in a breath and hurried on. "I was in the latrine with Adam, Moriddig's brother, the morning Moriddig was murdered. He tried to give me money so I would judge Patrick favorably."

Rhys couldn't be happier to be hearing such a secret, but it was a convergence of information in the wrong direction. "Did you take the money?"

"Of course not! I would never! I told Adam that Patrick was going to have to win or lose on his own merits. Then he laughed and said I'd passed his test. I was offended, of course, and asked what test he could be talking about. He said that the steward of the festival, Hugh, who is now dead, had asked him to try to bribe as many judges as he could. I thought that was ironic since Hugh had been notorious for accepting bribes, but Adam assured me those days were over." All of this came out in a similar torrent as before.

"Did you believe him?"

"He seemed sincere." Bedwyr's shrug was visible, even in the darkened field. "You know how Adam is, always cheerful, no matter what task is set to him. He implied that he had enjoyed the challenge. We sat talking for quite a while afterwards, right up until the warning bell for the start of the rehearsal, as a matter of fact. We were both expected to attend, so we had to hurry to finish our business after that."

A layer of ice settled on Rhys's shoulders that had nothing to do with the night mist forming over the field. "Was Adam wearing his blue hood when you talked to him?"

"In the latrine? No. It is a beautiful color, though, isn't it? You can pick him out in a crowd whenever he wears it. It's quite distinctive."

"Yes," Rhys said. "It truly is."

49

Day Six

Rhys

First thing the next morning, Rhys and Catrin approached Adam where he sat in front of what had been Moriddig's wagon, going through a box on his lap. As with every time they'd come to talk to him, he looked at them with a genuine smile of greeting. "You look exhausted! Didn't you sleep last night either?"

"We did try," Catrin said.

After Rhys's conversation with Bedwyr and Math's with Patrick, they had begun again working their way through the festival participants with intent. The pavilion had been packed with bards, judges, merchants, family members, and hangers-on of every stripe. Most were talking about the same three incidents that concerned Rhys, so it wasn't difficult to steer any conversation in that direction. He had enlisted every one of his compatriots too—Catrin, Simon, Miles, Hywel, Math, Jehan, and Ralph—for the endeavor.

When Adam made a motion with his head implying he'd had the same problem with the night too, Rhys added, "I'd like to ask you one more time about your movements the morning Moriddig was killed."

"Again with that? I told you." Adam rubbed his forehead. "I saw my brother at breakfast and then never again."

"Because you were in the latrine."

"Yes."

"We have since learned that you stayed there a long time," Rhys said, "and that you weren't alone."

For the first time in all their conversations, Adam looked wary. "That is true." His eyes flicked to Catrin for a moment.

She waved a hand. "I am not offended by the topic, Adam, and we need a few points of clarification. You spoke to Judge Bedwyr in the latrine. He has told us everything."

Adam's face paled. "What does that mean?"

"He said you tried to bribe him," Catrin said, "and when he wouldn't take the bribe, you told him Hugh had sent you to test him."

"And since Hugh isn't here to confirm my story, you think I lied to Bedwyr and really wanted to bribe him?" Adam's hand went to his throat. "Nothing could be further from the truth!"

"We are not accusing you of anything," Rhys said.

Adam let out a breath, like he believed him. "I really was doing it for Hugh and for everyone else at the festival. And for Moriddig too, with whom we discussed the idea before his death. He was wary of using Patrick as bait, but in the end we decided we had to use him to make the query credible."

"You and Hugh discussed this bribery test with Moriddig?" Catrin said.

"Of course. We wouldn't do something like that on our own; Hugh and Moriddig were nearly as close to each other as I was to my brother."

The ease with which he was speaking further confirmed to Rhys that they were on the right track. "We have since learned that you cut quite a swath through the judges. What would you have done if any of them had said *yes*?"

"I would have promised to pay him, and then told Hugh, who would have told you. As the king's quaestor, you could have arrested him."

Catrin looked at her husband. "It seems you also have cut quite a swath through the festival."

Rhys kept his eyes on Adam. "Back in the latrine with Bedwyr, where was your blue hood?"

Adam let out a laugh. "You too? I have had so many comments about that hood. It was a gift from Moriddig last year, in thanks for all I have done for him. But to answer your question, I left it on the breakfast table."

"You're wearing it now." Catrin gestured to Adam's head. "By the time I met you at Moriddig's wagon, you had it back."

"Patrick brought it to me at the rehearsal."

"So Bedwyr was right that you were in the latrine up until then? How long would you say that was?" Rhys asked.

"Nearly three-quarters of an hour, I expect." Adam's eyes went once more to Catrin, though this time there was amusement in them. "Poor Bedwyr. He was quite taken aback that I thought ill of him. I must apologize to him again."

"And thank him as well," Catrin said. "It is because he came to Rhys and confessed the incident that we are not arresting you for these murders. It has suddenly been made clear that you are not to blame."

"You really thought it was me?" Adam smiled as if they couldn't have been serious. "But if not me, who do you think did it?"

"You're not going to like the answer, I'm afraid." Rhys's expression turned grim. "We can only conclude now that it was your nephew, Patrick."

50

Day Six

Rhys

"A confession would be best." Prince Edmund leaned against the back of his chair, one of the few in the viewing stand because most of the spectators either stood or sat on benches to watch the contests. The king and queen had throne-like chairs, both of which were currently unoccupied. "I assume lack of any evidence other than hearsay is why you haven't put the boy in irons already."

Rhys could no longer be surprised that the king had insisted the festival continue, despite the deaths and the fire. King Edward had always been single-minded—hence his conquest of Wales—and was not interested in deviating from his set agenda. At the moment, however, there was still another hour before the events were to start. The festival was drawing to a close, with only one more day before the final contests, which would take place tomorrow afternoon. Once the chief bard was anointed, he would have the stage to himself to close the festival out.

Then everyone would start heading home. They were running out of time to make an arrest. Edmund knew it as well as Rhys.

"If we even had irons," Rhys said. "But yes, we need to be certain. All we know for sure is that Lady Joan can place a man wearing Adam's blue hood in Moriddig's wagon right before the start of the rehearsal."

"Have you spoken to Patrick about it?"

"We have not. We need to be sure before we confront him. As has become clear, he is an excellent liar."

"Does he wear a ring on his right hand?"

"He does not wear a ring at all."

Edmund grunted. "He could have taken it off."

"It has occurred to us that he could have been wearing his father's ring when he killed him."

"This is the ring that is missing?"

"Yes. Moriddig could even have given it to him that day, to make up for his disappointment at leaving the Poles' service."

"That's the working theory?"

"It's the best we can do without talking to him," Rhys said. "Adam is in shock and unable to give us any motive at all in his present state."

"Where was Patrick at the time of Hugh's murder?"

"Nobody admits to seeing him."

"And, unlike his uncle, he doesn't wear a distinctive hood."

"Just so." Rhys bent his head. "It's such a crush in the bards' pavilion, that even if he had been there, it isn't any wonder nobody remembers him specifically."

"And the fire at the castle?"

"Right before the fire, Math saw Patrick crossing the bailey with another youth, both staggering drunk. Patrick says he doesn't remember exactly where he was and what he was doing. When prompted, the guards at the gate remember seeing two people pass by, but every other coherent thought was swept away moments later by the fire. Patrick himself says he was in the latrine when the call came to come to the castle. I find it ironic that this was the same place Adam was when Moriddig died."

"And convenient."

"Adam himself was woken by his neighbors. At that time, Patrick was not in his tent." Rhys gave the prince a rueful look. "Patrick told his uncle that he couldn't bear to sleep in his father's bed. They met each other again in the castle."

"Again, convenient for Patrick." Edmund tipped his head. "It's a little daunting how easy it is for a man to walk about unnoticed. Could the pair of them, in fact, be working together?"

"As in, Patrick kills his father and Adam kills Hugh, so they both get what they want?"

"I was thinking more that Adam discovered his nephew had murdered Moriddig and Hugh so then set the fire as a distraction, in order to protect him."

Rhys gave a hard shake of his head. "We are guessing now, and that's all we can do until we confront Patrick."

A certain measure of amusement entered the prince's eyes. "So why come to me? Why aren't you having this conversation with Simon?"

"Because you have a facility, if you pardon me saying so, for deceit."

"I won't pardon you," Edmund barked a laugh, "but I won't argue with you either. If you are to arrest Patrick for these crimes, you need a confession firstly, and barring that, incontrovertible proof."

"So how do we get it?"

"You need to trap him, like you did Guy in Caernarfon." Prince Edmund tipped his head. "And I think I have a plan that might work."

51

Day Six
Catrin

Catrin had overheard at least three conversations that very morning speculating on who the murderer might be. None had mentioned Patrick. Although none mentioned Adam either, there was a strong desire to have it be *the Welsh* or some other outside group of marauders. There was no consensus on motive. In truth, it remained obscure, even to them.

Adam himself could give them no clues. In fact, he had been made more distraught by confirming his own innocence, and thus implicating Patrick, than by the fact that they had thought he'd done it. But if Patrick really had attempted to disguise himself as his own uncle in order to murder his father, that was more horrible still. Adam had told the truth and thus inadvertently pointed a finger at his nephew; Patrick's actions had been deliberate.

The next step was to prove it, and with Prince Edmund's blessing, they'd enlisted an unusual cast of characters, the first of which was Simon's niece Emma and her beloved, Stephen. The pair were betrothed despite their rocky beginnings, and it was that rough start that allowed them to be called upon to aid with the ending. They'd both seen Hugh's body. They knew what was at stake. The only hesitation had come on Stephen's part because he wanted to protect Emma.

Emma had given her beloved a pat on the arm. "This is nothing compared to what we saw in the barn, Stephen." And then she shot Catrin a rueful look. "I know I embarrassed myself by screaming. This is literally a stroll in a field compared to that."

Here, at the end of the day, few bards remained in the contest. Patrick, however, was among them. Despite his promise of a position in Owen's household as assistant steward, he remained focused on his last performances. In fact, he had squeaked into the top five contestants in vocal performance. Instead of celebrating with some of his fellows, he had retired to his wagon—apparently no longer squeamish about taking a rest in the same bed used by his dead father.

They knew he was in there because they'd been watching him for most of the day. They didn't want to unnerve him, but they also didn't want to be caught out were he to run before they were ready to spring their trap. While Rhys had told Catrin in no uncertain terms to stay out of harm's way, it was her job to keep an eye on the proceedings. She was among the few conspirators whom Patrick wouldn't find threatening if he saw her. Still, she was making sure to stay hidden, having found a spot from which she could watch behind a nearby tent.

Stopping a matter of five feet away from Patrick's wagon, Emma began in a loud voice, "I can't believe Adam killed his own brother. How could he have hated him that much?"

"Fratricide is as old as Cain and Abel. One never knows what is in another man's heart," Stephen said. "At least he's in chains now. They'll hang him before the start of tomorrow's events."

"But what if it wasn't him who murdered Hugh? When my father told my mother about Adam's arrest, she said he couldn't have done it since she saw him near one of the pavilions at the time of Hugh's murder! Even now, they are on their way to tell Lord Owen."

"Your mother is that sure she saw Adam?" Stephen asked.

"He was wearing his blue hood."

"Anyone can wear a blue hood," Stephen pointed out. "Still, it is worrisome. What if someone else is the real killer, and he's arranged things so Adam takes the blame?"

"That's what my mother said. Think of who else may have benefitted from Hugh's death."

"Maybe someone wanted to step into Hugh's place, taking bribes or what not." Stephen spoke even louder, as if the idea had just occurred to him.

Catrin blanched to hear it. They hadn't talked to the pair about the bribery scheme at all, even though it had been a parallel issue this whole time. On his own initiative, Stephen had started improvising.

Emma replied, again out of apparent inspiration, "I heard that Sir Reese is going to start a search tonight, wagon-to-wagon and tent-to-tent for Morrydig's missing ring and the knife that killed Hugh! We'll know soon if Adam really did it."

"I'm glad to hear that," Stephen said. "I've heard Sir Reese is the best at what he does. Adam might have murdered his brother, but I think there's more to the story."

At long last, he escorted Emma away.

Catrin stayed where she was. That had been the first step.

She heard nothing definitive from the wagon, however, and the quarter of an hour she waited before sending in Rhiannon, Gruffydd's wife, felt interminable.

Rhiannon, however, was in good spirits as she stood at the bottom of the steps to Patrick's wagon, having knocked on the side as if it were a door. "Patrick? Are you there? It's Rhiannon."

To Catrin's relief, Patrick pulled back the canvas. "Yes?"

Rhiannon had her instructions, which she followed to the letter: "I wanted to offer my condolences for the loss of your father and what has happened with your uncle."

She was kind and motherly, and he responded accordingly. "Thank you. It has been difficult." He didn't mention that he'd heard about Adam's arrest only moments earlier from Stephen and Emma.

Next, Rhiannon handed him a little pot of honey. "From our own hives. I thought a little sweetness might cheer you."

"Thank you again."

Patrick made to withdraw, but Rhiannon put out her hand to him, in what looked to Catrin like a very natural fashion. "I saw you the other day wearing your uncle's blue hood. Do you know where I could get fabric of that same color?"

"No, I'm sorry. I don't." Patrick retreated into the wagon, dropping the flap and effectively ending the conversation.

Catrin saw Rhiannon's smile as she walked away with long strides. The wait was shorter this time for the company of six riders to come into view, cantering down the track that ran through the grounds. Rhys was in the lead, and he reined in his horse in front of the wagon. He was up the steps and flinging open the canvas door in the same moment Patrick appeared yet again in the entrance.

"Your uncle has escaped custody! Have you seen him?" Rhys was still holding the canvas flap and now he hooked it open.

Patrick's eyes were as wide as Catrin had ever seen them. "No, I haven't."

Rhys turned to go. "Send word to the king's pavilion immediately if you do!"

The riders were off again.

Patrick didn't take the time to close the flap, such was his hurry to get down the steps, hardly waiting until Rhys and the other riders were out of sight. At a fast walk, he headed in the direction of the corral where the horses were kept. Catrin's natural thought was that his intent was to collect his horse so he could drive away in the wagon.

Then her brother Hywel stepped out from behind a tent three spaces down. With a nod to her, he followed Patrick at a more leisurely pace. At that point, Catrin came trotting out from her hiding place and up the steps into Patrick's wagon ... to discover it had been torn apart as if a windstorm had blown through it.

Patrick had been looking for something. Well, Catrin was looking for something too. When she'd gone through the wagon after Moriddig's death, everything had been neat and in its place. Patrick clearly had a different style. As quickly as she could manage, Catrin went through everything one more time, all the while noting that the secret bottom drawer was still closed. Patrick hadn't touched it, even if all the other containers in the wagon were open.

Catrin didn't go near it either, saving it for last.

Then, even with the mess, she noticed the only new element, a small, half-open satchel that hung on a hook at the entrance to the wagon. She snatched it up, not hesitating even for a heartbeat to look inside. Within it she found a number of small items—a woman's hair ribbon, a rock, a piece of charred wood—but also a knife with a gap for a gem on its hilt; a leather purse into which the letters H and C had been embossed; and, secreted in the very bottom of the bag, a ring that, from Adam's description, had been Moriddig's.

"What are you doing?" Patrick shouted as he ran towards her, having spotted her from some distance away. She saw no sign of Hywel anywhere.

Her surprise at finding physical proof of Patrick's guilt had her hesitating a moment too long. She shouldn't have gasped. She should have behaved as if she'd seen nothing untoward and just made some excuse to leave.

But it was too late. By the time she stuttered an inane reply of *nothing*, Patrick was at the bottom step, staring up at her with hate in his eyes.

52

Day Six
Catrin

"Stay back!" The knife was right there in the satchel. Coming to her senses, Catrin pulled the blade from its sheath and held it out in front of her. "Don't come any closer!"

Maybe she could have made more of his guilt if he openly attacked her, but she was not interested in a repeat of the events in the village of Hartford, when she'd been hit by one of the Justiciar of Chester's men.

At her cry of defiance, Patrick hesitated long enough for Catrin to set herself more firmly into place at the top of the steps, the satchel now at her feet. If looks could kill, she would be dead where she stood, but he knew better than to lunge upwards at her. She had the high ground and his knife. Although she was no soldier, she knew how to use it.

"Why did you keep mementos when you knew each and every one would implicate you?"

"I don't know what you mean." All of a sudden, Patrick relaxed, putting up both hands and laughing, as if their confrontation was just a big misunderstanding.

"I'm holding the knife you used to murder Hugh, and you also have his empty purse, your father's missing ring, and isn't that a charred piece of wood from the castle?" Catrin kept the knife pointed towards him, hoping to hold him off until help arrived.

"Why shouldn't I have my father's ring—" As Patrick said the last word, he surged up the last few steps towards her as if he intended to tackle her to the floor.

At that exact moment, Hywel appeared out of nowhere, captured Patrick around the waist, and fell with him off the steps to the ground.

The two men rolled around, arms and legs flailing. Although they were similar in size, Patrick was twenty years younger than Hywel, and Catrin feared for her brother's life.

But then Rhys was there again, as she was learning to believe he always would be, along with the rest of their friends and companions. The riders had circled around through the encampment to arrive back at the wagon. It was Catrin who'd changed the plan by entering the wagon on her own, not Rhys. *Of course*, they hadn't actually been conducting a search for Adam, who hadn't been arrested and certainly hadn't fled. That had been a ruse for Patrick's ears alone. Emma's mother and father hadn't been on their way to speak to Lord Owen either. Prince Edmund had said Owen couldn't keep a secret, and they hadn't shared their plan with him, though he would be among the first to be told of the results today, as was his right.

Math and Ralph dismounted and soon each had a knee on Patrick's arms to prevent him from moving. His upper left arm was also bleeding. In the heartbeat before Hywel had brought him off the steps, he had come close enough to her that she'd cut him.

"Are you all right down there?" Miles studied Hywel, who'd managed to end up on top of Patrick. As a bard, rather than a fighter, in the end Patrick's blows had been ineffectual compared to Hywel's. He'd also been on the bottom when Hywel had hit the ground and even now looked a little woozy from the blow to the head and perhaps from having the wind knocked out of him.

"I am now." Hywel was breathing hard as he pushed himself to his feet. "It's over. You have nowhere to go, boy. Stand down."

Patrick's face was screwed up in fury. "I have done nothing wrong. You have nothing on me. You are *nothing*."

"That may well be, but he—" Hywel tipped his head to indicate Rhys, "is the king's quaestor. You are charged with the murder of your father and Hugh."

Patrick's jaw remained tight as Math and Ralph got him to his feet. He had grass in his hair and dirt all over his clothes, as did Hywel. "There is a real villain here, but it isn't me."

"Is that so?" Simon was going through the items in the satchel Catrin handed to him. "What do you mean by that?"

"Did they not tell you what was stuffed into my father's mouth?" Suddenly, Patrick's eyes lit. "Have you not seen the lament to Llywelyn, written in Gruffydd's own hand? It is him you should be arresting. Not me." He tossed his head. "It is they who are keeping secrets, not me!"

Rhys stepped in front of Patrick to meet his gaze. "We found a paper stuffed into your father's mouth, but the writing on it was illegible. We really have no idea what you're talking about."

Patrick's mouth opened and closed as he struggled to find something to say.

Simon, meanwhile, turned to Hywel. "Has Gruffydd written a lament to Lewelen?"

"I would be very surprised if he hasn't." Hywel managed to answer with utter calm. "I have not heard any sung, however."

As with all lies, it was best to stick as close to the truth as possible. Now Math intervened, directing his question to Patrick. "Where did you get it?"

Patrick didn't seem to realize how thoroughly he'd condemned himself with his knowledge of the paper. "From Gruffydd's wagon. If you search it now, you'll find plenty more!"

Rhys stepped away from Patrick in order to say to Simon, in something of a conspiratorial tone, "Gruffydd often discards papers on the floor of his wagon. It is a well-known habit. Half the time, I think he doesn't even know what's there after a while, buried in all the layers."

Simon was looking to each one of them in turn. He was an intelligent man, and savvy to boot. Catrin couldn't be more grateful now that they'd made up the story of the poem being illegible. For Patrick to have proclaimed its existence, and them to deny it, would have put them in an untenable position. From the triumph in Patrick's voice, he also didn't seem to have yet realized how thoroughly he'd incriminated himself. He had worn his uncle's blue hood; he had stopped by Gruffydd's wagon. Strangling was often a crime of passion, but Patrick had just proved that, in his case, it was entirely premeditated. He had not only murdered his father, he had meant to do it.

As to the poem itself, Catrin would have preferred to drop the subject entirely, but since that didn't seem possible, she could at least deflect Simon from what she and Rhys knew.

"Moriddig also wrote secret poetry." She put her hand to her heart. "I should have said something when I found his papers the day he died, but I did not. I understand if I am condemned for not reporting it, but since Moriddig was already dead, he couldn't be punished more than he already had been. I just left them where they were."

Without waiting for a reply, or acknowledging the stunned look that had crossed her husband's face as she was speaking, she flitted up the steps into the wagon and popped open the secret drawer. The bag of silver coins was still there, making her think that Patrick hadn't found this hiding place—and maybe it was for the coins he had been searching the wagon so thoroughly. For now, she grabbed the first paper on top.

It was another poem about Cadwaladr, more complete than Trahaearn's had been, and not one she remembered ever hearing before. She held it out to Simon. Of course, it was in Welsh, so he required her to translate:

"There was a time when the people of Cymry,
Possessed wealth and peace before their sovereign king.
The people of Cymry
Found tranquility at his table.

But what is this?
Commotion in every land; a wasteland of desolate years.
The ambitious man raises his head,
The jealous man rises from his knees,
The righteous man lifts his hands in prayer,
Begging for deliverance.
The Cymry lost their bounty,
Choosing alliance with their enemies.
Who laid waste to our lands,
Demanding our pledge in trade for peace.

But see who rides forth, no longer hiding,
The dragon banner raised high,
Submitting to no one:
No foreign king, no Saxon, no creature from the depths of
Annwn.
See his men: Rhun, Bedwyr, Hywel, Dafydd, Goronwy.
Riding out of tales from another age,
Strapping their swords to their waists,
Setting their pikes in their rests,
Spurring forward,
Protectors of a ravaged country.

The land will be red with battle and strife.
None will stand against him.
All will fall to their knees before him.
The Cymry will rise,
When Cadwaladr comes."

When she finished, he looked at her for a long moment, before asking, "There are more of these?"

"Yes," she said.

"Does anyone else know about them?"

"Not that I know; not that anyone has said."

Rhys cleared his throat. "I will see to their disposal personally."

Simon turned back to Patrick. "This was your great weapon? To expose your father as a traitor to the crown, even after you killed him?"

"I-I-"

"You disgust me." Simon made a motion to indicate that Math and Ralph should take him away. "The gatehouse at the castle is still intact. He'll be safe enough in the basement."

As they hustled away, Simon picked up Patrick's satchel. "Are we sure about what each of these represents? Is there more in that wagon I should know about?"

"Not that I am aware." Catrin had kept hold of the dagger and now handed it to Simon, who returned it to its sheath. Once they were no longer standing in the middle of the festival grounds, they could see if the garnet Stephen had found amidst the coins on Hugh's belly was a match. She was confident it would be.

Even more convincing was the dried blood that remained on the leather sheath, separate from the swath of blood on the blade, which was new, from when she'd swiped at Patrick's arm in self-defense. Somehow, she couldn't feel bad about it.

"He had to know any one of these items would point an accusing finger right at him." Rhys seemed to be recovering from the shock of her revealing Moriddig's poem. "He thought he was smarter than everybody else."

"They always think that, don't they?" Simon said. "Let's hope the culprits we are after keep on thinking it. As long as they do, we will always catch them."

53

Day Six
Simon

"It's time for you to tell me about Patrick." Rhys brought a chair to the other side of the low table in front of Adam, turned it around, and sat with his arms across the back rail. They were all trying to be unthreatening. Adam was having a hard enough time as it was.

At the moment, he was sitting on a bench in Owen's receiving room off the great hall, leaning forward with his elbows on his knees and his head in his hands. Patrick was a stone's throw away in the dungeon-like basement of the gatehouse. The keep also had a basement, but at the moment it was being used to store everything they had salvaged from the fire.

Now that the younger man was in custody, they had let it be known that Adam had been a willing participant in the trap to catch his nephew. Prince Edmund himself had stood at Simon's side as he'd informed the king and Owen de la Pole of what they'd discovered. While Owen had appeared offended not to have known about the ruse in advance, the king had laughed and said to his brother, "You didn't trust me with the truth, eh?"

"That isn't it at all. As your quaestor could tell you, the smaller he keeps his circle of knowledge, the better."

"Looking out for me, as always." King Edward's words could have been mocking, even towards his brother, but they sounded sincere.

Owen had insisted on being in the room when Simon and Rhys interviewed Adam. At the moment, he was braced against the mantle of the fireplace, something of a glower on his face. Fortunately, he was not in Adam's direct line of sight.

"I can't believe any of this. Patrick has always been a sweet boy." Adam was practically moaning with unhappiness.

"But has he, really?" Rhys said. "I admit until he was arrested he presented himself well, but now we know the dark side of him and have seen it ourselves. Can you really tell me you haven't seen it too?"

The pause was long enough for Simon to know the answer before Adam replied. "I don't know. Moriddig drove him hard. Patrick is immensely talented, as you have heard, but he has always wanted to take short cuts."

"You told me he didn't apply himself to his learning the words to the songs," Rhys said. "When we spoke earlier, you implied he would do almost anything to avoid it."

"I have always tried to give him the benefit of the doubt. I do think he is smart enough, but if pushed, he pushes back. And if he isn't pushed, he does even less of what he is supposed to do and then gets upset when he doesn't do well. It's like he is incapable of understanding why that is. It drove Moriddig mad." Adam put out a hand. "My brother swallowed down the criticisms that rose to his lips more times than I can count. He tried to be understanding. We all had a hard time after Patrick's mother died. Maybe we spoiled him."

"There's spoiling and then there's murder," Rhys said. "Did Patrick ever give any indication to you that he was capable of killing his father?"

"No!" Adam shook his head. "It's inexplicable."

Rhys brought out the satchel. "What do you make of each of these?" He set the items in front of Adam one by one.

At first, Adam stared at the collection, which to many would have appeared innocuous. Then he picked up a little bell on a ribbon. "This belonged to our cat." He looked up at Rhys. "He kept it all this time?"

"It seems so."

Then Rhys took out the garnet Stephen had found on Hugh's body and set it next to the knife, explaining where it had come from. If Adam's face could have paled further, it would have been luminescent.

"It really was him," he said dully.

With that, Owen could contain himself no longer. "How could you not have known what a snake he was? He murdered your brother and Hugh! He set fire to my castle!"

Adam's face was back in his hands, and it occurred to Simon that maybe he had suspected what Patrick had done, but hadn't wanted to admit it. "Can you tell us *why* he would do any of these things, Adam?"

Although Adam shook his head fairly forcefully, he answered anyway. "I can only think he was more displeased than I thought to learn that we would be leaving Lord Owen's service."

Owen was outraged again. "You're saying the murders are *my* fault?"

Adam looked stricken, so Simon intervened. "Of course not, my lord. I don't think you'll find a more loyal servant in your retinue than Adam. But there are instigating events in every murder. Adam would be lying if he didn't point out one of them."

Owen subsided, slightly mollified, and Adam turned to him for the first time. "I am tainted by these crimes. I realize you will not want me serving you anymore."

"Don't be absurd. I need you now more than ever! It isn't your fault your nephew is a murderer." He wrinkled his nose. "And to think I intended to take him into my personal service too. The two of you together could have gone a long way to replacing Hugh—" He stopped. "Is that why? Was his intention simply to further his prospects, first by replacing his father, and when it was clear he wouldn't be offered the position of bard, to replace Hugh as steward?"

"If that was his plan, it was working," Simon said, "though I don't see how he could have laid it all out in advance. If he had the *sight*, he would have seen the end result was losing his life on a gallows."

"Thank you for speaking with us about Patrick, Adam." Rhys began returning the items to the satchel. "I think we know enough now that we can ask him."

54

Day Six

Rhys

Rhys set a large chicken leg, half a loaf of bread, and a portion of various vegetables in front of Patrick. "Care to talk?"

It was the end of a very long day. Simon had already tried to elicit something meaningful from Patrick without result. Patrick seemed shocked that exposing the existence of Gruffydd's poem hadn't achieved what he'd hoped and had refused to speak at all. They'd even brought in Adam to beg Patrick to just tell the truth. For once.

Given that the king had decreed Patrick would be hanged at dawn, he had nothing to gain from speaking. He wasn't Trahaearn, but an example would be made of him nonetheless. Rhys's window of opportunity to learn what exactly had gone on inside Patrick's head was closing. Why had he killed his father? Why had he killed Hugh? Rhys wouldn't be satisfied until he knew.

"Is this a bribe or a last meal?"

"Both." Rhys shrugged. "Neither. You killed your father. Why?"

Patrick picked up the chicken leg and sniffed it. It was hot and juicy, and Rhys would be happy to eat it if Patrick didn't. "It doesn't matter now."

"It does to me."

"Why?" Patrick started eating with a will, but then spoke around a full mouth. "I'm not long for this world, whether or not you hang me. See?" With his free hand, he unknotted the bandage around his upper arm, revealing a gruesomely inflamed wound, purple and tight. At Rhys's surprised expression, Patrick shrugged and went back to eating, leaving the bandage undone. "Your wife's blow, but my dagger."

The wound looked far worse than Rhys would have expected in a few hours, perhaps a product of wrestling about in the dirt and grass with Hywel. Patrick was right that it hardly mattered. "So, why were you at that barn? We already know it wasn't to meet Hugh."

Patrick kept eating, and Rhys was about to give up when he said, "I was meeting one of the judges there."

Rhys allowed himself an inward sigh. "You wanted to bribe him, didn't you? Who was it?"

Patrick sneered. "Like I would tell you." Then he shrugged. "He didn't come anyway, so it hardly matters. He chose the high road after all."

Good for him was Rhys's thought. With the contest all but over, they might never know his identity, though Rhys would make sure to speak to the head judge on the subject. "And Hugh?"

"He'd followed me to the barn. In recent months, he'd been growing more distrustful of me overall, and my father's death had him worried."

"He suspected you'd killed him?"

"He chose to confront me then and there. I tried to give him the money I'd meant to give the judge, but Hugh threw the purse back in my face. Why wouldn't he take it?"

It wasn't quite what they'd guessed. "And for that you killed him?"

"Did I say so?"

Rhys could see their meeting like it was being enacted in front of him. Whatever Hugh had said to Patrick, he had surely underestimated the evil within his friend's son. "After you killed him, you had your own purse and Hugh's. Why dump the money on his body?"

Patrick's upper lip lifted. "I wasn't there, but if I were, I would say it amused me to do so."

More than anything, Rhys wanted to wipe the smirk off his face. "Is that why you murdered your father too? He refused to do what you wanted? What kind of monster are you?"

"I'm not a monster!" The words burst from Patrick, the hope for which had been the reason Rhys had spoken that way. He'd meant to provoke him into telling the truth. And it worked. "I was about to lose everything!"

"How so?"

"He told Owen he was leaving his service. And then he told me that even if I came with him to the Bohuns, he wouldn't be ordaining me a bard this year. Or the next. Or ever, not without a change in attitude. I lay awake all night thinking about how he had ruined my life. He couldn't do that to me!"

"You could have changed your attitude."

Patrick scoffed. "He had no right to withhold from me what only he could give. He gave me his ring, as if that could make up for his failures. It's his own fault he's dead."

"We know you planned it." Rhys couldn't help but lean forward in his intensity. "You took Adam's hood and wore it. You took the poem from Gruffydd's wagon. You planned to kill him."

"I gave him one more chance, there in the wagon, to change his mind." Patrick was wholly unrepentant.

Rhys had just one more question, purely for his edification. "Why confuse the issue by stuffing Gruffydd's song into your father's mouth?"

Patrick wrinkled his nose, reminding Rhys sadly of Adam. "It seemed like a good idea at the time. I shouldn't have bothered. It isn't as if his lament is a secret."

"What do you mean by that?"

"Gruffydd sings down by the River Dee, thinking somehow we can't hear him. We all know the tune by now. Do you want me to recite the lyrics for you?"

Rhys put up one hand before he could start. "Best you don't."

"Because you'd have to report me to the king?" He sneered again. "I don't envy you; I don't have to live in this world anymore. For you, it's just beginning."

Rhys couldn't move off the topic fast enough. "Why burn Hugh's body?"

"Oh that." Patrick shrugged. "It was impulse, honestly. I lost a garnet from the knife's hilt in the barn. I figured it fell off when I stabbed him. If you found it, Adam would have recognized it, since he's the one who gave me the knife."

"I'd already found it. I was done, and the body was wrapped for burial."

"I didn't know that."

"It would surely have been easier just to get rid of the knife."

"It was *mine*." His emphasis on the last word was notable. "And again, Adam would have recognized the garnet regardless." He was entirely correct, of course, since Adam had recognized the garnet.

"When you told me you had accepted a position as assistant steward, you seemed genuinely pleased about it. Why not murder Adam while you were at it?"

"There was no need." Patrick appeared to have entirely forgotten he was supposed to be keeping secrets. "Adam was among the few in Owen's court who could read. I apprenticed to my father for over a decade. I could wait a year or two to step into Adam's shoes."

"You were that sure Owen would replace Hugh with Adam?"

Patrick scoffed. "Owen is nothing if not predictable."

"And then what? Why was a position in Owen's court so important to you?"

Patrick gazed at Rhys in astonishment. "It is where I belong; it's what I deserve."

Rhys thought back to everything Patrick had done and said so far, and in a moment of clarity, thought he finally understood what this was really about. "The judge you were trying to bribe ... that wasn't the first time, was it? You were going to start up Hugh's scheme again." When Patrick waggled his head, effectively admitting it, Rhys said further, "How did you even know about it?"

"Who didn't know about it? I had been a runner for Hugh since I was ten years old. I found him taking money from some poor farmer who wanted the upper hand in a land dispute."

Rhys was almost impressed. "You blackmailed Hugh?"

Patrick made a face. "Not exactly. I'm not stupid. I made myself indispensable and got paid for my efforts. A pittance at first, and then more as the years passed."

The last piece fell into place. "And then nothing, because Hugh had a change of heart, and there was no more money coming in. Did your father know? Was that the final straw? He was leaving the Poles because he was worried about you and your plans? Did he confront you?"

Rhys saw in Patrick's face that he'd finally reached the truth. He didn't know if ironic was the right word, but it was certainly *something* that Patrick had killed initially because his father had guessed he was going to take over Hugh's system of payments, and then murdered a second time because Hugh had guessed he'd killed his father.

Patrick settled his back against the wall behind him. "My father wasn't as smart as he thought he was. And neither are you."

"You keep telling yourself that." Rhys decided he couldn't stand his presence anymore and headed for the door.

Patrick spoke louder to Rhys's retreating back. "You won't be quite so smug when you find yourself in chains too."

Rhys didn't want to look back, but somehow he had to. "Why would I be in chains?"

Patrick's expression was smugger than ever. "I know you heard Trahaearn singing that first morning. I know you helped him flee. Set me free, and I won't tell anyone else."

He was guessing. He had to be.

"Tell whomever you want whatever you want. I am not afraid of you." They were brave words, firmly spoken. Rhys surely hoped Patrick believed him. As he pulled the prison door closed behind him, he was quite sure he didn't believe himself.

55

Day Six

Simon

Since Patrick's arrest, Simon's questions about his friends' lack of forthcomingness had been eating at him—to the point that he knew he had to confront them. If he did not, he didn't know that he could continue to call them friends anymore. And if that was the case, he was going to have to rethink his life.

After the conclusion of the events at Vale Royal Abbey, Simon had thought he and Rhys were in accord again, with each other and with the king. After the events here, he wasn't so sure again. Thus, he had enlisted Elizabeth to help with the conversation, and together they arrived at Rhys and Catrin's tent, where his friends were sitting together at a low fire.

He didn't think he mistook the identical wary looks they exchanged with each other as he came into the light. Catrin, in particular, had a hard time not showing her emotions. At the sight of Elizabeth beside him, however, she brightened and leapt to her feet. "I'm glad to see you again before you go."

"We thought it would be nice to have a last visit together. The children are finally asleep." Elizabeth took Catrin's hands and squeezed, while Rhys filled the silence between them by pouring Simon and Elizabeth each a cup of mead.

Simon just managed to force down a first sip. He had never told his friend how much he despised the drink. It was both too dry and sweetly cloying at the same time. Besides, he was here on a mission, and alcohol wasn't going to help.

In fact, he had every intention of getting straight to the point, but then Catrin got in ahead of him. "Rhys and I are glad you are here because we have something important we need to talk to you about."

"It's about the bards," Rhys said, "but even more, it's about what we didn't tell you over the course of this investigation."

Now, it was Simon's turn to look wary. He'd wanted to talk about this too and had rehearsed with Elizabeth how to begin. He'd known the conversation would be difficult. He hadn't expected his friends to be bringing up the subject first. But since they'd started, he was happy to let them continue. "I'm listening."

"After we arrested Patrick, I saw the look on your face when I told you about Moriddig's poetry," Catrin said. "You thought I should have said something to you earlier."

"Yes." Simon wasn't going to deny what was true. "Especially with what happened with Trayhern."

Elizabeth squeezed Simon's hand. Normally, she had no role in his work, but he always told her everything afterwards as a matter of course. This was the first time she'd been any kind of participant. She sat silent, however, not speaking, just listening.

Rhys leaned forward, his elbows on his knees and his hands holding his cup between them. "Here's the truth, Simon, as much as we haven't wanted to admit it. If we reported to you every person who expressed unhappiness with the king or his edicts, you'd be arresting ten people a day. As long as what they are doing or saying isn't public, we have been ignoring it."

Catrin chimed in. "We have known we would need to address this with you sooner or later, especially with what happened with Trahaearn. Yes, he was heard singing a forbidden song, but it was also at the crack of dawn, not in public, per se. He obviously saw the error of his ways very quickly or he wouldn't have fled. Our intent hasn't been to hide anything from you." She gave him a rueful smile. "We do want you to trust us. We understand if you feel you no longer can. If you need us to report every single instance we come across, we can do that."

"Or rather, we can try," Rhys said. "We are still not going to be perfect."

With a barking laugh, Simon sat back abruptly on his stool. Here, he had been thinking this conversation was going to be hard, and Rhys and Catrin had jointly gone straight to the main issue and diffused it. "No! Sweet Mary, no. The last thing I want from you is a blow-by-blow of everything you learn. Already, the king has had to divert one of his scribes from his usual tasks to deal with all the people reporting on their neighbors."

Rhys straightened. "We hadn't heard that. What exactly is happening?"

"No surprise you've been too busy to notice. He has recorded hundreds of names already, and it's been all of a week. Every man or woman with a grievance has suddenly decided this is the opportunity to air it. Many of the names of those who've supposedly offended the king's edicts aren't even Welsh! It's a nightmare to sort through all the claims and counterclaims." He paused. "Someone has even reported Catrin."

"Really?" Catrin blinked. "For what?"

Elizabeth put a gentle hand on Simon's arm. "What my husband is trying to say, somewhat inelegantly, is that he wants to know what you know if it affects the health and safety of the king. That is all."

"We would never not report such a thing." Rhys reached for Catrin's hand. "You know that."

"I do know that, and I do trust you." With an overwhelming sense of relief, Simon took a second sip from the cup of mead Rhys had given him. If asked, he might even say the taste was growing on him.

56

Day Seven

Catrin

A whisper of anticipation ran through the crowd as Gruffydd ab yr Ynad Coch stepped closer to the king to allow the chain of office to be placed around his neck. Then, once the king adjusted the ornament on his shoulders, Gruffydd bowed deeply.

Having turned to walk back to the lines of waiting bards, still nearly a thousand strong, Gruffydd beckoned to Adam to come out from amongst the crowd. Lifting the chain over his head, he held it out with great ceremony, as a knight might lay a sword in the palms of his hands to present to his liege lord. While Gruffydd had won, and Cadwgan had come in a close second, who was to say that Moriddig, had his son not murdered him, wouldn't have been standing with them too? Likely so.

Gruffydd had arranged for the scene in advance, in acknowledgement of Moriddig's long service and Adam's place in it. Catrin glanced at the king. He had been among those fore-warned, but that didn't mean he wouldn't take offense when it came to it. But he rocked back and forth on the balls of his feet, a contented smile on his lips.

"Are you sure we're going to survive this?" Catrin leaned into Rhys to whisper her query. They were coming to the part that only the participants knew about it.

"Does it matter?" Rhys didn't have time to say more because an ancient bard, one of the oldest at the festival, eighty years old if he was a day, hobbled to the fore.

"Oh king, we have one last song for you to hear." His voice didn't shake as much as his hands and, even in great age, was revealed to have a fine baritone.

Then he turned to face the assembled bards, lined up thirty men across and many rows deep, and raised his hands. With his arrival, the host of men had quieted. It wasn't so much that a pall settled over them, as an aura of determination.

Gruffydd retook his place in the center of the first row. Even so, it was the elderly bard upon whom everyone was focused. There was a moment's pause, like an indrawn breath, and then he pointed a finger high in the air. From somewhere in the back rose a beautiful tenor:

Cold my heart in fearful breast
Today I grieve
Our king, the oaken door of Aberffraw,
Our dragon

By whose hand the gold diadem was given
Is no more.

As he sang, the rest of the bards, a thousand strong, took up the lament. Their voices wove together, as if they'd practiced the song a hundred times instead of never before. Gruffydd's eulogy to Llywelyn was bold and beautiful and utterly terrifying. Finally, they reached the final words:

Can you not sense the turmoil amongst the oaks?
Do you not see the path of wind and rain?
And that the world is ending?
How could we value our own heads
when he has lost his?
We are left with only fear and surrender

Proud king, swift hawk, fierce wolf
True Lord of Aberffraw
our warlord, our dragon-king
Our Llywelyn ... is dead.
His only refuge
the Kingdom of Heaven.

As the last notes faded, the old bard who'd led them turned to face King Edward, and then, with effort, given his age, went down unsteadily on one knee. A heartbeat later, every bard behind him did the same, bowing their heads before the king.

They held the position through the silence that fell on the on-lookers. Catrin was holding her breath, along with everyone else. How would the king reply? Catrin was sure his next command would be to order his swordsmen, Rhys among them, to cut down every bard before her in a orgy of blood.

And then it occurred to her that Gruffydd had written the lament in Welsh, and the bards had sung it in Welsh. King Edward had no idea what they'd just said.

Out of the corner of her eye, she could see Simon fidgeting. She had thought for some time that he understood more Welsh than he let on. Maybe he had understood the words. Regardless, he wasn't stepping forward to translate them for the king. Neither was anyone else.

Catrin gripped Rhys's hand tightly, knowing what she had to do if they were to fulfill their promise to Simon and continue in their service to the king and queen. It was for this reason she'd accepted her position in the queen's household. It was why Rhys now served in the king's guard and as his quaestor. She didn't want to diminish the sacrifice these bards were making, but if ever her job was to stand between the king and her people, it was now.

Her first step brought her out of the ranks of onlookers. By the second, Rhys was at her shoulder. Together, with the bards still on their knees before the king, she and Rhys paced steadily to the front of the viewing stand.

Their position on the grass put them well below Edward's seat, since the stand was raised up to chest height. Unlike at Nefyn, when the king had moved off his throne to speak to Rhys at the conclusion of the archery tournament, this time he didn't budge, not even leaning forward so he could speak to them more privately. The song had been utterly moving, with those thousand voices lifted to the heavens like she'd never heard before, but Edward appeared to be as cold as ever.

The king spoke first. "That was a lament to Lewelen, was it not? I heard his name at the end."

"Yes, my lord." It was Rhys who replied, even if it was Catrin's doing that they were here.

"Was the song a fitting tribute to my fallen cousin?"

Neither of them was going to quibble with his use of the word *cousin*. Edward and Llywelyn shared no blood but had been cousins through Llywelyn's marriage to Elinor.

"Yes, my lord," Rhys said. "It was perfect."

"Was there any mention of David?"

He meant Dafydd, Llywelyn's brother, who had been more a brother to Edward than he had ever been to Llywelyn, except at the very end. Dafydd was the one who'd rebelled to start the 1282 war. Edward had hanged, drawn, and quartered him two years ago in Shrewsbury. "No, my lord. Not a word."

Edward spoke now in a resonant voice so everyone could hear. "Let it be known that this is the first and last time this lament to Lewelen will ever be sung."

"Yes, my lord." This time Rhys and Catrin spoke together, answering for themselves and the bards behind them.

The king got to his feet. He gazed out at the men before him for a long moment. Then he put his hands together and began to clap, albeit decorously, his approval. Within a few claps, the lords behind him were clapping too.

In that moment, Catrin was able to see the scene in two diametrically opposed ways. To the bards, they had sung their song, and then they had bent the knee, not in obeisance so much as in acceptance of their fate.

The king, however, as he had looked out over all those bowed heads of a thousand bards, plus the sea of onlookers, all of whom had their heads bowed too, was interpreting their behavior as submission.

The clapping continued, up until the king put out his arm to his queen and escorted her from the viewing stand.

At that point, the crowd surged onto the field, surrounding the bards, who finally got to their feet. In their faces, she saw an overflowing sense of relief that she herself shared.

They had survived the week. Gruffydd had sung his song. The world would go on.

And they would go with it, by the Will of God and of the English king.

Historical Note

ardd is based on real events. History has noted that, after visiting Vale Royal Abbey earlier in the month, King Edward summoned a thousand Welsh bards to him at Overton-on-Dee in September of 1284, for another opportunity to celebrate his conquest of Wales.

What happened at the festival is not recorded, but it is indisputable that it served as yet another step on the road to undermining, if not eliminating, the influence of the Welsh bards in daily life. A first step had been the near-destruction of the Welsh nobility, particularly in the north, since it was their patronage that had for centuries allowed the bards a living.

Hundreds of years later, in 1757, the English poet Thomas Gray published *The Bard,* a poem about a confrontation between King Edward and the last bard in Wales. In another document, Gray writes that King Edward had "hanged up all their Bards, because they encouraged the Nation to rebellion, but their works (we see), still remain, the Language (tho' decaying) still lives, and the art of their versification is known, and practised to this day among them."

Historians have found no evidence that King Edward actually massacred any bards, but that hasn't stopped the legend that he did from growing. A massacre of five hundred Welsh bards is further memorialized in a poem titled, *The Bards of Wales*, which Hungarian school children are taught to memorize even to this day.

What is uncontested is that King Edward's efforts to limit, contain, and even eliminate the power and influence of the Welsh bards were extended throughout subsequent centuries. In 1402, the English Parliament enacted the Welsh Penal laws, which read, *In order to eschew many diseases and mischiefs which have happened before this time in the Land of Wales, it is ordained that no waster, rhymer, minstrel nor vagabond be in any wise sustained in the land of Wales to make gathering upon the people there.*

The law was enacted to prevent bards from singing of a glorious Welsh past and encouraging the people to support Owain Glyndwr's rebellion against England.

And yet, despite the best efforts of King Edward and those who followed him, the Welsh musical tradition continued. To this day, the annual National *Eisteddfod* of Wales, which includes eight days of performances with upwards of six thousand competitors and one hundred and seventy thousand attendees, is the largest musical and poetry festival in Europe.

... and the Cymry will rise.

About the Author

With over two million books sold to date, Sarah Woodbury is the author of more than forty novels, all set in medieval Wales. Although an anthropologist by training, and then a full-time homeschooling mom for twenty years, she began writing fiction when the stories in her head overflowed and demanded that she let them out. While her ancestry is Welsh, she only visited Wales for the first time at university. She has been in love with the country, language, and people ever since. She even convinced her husband to give all four of their children Welsh names.

Sarah is a member of the Historical Novelists Fiction Cooperative (HFAC), the Historical Novel Society (HNS), and Novelists, Inc. (NINC).

She makes her home in Oregon.

www.sarahwoodbury.com

Thank you for reading *Bardd*!
It's readers like you make my job the best in the world.
Feel free to sign up for my newsletter
https://www.sarahwoodbury.com/
Or email me directly at sarah@sarahwoodbury.com
Happy reading!

www.ingramcontent.com/pod-product-compliance
Lightning Source LLC
Chambersburg PA
CBHW021239190726
48289CB00005B/1397